Jean Pau

MW01674216

Walt and Vult

SALZWASSER
VERLAG

Jean Paul Friedrich Richter

Walt and Vult

Reprint of the original, first published in 1863.

1st Edition 2022 | ISBN: 978-3-37500-348-7

Verlag (Publisher): Salzwasser Verlag GmbH, Zeilweg 44, 60439 Frankfurt, Deutschland
Vertretungsberechtigt (Authorized to represent): E. Roepke, Zeilweg 44, 60439 Frankfurt, Deutschland
Druck (Print): Books on Demand GmbH, In de Tarpen 42, 22848 Norderstedt, Deutschland

WALT AND VULT;

OR,

THE TWINS.

FROM THE GERMAN OF

JEAN PAUL FRIEDRICH RICHTER,

TRANSLATED BY

The Author of "Life of Jean Paul."

VOL I.

NEW YORK:

1868.

BY THE SAME AUTHOR.

REMINISCENCES

OF THE

BEST HOURS OF LIFE

FOR

THE HOUR OF DEATH.

PRICE, 38 cents.

TRANSLATOR'S PREFACE.

THE following work, although one of the most pleasing, is not one of the most powerful or exciting of the remarkable works of fiction of this author. *Hesperus*, and *The Titan*, are more elaborate and finished works. They contain scenes that descend deeper into the heart, and are of a far more exciting interest; yet, *this* seems to the translator the work most free from objection, most purely artistical, and the gentlest expression of the personal character of Jean Paul, which he has left.

One might, before reading, ask what is the object and character of the work? It would be difficult to answer. But it may be called a series of pictures, describing the successive moods of mind of the *poet;* and from these moods of mind, arise, scenes of comic, tender, or pathetic interest. It contains Jean Paul's own view of the value of his own art; that of an imaginative writer, and the adaptation of such a pursuit to the actual world. It probably throws more light on the personal character of the author than any other of his works.

His most authentic biographer tells us, that Richter, "in the combined characters of his *twins* intended to embody the characteristics of the true poet." The truthfulness, generosity, tenderness, and hopefulness of the poetical temperament in Walt, wrought in and blended with humor and satire; with a cold, sarcastic dissection of character; with a penetrating knowledge, and a keen sense of all that is false and hypocritical.

This is a union belonging to the highest form of genius; to Shakspeare, Cervantes, Burns; preëminently to Jean Paul himself.

The true poet can be enchanted only with the highest and most lovely in woman. The brothers both love the high-born Wina; but it would be a violation of all German conventionalism to bring the love of either to a happy termination; and, in accordance with the nature of the true poet, Walt is left, still aspiring to reach the highest; the *ideal* is still before him, — and the reader is left with the hope, that he will not forever wait at the gate of paradise.

Wina's character runs through the whole book like a sweet undertone, heard only at the intervals when the clang of the other instruments pauses. Or, she is like an exquisite perfume, which seems always to come to us, as it were a *remembered sense;* evanescent, but associated with the fairest and purest hours of existence.

Wina, like a true woman, loves the tender, the spiritual, the poetical in Walt, but is only brought to acknowledge her love to the society-refined and accomplished Vult; when he exhibits to her his culture and knowledge of the world, and by his address draws from her unsophisticated character its deepest secret.

It seems also to us, in a country where it is difficult to sympathize with the wide gulf between the noble and the commoner, that the whole book is a satire upon the absurd distinctions of rank; the conventional discrepancies, which, while they call upon the poet and the man of education to instruct and entertain, forbid him to sit down at the table of the nobleman.

The change of name may require an explanation. There is no English word that gives correctly the meaning of *Flegeljahre*. Mr. Carlyle translates it *wild oats*. It might be translated the *winged year*, or the year of trial, but the time of trial through which Walt passes is scarcely six months; and as Jean Paul's friends, when writing to him of this book, called it "*die Zwillinge*," *the Twins*, I felt that it would not be violating the fidelity of a translation to name it, in English, THE TWINS.

In some instances I have left out pages; and sometimes a few words, or lines, in the translation. There are one or two other scenes which I would have omitted; but I felt it my duty to the author to omit nothing, which developed or threw light upon character.

Mrs. Austen, the accomplished translator, who more than any other has made a "dwelling place" for German thought in the English language, says of Jean Paul:

"The difficulty, almost the impossibility of translating him, arises from the uncouthness, irregularity and oddness of his style; from its powerful eloquence; from the chaotic profusion and confusion of his images, and his deep-dyed local color."

I do not quote Mrs. Austen to enhance, in the estimation of others the difficulty of my work, but to apologize for the many defects which I am conscious remain in my translation.

BOSTON, December, 1845.

CONTENTS

OF

VOLUME THE FIRST.

WALT AND VULT,

OR

THE TWINS.

CHAPTER I.

THE WILL.

No event had excited such curiosity since Haslau had been a princely residence (the birth of the crown prince excepted) as the opening of the Van der Kable testament. Van der Kable might be called the Haslau Crœsus, and his life a festival for coining money, or a gold washing beneath a golden shower, or anything the wits would think a more appropriate celebration. Seven distant relatives, the survivors of seven of the far-off kindred of Kable, cherished great hopes of a place in the will, because Crœsus had assured them he would not forget them; but these hopes did not amount to entire confidence, as he managed his own affairs with the severe morality and disinterestedness of which the said relations were deficient, but also the whims and eccentricities that often appeared to influence his conduct, made it unsafe to rely entirely upon his favor.

The perpetual smile about the temples of Van der Kable, his thick lips, and his peevish, treble voice, impaired the favorable impression that was made by his nobly formed countenance and liberal hands, from which benefits and favors and new-year's gifts were continually falling. The human birds of passage that rested and fed upon this ever living service tree, declared it to be only a trap, where snares were concealed under the berries.

Van der Kable had made his testament between two paralytic strokes, and entrusted it to the city council; but when on his death bed, as he delivered the receipt for the deposited will to the seven presumptive heirs, he said to them in his old way, that he hoped this sign of his near approaching decease would not entirely overcome firm men like them, for he had much rather think of them as laughing, than as weeping heirs. One of the heirs only, Harpretch, the cold, ironical police inspector, answered to this singular address, "that it was not in their power to express their sorrow at such a loss."

At length the seven heirs appeared at the Townhall, with their own receipt for the will. These seven heirs were the consistorial counsellor, Glanze; Harpretch, the inspector of police; the court agent, Newpeter; Knoll, the attorney; Pasvogle, the bookseller; Flachs, the morning preacher; and Flitt, from Alsatia. All insisted upon the immediate opening of the will by the magistrate, and the reading of the constitution left by Kable. The mayor himself was the principal executor, and the other members of the city council were to act as assistants. The will and the constitution were brought from the archives into the council chamber, that the collected heirs might see the city seal, and that the State registry of the will might be read aloud by the city secretary, and all informed that upon the day of the registration the departed Kable was in full possession of his reason, and that the seven seals which he had himself impressed upon the will remained unbroken. After the city scribe had made a short registry of this fact, the will, *in God's name*, was opened and read aloud by the Mayor to the listening and eager heirs.

"I, Van der Kable, upon this seventh of May, in the year 179–, here, within my house, in the Hundstrasse of Haslau, declare this to be my will; and although I have been a German notary and a Dutch schoolmaster, I do it without many millions of words. I believe I am so much at home in the craft of a notary, as to be perfectly able to make a true testament. Testators usually preface their wills with the moving causes of the testament; these are with me my approaching dissolution, and the estate coveted as usual, by so many. It would be too foolish or too affecting to speak of interment and the things connected with it; but may the Eternal above all, remove that which survives the body to no cold and dark winter, but to a perpetual spring.

"For bequests to pious institutions, after which

the notaries have to look, I bequeath so far as to give to 3000 of the city poor of every condition in life as *many* light Gulden; for which purpose they shall meet next year upon the common, provided it is not occupied by the yearly parade, pitch their tents, and spend their money joyfully, and afterwards clothe themselves with the tent-linen. I also give to every schoolmaster in our Principality, to a man, an augunt d'or; and my pew in the Royal chapel to the *Jewish* corporation of this city. As my testament is divided into clauses, this is the first.

"Clause second. Inheriting and disinheriting are commonly thought the most essential objects of a will. Consequently, I leave to the following gentlemen, — the consistorial counsellor, Glanze; the police inspector, Harpretch; the court agent, Newpeter; Knoll, the attorney; Pasvogle, the bookseller; the morning preacher, Flachs; and Flitt, from Alsatia, — provisionally, *nothing;* not because they are relations, extremely distant, or that they will themselves have enough to bequeath, but because I know from their own lips that they hold my humble person, small as it may be, dearer than the whole of my estate, and on this account I leave them *directly* as little as they have desired."

Seven long faces now were seen to awake, like the seven sleepers of old. Glanze, especially, the church counsellor, a man, although yet young, already celebrated throughout Germany for many preached and printed sermons, felt himself particularly offended by such irony. The Alsatian, Flitt, forgot himself so far, as to walk about the room with many light, snarling curses on his lips. The morning preacher lengthened his chin till it looked like a pointed beard.

Many gentle exclamations upon the deceased, Van der Kable, such as heathen, fool, and shabby fellow, now reached the ears of the Senate, but Kuhnold, the mayor, made a sign with his hand, and the court agent and the bookseller wound up again the elastic springs of their faces, while he went on with increased earnestness.

"Clause third. I give my present house in the Hundstrasse, by this third clause in my will, exactly as it now stands, to that one of my seven above-mentioned relations who in half an hour from the reading of this clause shall first shed one, or a couple of tears over me, his deceased relative, in the presence of the honorable mayor, whose duty it will be to record the fact."

Here the mayor shut the will, and remarked it was true the condition was very extraordinary, but not contrary to law, and that the Judicial Court would assign the house to the first one among them who really wept. He laid his watch, that pointed at half past eleven, upon the session table, and sat quietly down to observe, as executor, who first would shed the desired tear over the departed testator.

Since the world stood, there was never such a singular and troubled Congress as of these seven dry provinces united for the purpose of weeping. At first, many valuable minutes were lost in confusion, astonishment, and laughter. The Congress found itself in the situation of a hound that in the midst of the warmest pursuit is suddenly startled with the cry to halt! back! and waits arrested, with the fore feet in the air, and the white fangs all visible. It was evident to all, that of a sudden shower no one could dream, but yet in twenty-six minutes something might happen. The court agent, Newpeter, asked if it was not a cursed fooling for a sensible man to make such a foolish condition. Knoll, the attorney, distorted his face till it looked like that of a poor journeyman mechanic, who on a Saturday night by a cobbler's rush light has his chin shaved by a barber's apprentice. He was fearfully angry, and came near to shedding tears of rage at the misuse of the word testament. The cunning bookseller instantly applied himself in silence to the thing itself, and quietly recalled to his memory the touching passages he had read as editor or commissioner, hoping thus to brew a tear or two out of them all; but although it produced no other effect, it made him look like a hound to whom the dog-physician in Paris had given a dose of nux vomica. Flitt, from Alsatia, danced about the room, looked laughingly at all the long faces, and declared that although he was not the richest among them, he could not, for all Strasburg and Alsatia together, weep at such a joke.

At last the police inspector looked at him very significantly and said, "If Monsieur hopes to succeed by laughter, that well known process which expresses the desired drops from the tear gland, and thus thievishly to win the property of others, he would gain as little as if he were to sneeze, and expect to profit by it; for it was well known that in this last process more moisture passed from the eye through the nasal passage, than was usually elicited by the best funeral sermon. The Alsatian assured him he laughed only at the joke, and not with any serious views.

The inspector knew on his own part that with his petrified feelings, something external only, a floating mote or spark could ever bring tears into his eyes; he therefore held them staringly open, hoping by this means to gain some passing good fortune. Flachs, the morning preacher, looked in his sorrow like a travelling Jew beggar, and as his heart, from domestic and church griefs had collected many melting clouds about it, he could perhaps, like the sun before the rain, have drawn the necessary drops from them, had not the coveted house, like a fair prospect, always come between.

The church counsellor Glanze, who, from new-years' celebrations and funeral sermons knew his own temperament, and that if he would soften himself he must address the most affecting images to others, stood up, and looking round upon the aridity of the whole company, he said with much dignity, "That every one who had read his printed works must surely know that he bore a heart in his bosom, and that he would rather repress that sacred sign of grief, tears, than do anything from selfish or interested views to draw them out. This heart," he continued, "has already shed them, but secretly, for Kable was my friend!" And he looked feelingly around.

He remarked with satisfaction that all there sat as dry as touch wood, and just at this moment it would have been easier for crocodiles, elephants or ravens to weep, than these heirs thus disturbed and irritated by Glanze.

Flachs meanwhile endeavored secretly to excite himself by hastily holding before his mind the benevolent deeds of the blessed Kable; the threadbare coats of the men, and the gray locks of the old women who came to the early morning service, Lazarus and the dogs, the sorrows of Werter, a small battle field, his own coffin, and of himself, fearfully exerting himself here in his own young years about this very clause in the testament, so that it requires but three more strokes of the pump-handle to bring water to his eyes, and the house into his possession.

"Oh Kable, my Kable," exclaimed Glanze at this very moment, almost weeping for joy at the near approach of the tear of grief. ——

"I believe, reverend gentlemen," suddenly interposed Flachs, rising with overflowing eyes and looking round, "I believe I weep." He sat down again, and with much satisfaction suffered his tears to flow. He soon dried them, for in the eyes of the executors he had, as it were, robbed Glanze, who was now very angry at his own exertions, of the house; but the emotion of Flachs was proved and duly registered, and the house in the Hundstrasse assigned to him and his heirs forever. The mayor with his whole heart gave it to him. It was the first time in the Principality of Haslau that the tears of a school or parish teacher had been converted, not like those of the Muses into the amber that imprisons insects, but like those of the Goddess Freia into gold.

Glanze congratulated Flachs, and remarked with apparent joy that perhaps he had himself helped to call up his emotion. The others were divided in opinion, whether it should have been assigned to Glanze or to Flachs, but were at present more intent upon the remaining clauses of the will. The reading continued,—

"Clause fourth. I have desired above everything else in the heir to my personal property also to my garden before the Sheepgate, my small wood upon the mountain, my eleven thousand George d'ors invested in the Berlin South Sea Company, and also to both my feudal soccagers in the village of Elterlein, and the piece of ground belonging to them; I have desired, I say, of my heir, much temporal poverty, together with spiritual riches; and at length in my late illness in Elterlein I have met with such a subject. I believe that in a dozen Principalities there does not exist a man more miserably poor, yet thoroughly good and simply happy; one who loves best of all those who truly love their fellow men. He once said a couple of words to me, and has twice performed a deed in secret that would make me rely upon the youth firmly and forever! Yes, I believe it would be an affliction to the youth to know that he was my general heir if he had not poor parents. Although he is at present a candidate for a justiceship, he is entirely without duplicity, pure, naive, childlike; apparently a truly pious youth of the times of our fathers; besides all this he has thirty times more brains than he thinks he has. But he has three faults; first, he is somewhat of a bombastic poet; secondly, like many states that should be acquainted with moral institutions and political economy, he loads the powder on the top of the ball; and thirdly, he advances the hour hand of a watch for the purpose of turning the minute hand. It is not probable that he can learn to set aright a student's mousetrap; and how entirely a trunk cut from a carriage would be forever lost to him, appears from the circumstance that he could not specify the contents of one thus lost from the Post-wagon, nor how it looked.

"The name of this my general heir is Peter Gottwalt Harnish, son of the justice of Elterlein, a fair-haired, well-formed and rather delicate, but dear youth."

The seven presumptive heirs were nearly beside themselves with curiosity, although they were obliged to continue to listen.

"Clause fifth. He has, however, first, nuts to crack! It is well known that I inherited this my inheritance from my never-to-be-forgotten adopted father, Van der Kable of Brœck of Waterland, for which I have never been able to give him anything but two miserable words, Frederic Richter, my own name. Harnish shall inherit the name also if he lives and repeats the life that follows

"Clause sixth. It may appear to this poetic youth a mere joke that for this purpose I demand and exact the following conditions; I have myself done all that follows, and for a much longer time than I require from him. I demand,

A. That for one whole day only, he shall tune pianos.

B. Superintend for one month my garden as upper gardener.

C. Practise the business of a notary for a quarter of a year.

D. That he remain with a game-keeper till he has run down a hare, whether it last two hours or two years.

E. That he shall correct the press of twelve printed sheets.

F. He shall serve Herr Pasvogle the bookseller through one week of the fair, if he will consent to accept his services.

G. He shall, unless they shall themselves decline it, live one week with each of the gentlemen presumptive heirs, and for the time comply with the wishes of the host whenever they are consistent with honor.

H. For a couple of weeks he must keep school in the country. Finally, he must become a pastor, and he shall enter upon his inheritance at the same time he enters upon his vocation. These are the nine conditions.

" Seventh clause. A joke I said above will it appear to him, especially as I allow him to reproduce my own life in his own way. For instance, to enter the school-room earlier than the fair, but he must finish with the pastor.

" But, friend Harnish, I attach to the testament in all its parts a sealed regulation tariff, called the *secret* articles, which in case you should load the powder on top of the balls, that is, in short, for the faults that I myself committed, a deduction shall be made, or the possession of the inheritance delayed. Be wise, young Poet, and think of your father, whose estate, like that of a Russian nobleman, consists in peasants, yet only in one, that is, in himself. Think of your vagabond brother, who perhaps before you dream of it will return from his Wanderjahr, and stand at your door with half a coat, and say, ' Hast thou nothing worn out, nothing for thy brother? Look at these shoes!' Be therefore careful and prudent, universal heir!

" Clause eighth. I desire the counsellor Glanze, and all the gentlemen, including the bookseller and Flitt, to consider how difficult it will be for young Harnish to earn the whole inheritance, if they weigh only what is here attached to the margin of the will,—a poem, where the poet describes a favorite wish of his own, that of being a pastor in Sweden." (Here the mayor asked if he should read the poem, but all thirsted for the remaining clauses of the will.) "I therefore beseech the gentlemen, my dear relations, for which indeed I do little but express my gratitude, to accept ten per cént. of the interest, as my funds and estate shall be valued as long as Harnish, according to the sixth clause, shall be prevented from entering upon the inheritance. I, the Christian, beseech them, as Christians, sharply to observe the young heir, and not to allow the smallest false step by which the inheritance may be delayed, or drawn off to be overlooked, but every one to be justly observed and duly registered. This will serve to keep the careless young poet awake, or to wake him from his dreams. If it be true, that my seven relatives value my person only, let them show it by watching over my representative, and although in a *truly Christian* manner, let them chicane and vex him as much as is consistent with their *Christianity*. Should he have to suffer, that is, to wait, so much the more salutary will it be for him,—or for them.

"Clause ninth. Should my universal heir be so deserted by all good angels, or so possessed with the devil, as to bring disgrace on a married woman, he shall forfeit a quarter of the inheritance; a sixth part also if he should seduce a maiden, and this reduction shall fall to the seven relations. Days' journeys or days of imprisonment cannot be deducted (and only the time lost upon a bed of sickness or death) from the time of receiving the full inheritance.

"Clause tenth. But should the young Harnish my heir die before his twentieth year, the inheritance must go to the pious institutions of this city. After he is examined and approved as a christian candidate, he may draw ten per cent. together with the other heirs until he is nominated, that he may not starve in the intervening time.

"Clause eleventh. He must take an oath not to borrow upon his future inheritance.

"Clause twelfth. As I took the name of Van der Kable, it is my wish, although not my will, that at his entrance on the inheritance, my heir should take the name of Richter. It may, however, depend on the wishes of his parents.

"Clause thirteenth. If there exist a skilful and already well harnessed author, furnished with gifts original and acquired, the proposal shall be made to the venerable man to write with his utmost ability the history and time of trial of my apparently adopted son; not only the heir, but also the testator will receive honor from that excellent but yet unknown author, who I request will take as a faint memorial of me, a *Number* from the articles in my cabinet of art and natural history, as a reward or salary for each chapter. He shall be admirably furnished with these specimens.

"Clause fourteenth. Should the young Harnish forfeit by his mistakes and errors, it will be the same as if he had committed the crime of seduction, or as if he were dead. The ninth and tenth clauses will then take full effect.*

"Clause fifteenth. I name as executors of my will the same highly honored persons of the common council, to whom the will has been entrusted, and the mayor Herr Kuhnold as the principal executor. He alone shall open the secret articles of the regulating tariff, in which the duties of my chosen heir are exactly defined. In this tariff it is set down in the most exact manner, for instance, how much Harnish shall receive while he is a notary, for how otherwise can he live? how much each person connected for the time being with the heir, for instance, how much Herr Pasvogle shall be remunerated for his seven days' board in the week of the fair. All shall be satisfied.

"Clause sixteenth. Volkman, upon the 276th folio page of his fourth revised edition, demands of testators an ever continued providence, and therefore I establish in this clause, that if either of the *presumptive* heirs seeks to dispute or break this my will, he shall not receive a farthing of the ten per cent., which ten per cent. then belongs to the other heirs; but should all unite in the process, then it shall go to my general heir.

---

* See ninth and tenth clauses.

" Clause seventeenth and last. I need not open myself further to this world, which the approaching hour of death will soon close upon me.

(Signed) FREDERIC RICHTER formerly;
at present VAN DER KABLE."

So far the testament. The seven heirs found all the formalities of signing, sealing and witnessing faithfully observed.

No. 1. *A vein of Lead.**

* I have taken the liberty of placing the Numbers from the *Cabinet of Art and Natural History*, which the author received as the reward of his Chapters, at the end rather than at the beginning of each chapter. — Tr.

CHAPTER II.

J. P. F. R.'S LETTER TO THE CITY COUNCIL.

The author of this history was chosen by the executors, especially by the excellent mayor Kuhnold, to write the life of the heir. At receiving this honorable offer, he sent the following answer.

"Gentlemen: I have the honor to describe to his Excellency the mayor, or the excellent executors of the will, the pleasure I felt that, according to the clause, 'Let a skilful, and for that purpose well harnessed author,' &c., I had been chosen from the 55,000 authors of the present day as the historian of a Harnish. I am unable at present to describe the satisfaction I shall have in such a work, and with such companions, having had to remove the day before yesterday with wife and child, and all my household goods from Meinungen to Coburg, and having had things without number to load and unload. Nay, scarcely had I entered the gate of the city and my own house door, than I again went out and upon the mountains, where many beautiful views may at once be seen. How often, said I to myself, wilt thou in future be upon this Tabor inspired!

"I here enclose the first number, *a vein of lead*, to the mayor, but I pray the excellent executors to remember that the future numbers will be richer and more finished, and that I shall show my power more than in the first, where indeed I had nothing to do but to transcribe my copy of the testament. The next chapter will contain this letter, and a title for the work, which shall be neither too common nor too eccentric. It is to be called *The Flegeljahre.*

"As to what concerns the work itself, the Author pledges himself to the noble city council that one shall be produced that may be boldly exhibited to every master in the art, be he a city or free and honorary master; and more especially, as I am perhaps related to the departed Van der Kable, who was formerly Richter. The work, to say a little of it beforehand, shall contain all that is found scattered about in libraries; it shall be a supplementary volume to the book of nature, and a preliminary, or sheet *A.* to the book of the blessed.

"Domestics, lads advancing in life, and growing daughters, as well as countrymen and princes, will read therein *Collegia conduitica*, and the whole will be a lecture upon good style. The taste of the most remote, even the most uncultivated people, will be cared for. Contemporaries and predecessors will be able to find their account in it, as well as posterity.

"In it I shall touch upon vaccination, the book and wool trade, the monthly periodicals, Shelling's double system of magnetism and metaphors, the new territorial boundary marks, with the illegal duties; also, field mice and caterpillars, and Buonaparte. These last I shall touch only cursorily, and as becomes a poet. I shall express my opinion of the Weimar theatre, and the no less important theatre of life and of the world. True wit and true religion will enter into it, although the last is as rare as a curse among the Moravians, or a beard at Court. Bad characters, (for the noble Rath assures me of them), will enter into it, and will be treated boldly, but without personalities or abusive epithets, for black hearts and black eyes, when observed closely by the last, are found to be only brown, and demi-gods and demi-monsters may well be furnished with the other half, namely, the human. Is it necessary that the whip be as thick as the skin?

"Dry reviewers, with exceptions, however, will be so affected through the recollection of their golden youth and all that they have lost, that they will shed tears, as the old relics of Saints are exposed to implore God for rain. It will speak freely of the seventeenth century, humanely of the eighteenth, and the present will be thought upon, but very freely. Even the typographical mistakes will hide some wit, and the list of them at the end of the book will contain some truths.

"The little work will climb daily higher and higher; from reading libraries to lending libraries, and from these to city council libraries, the last honor and parade bed of books, the widows seat of the muses! But I can more easily *keep* than make promises, for an *opus* it will be!

"Oh, noble city council! Gentlemen executors! Should it be granted me in my old age to see all the volumes of the Flegeljahre about me, printed and packed up in large bales ——! Until then I remain with high esteem,

Your obedient servant,

J. P. F. R. LEGATIONSRATH.*"

No. 2. *Mica, from Thuringia.*

---

* Much of the wit and satire of this chapter is lost to us, as it relates to the German and local literatüre of the time. The translator has therefore omitted some parts.

CHAPTER III.

THE SWEDISH PASTOR.

After the reading of the will was finished, the seven heirs showed in different ways in their faces the utmost astonishment, although they said little about it. They could indeed say nothing against it. Each asked of the other if he knew the poor youth? But to the court fiscal, Knoll, who was the attorney of a certain Polish general in Elterlein, the question was principally addressed.

There is nothing wonderful about the young heir, he answered; his father loves to play the Justice, and to be in debt to me and to all the world. In vain the seven heirs inquired of Knoll, *he* merely demanded a copy of the Will and the Inventory from the mayor. The other richer heirs also asked for copies. The mayor announced that he should cite the young man and his father before him on the next Saturday. Knoll answered, that as on the morning of the thirteenth, that is, on Wednesday, he should have Justice business in Elterlein, he would in due form summon the young Peter Gottwalt Harnish to appear in his presence. It was granted.

As all the business was finished, Glanze the

church counsellor desired to have a short minute for the poem in which Harnish had described his wish to be a Swedish pastor. It was granted him, and he began to read. Three steps behind him stood the bookseller Pasvogel, and read the page twice before the counsellor was ready to turn over. At length, as all placed themselves one behind the other in his rear, he looked around and said it would perhaps be better if he read aloud.

THE HAPPINESS OF A SWEDISH PASTOR. A POEM.

"Unreserved shall be my endeavor to paint the theme of these words, and to represent myself under the image of this pastor, that when in future years I recur to this my effort, it may retain the power to warm and inspire me. A pastor is in himself most happy, how much more blest he of Sweden. The Swede enjoys, without long and unpleasant interruption, a perfect summer and a complete winter. After a prolonged winter, the full ripe summer, heavy with blossoms, red and white, comes upon him. In the summer's night one half of Italy is his, and in the winter a second and brighter world comes down to him at night. To begin my Poem, I will describe the winter festival of Christmas. I will suppose the pastor to come from Germany, from Haslau, and to be selected for one of the most northern parts of Sweden. He rises at seven, and till nine trims his feeble lamp; at this time the stars shine clearly, and the moon, magnified as it departs, lingers in the heaven. The constellations, unseen in Germany, that linger above the sky till noon, rather inspire emotion than impart light, from the astonishing novelty of their appearance.

"Now I imagine the pastor meeting others of his parish, each with his little lantern, as they wend their way to the early service. The numerous little tapers carried by the common people, unite the whole community like a family festival within the church, and place vividly before the pastor the festival of his childhood, when every one, even the youngest child, had his little taper. From the height of his pulpit he speaks to his beloved hearers of simple things, whose words are from the bible, for God prefers an honest mind to the most subtle reasoning. He secretly rejoices at the opportunity of having them all draw near, so that by the help of the lamps he can look in the face of every one of his parish, and divide as to children the food and the refreshing draught of the holy supper. As he longs for the more frequent recurrence of this feast of love, I believe it must be permitted him every Sunday" ——

At this place the church counsellor looked round among his listeners with an inquiring glance of reproof, and Flachs, the morning preacher, nodded his head, but as he was thinking of his house, he understood little that had been read.

"When, the service over, the pastor and his large family leave the church, the Christmas morning sun is just rising above the horizon, and darts its morning beams in the face of the worshippers. The gray old men, so numerous in Sweden, look young in the rose-colored light, and the pastor, as he looks upon the frozen lap of his mother earth, where the flowers and the dead lie buried together, forms his thoughts in the following verse: 'In darkness and silence rest the dead children in the arms of the cold mother, but at last, when the sun of eternity rises, they shall arise, and she too shall bloom again.'

"At home he meets a warm and comfortable summer, and a streak of sunlight on the book-shelves welcomes him. He spends a lovely afternoon, for he scarcely knows which he shall select, from the midst of a whole flower-stand of joys. Is it the sacred festival of Christmas, he preaches again, and his theme is of beautiful Eastern lands, or of the sunlight of Eternity, for it is now twilight in the temple, and the tapers on the altar throw long strange shadows through the church, and the angel of the baptismal font appears to be descending upon the altar. The silent stars and the moon look in upon them. In the increasing darkness the excited preacher is no longer restrained by diffidence, but with tears and melting voice thunders down, as from the night of his pulpit, of this world and of heaven, and all that powerfully swells the heart of man. When, about four o'clock, the sermon is over, the pastor returns beneath the fluctuating northern lights, that to him are like the aurora of the South, or the burning bush of Moses near the throne of God.

"Is it the afternoon of a common day, guests with their well-behaved young daughters dine with him at about two o'clock, like the great world at the setting of the sun, and drink their coffee by moonlight, so that the whole parsonage looks in the changing light like an enchanted palace. Sometimes he goes to the schoolmaster during the afternoon school, and like an aged grandfather collects the children of the parish school around his knees, and by the light of the fire instructs and amuses the youngest among them. But if all this does not happen, he walks in the warm twilight of the strong moonlight backwards and forwards in his own apartment, and by the help of a little sugared orange upon his tongue, brings the beautiful southern climates, with all their orange gardens, before his senses. Can he not imagine that the silver shield of the moon hangs in Italy, among the verdant trees? Can he not remember that the lark and the windharp, music and the stars, even children, are the same in all climates, whether warm or cold? If the travelling post-boy, bringing news perhaps from Italy, can by a few notes from his horn, as he passes through the village, blow a whole climate of flowers upon the frozen window of his study; if when he takes some faded leaves of the last summer flowers in his hand, leaves of the rose and lily, or the gift of a feather of a bird of paradise, he scarcely remembers that he is in Sweden; and if the cherished sounds of *cherry time*, *rose bloom*, the *Virgin's day*, touch his heart, he looks doubtfully around the strange apartment when the lights dissolve his visions. But would imagination go still further, he has only to kindle the end of a wax candle to spend the whole evening in the great world from whence it came, for at Stockholm, as at other courts, the ends of wax candles that have been burnt upon silver may be had from the courtiers for gold.

"After the course of half a year the splendidly rich, longest day, more beautiful than Italy itself, where the sun sets earlier, knocks at his breast, and an hour after midnight holds the rose-colored morning, full of the songs of larks, in his hand. Between the hours of 1 and 2, as the sun is rising the above named agreeable guests enter the parsonage and propose a pleasure excursion, to which the pastor's company is indispensable. They go forth at two o'clock, when the open flowers smile upon them, and the woods schimmer in the morning light. As thunder and sudden rain are almost unknown in Sweden, the warm and fervid sun threatens no storm. The pastor, like the others, wears the costume of Sweden. The short doublet confined by a broad sash, with a short cloak hanging over it, becomes him well. With his broad-brimmed hat with waving feathers, and shoes tied in variegated ribbons, he looks like a Spanish knight or Southern minstrel, especially when with the other young people he roves through the woods, under branches now luxuriant with the blossoms and leaves of their rapid verdure.

"It is easy to imagine that this longest day of pure air, sunshine and flowers, passes more quickly than the shortest of the year. About 8 o'clock in the evening the sleepy flowers begin to close their petals beneath the sun's moderate beams. At 9, the sun itself withdraws its beams, and seems bathing in the blue ether, as it rests upon the horizon. The pastor becomes strangely moved with tender melancholy as he returns to the village, and sees the reflection of the weary sun upon the window panes of the humble houses, while all within are hushed in the quiet of deep sleep, and even the birds slumber on the tree tops; and at last the sun itself goes down, like the rayless moon, and all the world is silent. A rose-colored world now opens to the view of the romantic pastor, where dwell fairies and spirits, and he would scarcely be surprised, if in this spirit's hour his brother who left him in childhood should enter, as if fallen from this enchanted rose-colored heaven.

"His friends, however, must not leave him after this day of pleasure. They can repose in the garden during the short mild hour before the rising of the sun, and all who are inclined can slumber in the sheltered arbors. The invitation is accepted, and many beautiful pairs of friends *seem* to sleep as they hold each others' hands, because slumber will not allow them to be withdrawn. Cool and silent a few stars look down upon them; the night violets and wall-flowers open their petals, and although the light grows clearer, they give out a stronger perfume. As the pastor walks through his beds of flowers, an eternal morning surrounds the northern pole, and sheds upon him a golden twilight. Full of silent emotion he thinks of the far-off village of his childhood, of the varied life and the vain longings of men; but the morning sun, after its hour of absence, again asserts its empire: many would fain believe it were the evening sun, and close again their weary eyes; but the lark is awake, and the groves are alive with music, the pleasures of yesterday, although they differ scarcely a flower's leaf from the former, are renewed."

Glanze, whose face was the most favorable commentary upon his own printed works, looked round with triumph at such a production as this. Harpretch, the police inspector, observed, with a whole Swift in his face, "that this rival, with his wit, may yet give us something to do." The court fiscal, Knoll, and the court agent, Newpeter, had long before retired with disgust into a recess of a window, and with Flitt were talking of something reasonable.

All now left the justice room. Upon the way Newpeter said, "I cannot yet understand how so grave a man as our departed cousin, while just on the brink of the grave, could endure such nonsense." "But perhaps," said Flachs, who was the possessor of the house, in order to console the others, "perhaps the young man will not accept the inheritance, on account of the difficulty of its conditions."

Knoll answered roughly, "Difficult as they are, they are more stupid for him and for us, for according to clause fifth, if Harnish should refuse the conditions, three quarters will go, not to us, but to pious institutions; but if he accepts it and commits nothing but blunders,"——God grant it, said Harpretch. But if not blunders, said the others, we have the clause where the testator calls upon the church counsellor and all the gentlemen to watch over the conduct of the heir. We have also the ninth clause. Here the Herr Glanze can do much for us. They collectively chose him as protector of their interests, and commended his prudence and memory. I remember also, said the counsellor, he has to succeed to a spiritual office, although he is yet only an attorney.

They separated. The court fiscal Knoll, followed the court agent Newpeter, whose attorney he was, home, and told him that he guessed the young Harnish had for a long time known something of the will, as he wished to be a notary and then come to the city, and that on Thursday he should go to Elterlein to nominate him. Knoll was Pfalzgraf.*

You can then arrange, said the agent, that he may lodge at my house; I have a poor useless empty garret at his service. "Very easily," said Knoll.

The first thing he did, when at home, was to write

* Pfalzgraf is the title of an attorney who fulfilled the duties of a sheriff.

a note old Justice in Elterlein, in which he signified that the day after to-morrow, which was Thursday, on his return from his circuit, he would stop towards evening at his house, and create his son a notary, and also that he had prepared for him excellent and cheap lodgings with a respectable friend of old standing in the city. Knoll had already made a verbal agreement with the mayor to receive the fee for creating a notary from the mayor, but he secretly determined to receive it also from the parents. In all the verbal agreements and relations that did not come into actual practice, Knoll was extremely exact; but he was like those animals of prey who only feed in the night, and his night was created by the self-deception of an advocate and a fiscal.

No. 3. *A wonderful piece of Saxon clay.*

CHAPTER IV.

THE MAGIC PRISM.

The burial of old Kable was like an earthquake under the quiet sea of Haslau; like waves hither and thither in restless motion ran all the souls therein to learn something of young Harnish. A little city is a great house, the streets are only steps. Many young gentlemen, merely with the hope of seeing the heir, took horse and rode out to Elterlein, but he was always in the fields, or wandering upon the mountains. General Zablocki, who had an estate in the village of Elterlein, ordered his servant to make inquiries about him in town. Many contented themselves with taking a flute-playing artiste of the name of Van der Harnish, who had just arrived in Haslau for the true heir, especially people who were deaf with one ear, and who hear only half that is said.

On Tuesday the will had been opened, and on Wednesday evening the city received light from the host of the Crab, an Inn in the suburbs.

Respectable officers of the administration sometimes, even in the very ink of their daily toil, came there for an evening draught of beer, to dilute that dark color of their lives. *Here* had the father of the heir, old Justice Harnish, for twenty years regularly turned in; the host could therefore tell them at least something of the father, such as that he ran every week to the public offices to ask empty questions of the Government, and returned to repeat with interminable tediousness the old history of his different offices, his judicial views, his books, his double domestic jurisdiction, and his twin sons, without ever consuming in his whole life more than a herring and a mug of beer. "It is indeed true," continued the host of the Crab, "that although the justice makes use of the most lofty and high sounding words, he is at heart but a hare; for in all important cases, or whenever he makes a petition, he sends his wife; he has also a too susceptible nature, and can be deeply mortified and made ill for a whole day by an unkind expression or a look askance." Of the sons he concluded by saying, he knew nothing except that the rogue Vult, the flute-whistler, when about fourteen years old, went through there with such a gentleman, and he pointed to Herr Van der Harnish, who had just entered the Inn. Of the other, the heir, there was a gentleman present, and he indicated one with black buttons and button-holes, who could certainly give the best information, for he was the schoolmaster in Elterlein, and formerly his instructor.

The candidate,* Herr Schomaker, had a piece of

* A candidate for the ministry is so called till he is placed, or presented to a living.

waste paper in his hand, upon which he had just been correcting errors of the press with a pencil, and in which he was folding about an ounce of arsenic. He did not answer, but kept folding white paper over the printed, sealed it, and wrote upon every fold *poison;* he kept on enclosing until he had made a packet as large as an octavo volume. Then he arose, a tall, broad, strong man, and said very timidly, placing commas and other notes of punctuation between his words as if he were writing: "It is true, he has been my pupil; it is sufficient, he is so noble as *that;* and secondly, that he makes excellent poetry in a new measure, which he calls Streck verse, but which I call polymetre."

At these words the performer on the flute, Van der Harnish, who had been coolly walking up and down the room, became much excited. Like other artists, he had brought from great cities a perfect contempt for the smaller; on the contrary, artists delight in a village, for there the council-house cannot pretend to be an Odeon, nor the private houses to contain picture cabinets, nor the churches to be ancient temples. He obligingly invited the candidate to continue his communications.

"If my duty commands, the latter answered, that on my return home I should communicate to the heir what has not yet been communicated, the opening of the Van der Kable will, for it was only on Saturday evening that the government gave its consent, how much more severely does it demand that I should not recall without his consent the history of a living man; — but good God! he added, which of us will be the next corpse?" as he heard the passing bell striking in tones of prayer, and immediately seized upon and read most devoutly the account of a battle in the newspaper, for nothing fortifies a man so much for a cool approach to his own peaceful death-bed, as a couple of square miles covered with innumerable bleeding and dead bodies.

The flute player made a very contemptuous face at his religious scruples, and drawing a prism from his pocket, asked for four lights. "I can soon tell who will be the next corpse, he said, but I will rather tell you, sir candidate, from the revelations of this enchanted glass what you will not tell me. The prism encloses four different kinds of water collected from the four corners of the world. Let one rub it warm upon his heart, and demand softly whatever he wishes to know, either from the past, or of the present, or of the future, and if he has undertaken anything which, without imminent danger of the punishment of death, he dare not disclose; a secret which is never imparted except by dying men or suicides, then the four waters will be evolved in mist, which, after many evolutions, will take the precise form of a human being, who, as the spectator wishes, either repeats the past, reveals the present, or takes the form of the future."

The schoolmaster remained tolerably indifferent and self-possessed, for he believed that no devil had power against him as long as he said his prayers. Van der Harnish drew from his pocket a thick veil, placed it over his head, and kept quite calm beneath it. At length they heard in a low voice the words *Shomaker's apartment.* He threw back the veil, looked alarmed into the prism, and described in a monotonous voice everything in the quiet apartment of the old bachelor, from a printing press to the little birds that hung behind the stove, and the mouse that ran frightened about the floor. No hair started upon the head of the candidate, but when the seer said, "In the empty apartment the shadow of a spirit plays your part, wears your night-frock, and lies down in your bed," a cold shudder ran over him; "*this*, said the virtuoso after a pause, is only something of your present, now a little of the past, and only so much of the future, as perhaps to know whether you will be the next corpse." The candidate in vain urged upon him the immorality of penetrating the past or the future; he only answered that he left all responsibility to the spirits, and began to find revealed in the prism that the candidate, when a young man, had refused a situation as morning preacher, and had broken a marriage contract on account of only eleven thousand conscientious scruples.

The host now said something in the ear of the tormented schoolmaster, in which the word flaggellation only was heard. Shomaker, who dreaded rather to hear of his future than his past, and was willing to get rid of the spirits at the cost of what he called his *duty*, now said, "he would give the history of the Harnish family, which, through Kable's will, had become so interesting, and that Van der Harnish could, if he pleased, help him out by looking into the prism." This was all the artist desired. Together, they worked out the short history of the hero which appears in the next chapter.

No. 4. *Mammoth bones from Astracan.*

CHAPTER V.

ANTE-HISTORY.

Justice Harnish, father of the universal heir, had in his youth aspired to be a journeyman mason. By his inclination to mathematics, and sitting idly in his room, except on Sundays, when he read in the open air, he would have so far succeeded, if upon a festival day he had not been caught in the fly-trap of the recruiting service. The next morning, it was in vain he tried to draw his neck from the narrow noose, they had him fast within. He was undecided,—should he slip out to the kitchen and there strike out his front teeth so as to bring none to the cartridges of the regiment, or should he, for even in that case he might be taken to serve the artillery as powder-boy, should he from the window of the recruiting house represent himself as the turnspit of the inn, characters, at this time ignominiously held free from the obligation to serve their country. He preferred to keep his teeth and endure the ignominy. The turnspit would keep him from the recruiting officer, but like a cerberus it would devour his golden harvest.

No, no, said Lucas, as he considered the two pictures rather a slit torn in the stocking than a shot in the body, and like a philosopher he fled from the army.

Just at this time, his father, also a justice, died. He went home as the heir of the house, and heir apparent to the domain, although his estate consisted in state debts, and in a short time he very considerably increased this apparent revenue of debt. He then threw himself body and soul upon law business, devoted his canonical hours to borrowed acts and books, prepared for both sides, useless responses of whole sheets in length, sent in every act of business in writing, and wrote every report with beautiful broken fractures and fine flourishing capitals. He enquired as a justice into every abuse, and governed the whole day long. By these means the village flourished more than his own fields, and the office lived by him, not he by the office. The sensible Elterleiners agreed that without his managing wife, a healthy, reasonable element *in corpore*, who in the same morning cooked for man and beast, mowed and gathered hay, he might long since, with the justice's sceptre in one hand, and the beggar's staff in the other, have fled from the government of his house and court, where he was only the tenant of his creditors. There was only one remedy for him, namely, the resolution to part with his house and his justiceship; but he would as willingly have suffered himself to be beheaded as to take this poison draught for his whole future life. In the first place, the village justiceship, from time immemorial, as was proved from history, had been in his family. His heart, nay, his eternal happiness hung upon it, for he believed that in the whole village no jurist so good for the office, so suitable to fill this post existed as himself, although competent judges declared that nothing more was required for this office than for that of Roman emperor, which, according to the golden bull, demanded *homo justus, bonus et utilis.**

As to his house to which he clung so fondly, there was about it this striking peculiarity. The village of Elterlein belonged to two lords; on the right hand of the brook were the tenants of the prince, on the left the possessions of a nobleman, although in every-day conversation they merely said, "*the right, the left.*" Now from all doomsday books and all demarkation treaties the dividing line of the brook ran close along side of the justice's house; but the brook had changed its bed, or a dry summer had exhaled it to heaven; in short, the Harnish dwelling had been so much extended, that not only the foundation timbers, but the ceiling of one apartment, nay even a rocking chair, if so placed, leaned upon both territories. From this cause the house was to the old justice a legal vision of heaven, while it was at the same time his financial purgatory. With inexpressible satisfaction he often looked around his sitting-room, on the wall of which leaned a post with the arms of the prince to mark his boundary, where he

---

* Aur. Bull II.

could cast his eye sometimes upon the prince's territory, and sometimes upon the floor, which was in the nobleman's possessions. He said to himself, in the night I am in the right, because in bed I belong to the prince; in the day time only, I am a *lefter*, because my table and stove belong to the nobleman. His sons often observed, that on Sunday, when he had thought much, he was more cheerful at the evening supper, that he repeatedly shook his head and said in an under tone, "My house is as it were expressly built for a thorough lawyer like myself, other men would not respect the important law difficulties occurring in it, not being at home in them, nor able to arrange them as I am. And that *I*, an old honest lawyer, should give it up! sell it! think of that, Veronica!" and sometime afterward he would say, "no, never!" without listening to what Veronica answered.

If, however, he withdrew, to avoid his creditors, into the citadel of his own house, and like other conquered commanders abandoned to them not only the field, but the fields of his possessions, and postponed to sell or to fortify the house, at the same time the post of his justiceship and the theatre of his knowledge, it was because this house was the bridge upon which were stretched the musical strings of his whole life. He had in his view four hands, formed by himself, who would help to repair and replace the chords and discords, namely, his twin sons.

When Veronica began to feel the pains of their

birth, he kept in her presence, as though she had been a Sicilian or an English queen, witnesses of the birth, who might afterwards be directed into witnesses at the baptism. The bed had been shoved into the territory of the nobleman, because she might bear a son, and through this artifice he would be withdrawn from the subjects of the prince, who would make him a soldier, instead, as already decided by his father, binding his brow with the laurel of Themis. In fact, as a citizen of the territory of the nobleman, Peter Gottwalt, the hero of this work, saw the light.

But the pains went on increasing; the father felt it both duty and prudence to replace the bed of the suffering mother in the territory of the prince, that each might receive his rights. "It cannot be worse than a girl," or he said, devoutly, "*Quod Deus vult;* What God wills!" It was the last, and no girl; therefore the boy received, from Shomaker's translation, the name of the Bishop of Carthage, namely, Quod Deus Vult, or Vult, as he was familiarly called. There were now established in the apartments sharp dividing lines and boundary treaties between the territories. Cradles, and all else were separated. Gottwalt slept and woke, and drank from his mother's breast as the Left; Vult did the same as the Right. Later, when both began to creep a little, Gottwalt was divided from his brother on the noble side by a little wicker-work fence, brought from the hen-house and manger, and placed before the doors of his apartment. But the wild Vult sprang so agilely behind these barriers, that with every effort he had the appearance of a leopard springing backwards and forwards behind his cage.

At first, with long and severe trouble, Veronica effected the ridiculous division between the children; for the old Lucas, like every merely pedantic learned man, had a wonderful obstinacy of opinion, and withal an insensibility to everything that was humorous or ridiculous.

It was very soon apparent that the philosophical fold would be the future fold of Gottwalt. Without any parental partiality it was easy to see that he was fair-haired, tender, soft-voiced, of a gentle stock; and when he had been a shepherd's boy for a whole summer, yet was he so fair, so lily and snow white, that his father said one might as well sole his boots with the inner white skin of an egg for sole leather, as try to educate this boy for a peasant. For he had a nature so credulous, timid, tender, pious, docile, enthusiastic, dreaming, at the same time so ridiculously eccentric, so wildly aspiring and elastic, that it displeased his father, who wished to educate him for a justice; but every one, even the old pastor, said he must be like Cæsar, the very first in the village, namely, its future pastor. How? they asked, Gottwalt, the blue-eyed blond, with fine ash-grey hair, delicate snow-white skin! How? shall he be a criminal prosecutor, and serve under the great Carpzow, who, even with his penknife, sharpened to become the sword of justice, can hew down twenty thousand men. "Let them, merely as an experiment," they continued, "send him with the seal of justice to a poor widow, who pale and with folded hands sits on her low stool and directs the tender creature to the remnant of her poor effects, and gives him free leave to seize all her old doors and cupboards, and the last memorial of her husband, for the benefit of his creditors, and see if his own compassionate and beating heart will allow him to do it. But the younger twin Vult, they cried, joyfully pointing him out, the strong, black haired, black eyed villain, who is always rambling about, quarrelling with half the village, and is in his own person a whole theatre *aux Italiens*; he who can imitate every physiognomy and every voice,— this is quite another thing. He could carry the criminal law in his hand, and the whole assizes on his back." When Walt in the dancing school, upon a festival evening, supported the fiddle of the master with his own little bass viol, and could leap only with his inspired and happy countenance, Vult sprung round alone with a penny whistle in his mouth, and found time for a thousand malicious tricks. Should not such talents be used for the law? The justice considered ——

"They shall," Lucas answered, "and Gottwalt shall be placed upon the ladder to heaven, as a future candidate for the consistory, or pastor. Vult, on the contrary, shall descend into the delphic depths of the law, in order to rise afterwards upon that ladder, and draw his father out of the embarrassments into which his law has involved him, and this poisoned mine may at the same time yield gold and arsenic from its veins."

But there was only this extreme objection to Vult, that he could never learn anything from Shomaker, and always drew the displeasure of the schoolmaster upon him because he would be perpetually blowing upon a penny flute; and since his fourteenth year he had always placed himself during mass under the musical clock of the castle, and took lessons by the quarter of hour, if not by the hour, of this his first teacher. Here, that problem was decided, that men may learn more in quarters of hours than in hours. In short, when his father one day took him to town, where recruiting was going on, he ran after a drunken musician who could rule his instrument but not himself. Vult followed him into the wide world! He did not return!

Gottwalt must now become the lawyer. Alas! everything opposed it. As he was always reading, or rather what the people called praying, as Cicero *religio ex relegere*, it ran through the tongues and the hopes of the villagers that he was to be the little pastor. A butcher from the Tyrol even called him sometimes the parson's boy, sometimes the little deacon, for he was in fact an embryo chaplain, or little sexton. Was he not the coadjutor of both, and willingly bore the great black bible to the pulpit, the communion cloth to the altar, and held the oblation plate and the cup. In the afternoon service, when Shomaker slipped home, he played the organ, and was an industrious church-goer at all the week-day baptisms. Ah yes, when he saw the pastor, after his daily studies, sitting at his window with a white nightcap on his head and a pipe in his mouth, did he not hope that he should arrive at the honor of sitting with an empty pipe, for he could not bear tobacco, and a white cap on his head; which last indeed would have turned the boy's pale face into one of the old stone fathers of the church. Did he not one cold winter's evening, take the hymn book under his arm, and in the place of the minister visit an uninteresting gouty old woman, a tailoress, as old as the hills, and begin to read to her the sublime chant, "O eternity, precious and joy-giving word;" and when he came to the second verse, was he not so overcome, not by the emotion of the deaf old woman, but by his own, at the sublime words of the litany, that he burst into tears.

Shomaker took so cordially to his favorite, that he went one evening to visit the Schulze (I would rather you called me judge, said Lucas), and freely declared that he thought the young man was intended, on account of his tender nature, for the spiritual office.

As the candidate had as yet arrived at no preferment, and was minus his own vacant place, the justice merely answered him with a polite sort of murmur and nod, and went on to the old story of a professor of law, who addressed his students in this manner: "My highly reverend gentlemen, ministers of justice, cabinet counsellors, privy counsellors, presidents, syndics, finance and other counsellors, for I know not what you may all be!" He went on. "In Prussia," he said, "merely an hour's work of an advocate is paid, according to the law itself, with forty-five creuzers, and what would that come to for a whole year? besides, a true jurist could beat the devil himself——" * * * *

As usual, his talking did no good. But the sensible Veronica, the mother, contrary to the usual nature of women, who in domestic debates always take the side of the spiritual against the worldly counsel, she impelled her son from the spiritual sheepfold to the butchery of the law; and that, merely because she had once served a city preacher, and knew, as she said, how they fared.

One day when she was alone with her son, for he cherished and relied much more on her than his father, she said to him, "My Gottwalt, I cannot compel you to follow your father's profession, but listen to me; — the first time that you ascend the pulpit to preach, I will put on my mourning robe and white veil, and go into the church and bend myself low, and weep during the whole sermon, as at a funeral sermon; and if the women inquire why I mourn, I will point to thee, my son!"

The picture of his weeping mother seized so powerfully upon Walt's imagination, that he cried out, No! no! to the mourning veil, and Yes! yes! to the advocacy.

Thus our actual path in life, as well as the course of our ideas, is often *indicated* by accident; the continuance only, and establishment of the one or the other, is dependent on our free will.

Walt now learnt to speak for himself. His father was overwhelmed with joy, for villagers, as well as scholars, find merely upon the *tongue* the difference between the learned and the laboring classes. The delighted father therefore built him a study with his own hands, and he now frequented the Lyceum *Johanneum;* afterwards, he was sent to the Gymnasium *Alexandrinum*, both of which were no other than in collegiate harmony, the candidate Shomaker, who was called John Alexander. In the beginning had Walt and Vult, before the latter ran away, represented the lower and the higher classes; but afterwards Walt was obliged to make out the whole of the *prima* and *secunda* without the piper, in both of which classes he was compelled, as is the general custom, to learn something of Hebrew. In his twentieth year he was sent immediately from the gymnasium, or rather the gymnasiarch, to the high school of Leipsic, where for the want of a higher he continued daily, as long as his hunger would hold out. Since Easter he has been with his parents, and tomorrow evening, in order to live, he will be created a notary. Thus the candidate concluded the pretty little history.

No. 5. *Marble, from the Province of Vogtland, with mouse-colored veins.*

CHAPTER VI.

QUOD DEUS VULTIANA.

AT the conclusion of this history the flute-player turned with an angry countenance to the anxious schoolmaster, and said, "Do you not deserve that I should look into the prism and see you a tall, horrible corpse within it. This is your moral microcosm! your moral *esprit du bagatelle!* How? Your alarm at my prophesy could frighten you to betray, against the voice of your conscience, the secrets of these respectable brothers and their parents. You will repent of it when I tell you that I also know the secrets of this family, not from the prism, but from the wandering Vult, the musician himself, who is a far different person from that which you describe him. I have been with him in the village of the same name with this; Elterlein, of the mountains near Annaberg, where we have blown the flute together, and I will be d—— if I do not know his history, and have heard it from himself."

This was no perjury; he was that vagabond Vult himself, and as fond of a joke as ever. The candidate took it quietly. There was nothing he hated so much as to be thrown, without preparation, into a new and unlooked for situation, where want of time did not allow him to elaborate his moral laws of conscience. There were few casuists or pastoral theologians, including the Talmud, that to avoid sinning and its punishment he had not studied. He compared his own person with the description in every warrant of arrest, in order to be prepared if there should happen to be some likeness between himself and the escaped prisoner. Thus he often secretly accused himself, merely for the joke, of murder and other crimes, so that if he ever met with such a criminal he might be prepared to know how he felt. He therefore answered, "that he could not carry more joyful intelligence to Walt than that Vult was living, for the fugitive, as he well knew, had always been infinitely dear to his twin brother."

"Well," said the host, just then entering, "so the flitter still lives. How does he look, gnadiger Herr? We all thought he had died long since."

"He looks much as I do, gentlemen," said Vult, with a side glance at the officers of the government, who quietly sipped their beer. "He is, but without indeed knowing it, the most agreeable, the most beautiful person I have ever looked in the face. He is far too grave and learned for a musician. You should see him, or rather hear him, and yet, as I have already said, he is far too modest to be known. With all my playing, he once said to me bowing, and laying his flute aside, I shall never be the music director of the spheres; and yet every one could speak as familiarly with him as with an emperor of

Russia, who appears in imperial splendor on the stage, and feels that Kotzebue has created him, and he Kotzebue. He was good-hearted and full of love, and only hated mankind in general. I knew him to pluck one wing of the flies that teazed him, and throw them on the ground with the words, Go! the room is large enough for you and me; while he has looked many ancient gentlemen in the face and told them they were seven-fold villains; old, although like herrings soaked in milk, they gave themselves out for fresh and innocent; he, however, added, he hoped they would not take it ill, and showed them all possible civility. I wish he were with me here, that we might together visit his family. I have such a wonderful partiality for the Harnishes, my cousins by name, that in the Leipsic Advertiser I entreated them to come out decidedly with their genealogical tree and all its branches; but without effect."

Vult now retired, mildly and politely, like a man of the world, who had courteously done all day long only what he liked to do, although on the contrary he had only followed his eccentric fancies. As he came through the village he had smelt in passing, without the least hesitation, the flowers blooming in the window sills. He reproved a young Jew in the market-place for his bad style of begging, and told him before all the people how he could succeed. At the gate he refused to translate his French passport into German, merely to put the custom-house officers to quarrelling about phrases, while he stood calmly by and said that he should rely on the words of the passport only. Alone in his chamber, he called up, by his art of ventriloquism, such a violent dispute, that the passing watchmen swore four or five men were fighting in the second story, and when they rushed up and tore open the door, Vult turned his face, covered with lather from his shaving-glass, with his razor in his hand, and much astonished and displeased, asked them what they sought? He could not bring himself to endure in these small places, which had not seen him in his shining days in the great cities, to appear as the peasant's son from Elterlein: he would make himself a nobleman with his own hand. He had come to Haslau to give a concert, intending to run to Elterlein incognito, to see his brother and his parents, but not to be seen by them. Impossible was it for him, after ten years of absence, in which, like an electrical spider, he had whirled over Europe without spinning or weaving, to appear before his needy parents, oh! heaven, just as he was? A poor musician, in long stocking pantaloons, a faded student's spencer, and a green travelling hat, with nothing in his pocket except some few dollars and the entrance tickets to future flute concerts. "No," he said, "before I do that, I will drink verdigris for my wine, feed a sea otter on my breast, read a Kantian mass, or listen to one for Easter." If for a moment he could hope to soothe his fantastical father with wonders from strange countries, or with the salary of a few musical lessons, there was the unalterable mother, with her cold, clear blue eye, her penetrating questions, which, with their inflexible anatomy, would divide his past, his present, and his future.

But this evening, the results of a hundred other hours had worked within him a complete change. He brought from his chamber the calm surface of a stormy sea, that had been all night raging within him. Walt's love for him had penetrated his inmost being. He would observe nearer this morning star of poetry, measure its diameter, its light and warmth. Besides, Kable's testament gave some importance to the poet. In short, Vult could scarcely wait for the dawn, to hasten to Elterlein, there to be secretly present at Walt's examination for notary, to listen to and observe everything, and at last, if he deserved it, to discover himself to his brother.

No. 6. *Copper Nickel.*

CHAPTER VII.

THE VILLAGE OF CHILDHOOD.—THE GREAT MAN.

VULT VAN DER HARNISH left the suburbs of Haslau for Elterlein, just as the sun, half-risen, shed its beams fresh and horizontally over the dewy fields and the flowery meadows. The sun had passed that day from the twins into the crab. He fancied a resemblance with his fate, and thought that among the four twins, the star twins and the brother twins, his was the most glowing nature.

In truth, when he was in the mountain village of the same name near Annaberg, his longing for his native Elterlein had begun, and had continued through the whole journey. How does it press warm upon the heart to meet a man of your own name! how much more interesting is the place with the same name as that of your birth-place! In the animated street of Haslau, which was indeed only a continued market-place, he took his flute from his pocket, and threw all the passers-by into ecstasies with flute and concert harmonies; then he would change these harmonies into horrible discords, and suddenly breaking off, seek his pocket handkerchief, or look unconcerned around him. The landscape now arose sometimes into wild heights, then sank into broad plains and grassy lakes, where corn-fields and pasture-ground represented the waves, and clumps of trees the ships. On the right, eastward, ran, like an elevated misty coast, the distant mountain chain of Pestitz; on the left, the western plain sank down, as though it would follow the evening sun.

As Vult intended not to arrive before evening, he stopped many times on the way. His hour-glass for a July day was the meadows under the scythe of the mower,—a Linnean flower-clock, formed of grass. At four o'clock in the morning, the grass was standing upright and firm; from five till seven, it lay upon the ground like ant-hills; at three in the afternoon, it grew to hills; and when they had become mountains, it was night. He had, in his former long foot-journeys, so fatigued his over-sated eye, that he looked for the first time with pleasure upon this index of rural work. As the heaps in this hour-glass became highest, and their shadows lengthened, he drew near the cherry and apple orchards of his home, and the produce of the harvest became more frequent. The little brook, that sometimes danced through Elterlein, now ran a silver line through the dark green meadows before him. As he ascended an eminence, he saw the sun gilding the tops of the thin grove of pine trees, from which the boards of his cradle had been sawed, and from which he could look down into his native village. He entered this pine wood, and the golden sunlight became again the aurora of his childhood. Now he heard the well-known little village clock, and the sound penetrated so deeply into the past and into his own soul, that he fancied he was again a school-boy, and this a holiday afternoon. Yet sweeter to the ear of memory came the bells of the herds, as they returned from their pasture.

The little scattered pale and red houses wavered through the sunny stems of the trees. At length, he looked steadily, and Elterlein lay at the foot of the hill before him. Opposite was the clock of the sloping white tower, and the flag on the top of the may-pole; the high castle, environed with a wall of fruit trees. Beneath him ran the post road, and just there the brook spread itself through the open village. Upon both sides of the stream stood the scattered houses, each with its motionless fruit trees, that looked like sentinels of honor. Winding all around the village, like the tents of a parade ground, was the fragrant camp of hay-cocks, the centre filled with wagons and people. Above them flickered pale yellow torches, made from the oil of colewort and beeswax, that shed a cheerful light over all.

As he descended the hill to the dear scene of his childhood, he heard behind the hazle bushes in the meadow a well-known voice, saying, "Fellows! bind your cattle by the foot; have I not ordered you to do it a hundred times? Boy, tell your people at home that the justice says, to-morrow, without delay, the cloister meadow must be mowed by two bondmen." It was his father,—the heavy eyed, meagre, pale faced man, but upon whose countenance the warm mowing day scattered some spots of color. He stepped, with a shining scythe upon his shoulder, from the hedge into the street. Vult had to turn aside, for fear of being recognized by his father; but he approached him from behind, throwing from his flute, as he remembered his father's fondness for anthems, sounds that might have come from paradise.

Lucas walked yet slower, that he might hear longer, and the whole world became beautiful to his heavy eye. Sun-burned maidens, with dark eyes and white teeth, shaded their eyes by placing the sickle above their brows, that they might look undazzled upon the flute playing student. The herdwomen accompanied him, walking on in unison with the bells of their flocks, on both sides of the brook. Lucas, as the choral sounds filled his eyes with tears, looked only the more earnestly at a loose horse in the meadow. From the castle, the parsonage, and the parental dwelling, the gilded columns of smoke rose in the stillness of evening far into the deep, cool, blue sky.

Thus Vult came down into the overshadowed Elterlein, the village where, as a little boy in that first bed, he could lie at his ease to dream that foolish, unknown dream, the long dream of life. In the village, where old things remained the same, were the old women, who in this mowing day had remained at home. The large house of his parents, on the other side of the brook, stood unchanged, with the date, 1784, in white slates upon the dark gable. He reclined against the smooth may-pole, and blew upon his flute the evening prayer, "Let God dispose of all." His father went more slowly, as though he were looking around over the foot-bridge of the brook, to his house, and hung his scythe upon the wooden peg near the doorstep. His active mother stepped out of the door, in a loose gown, and, without attending to the flute, shook the rejected leaves of the salad from the measure; both said to each other, like country spouses,—nothing.

Vult went into the little inn, near by. From the host he learned that the Pfalzgraf Knoll had gone with young Harnish to look at the fields, and the notary-creating business would not take place till late in the evening. "Excellent," thought Vult, "it will be quite dark, and I will place myself at the back window, and look at their creations."

The old Lucas stepped out at that moment in his shirt sleeves, but already powdered, and dressed in a large flowered damask vest, to whet upon the door-step the knife which was to carve the notary supper. Vult could not understand why, but he felt an intense yearning towards his parents and brother, and especially for his mother. "It has not been the case," he said to himself, "upon the whole of my journey." The host seized him by the sleeve to show him the Pfalzgraf, who was just entering the house of the justice, but without Gottwalt. Vult hastened out, that he might see all that was going on. There he found the village so full of the sweet twilight, that he seemed to have gone back to the clair-obscure of his childhood, and his earliest innocent feelings fluttered about him like night butterflies. He waded through the dear old brook close to the foot-bridge, that he might turn up the old stones again, under which he had taken gudgeons in his childhood. He took a circuitous course through some peasant's fields, that he might enter the garden at the back of his father's house; at last he came to the window over the oven,* and looked into the wide room. There was no soul in it, excepting that of a chirping cricket. The doors and windows stood wide open, but all appeared to him hewn in the adamant of eternity. The red table, the benches around the room, the iron spoons and ladles hung upon the wall, the frame placed near the stove for drying clothes, the deep beam of the ceiling, from which hung the almanac and the smoked herrings, all and everything, even the ancient poverty, had passed untouched and unchanged over the dark and troubled sea of time. He would have remained longer at the window, but he heard people in the room above, and

* In German houses the oven is built out from the house, forming in this case a sort of dome, over which waved the branches of the apple tree.

the light shone upon the old apple tree from the windows of the upper apartment; he climbed the tree, upon which his father had placed a platform and steps, and he could thus look directly into the room beneath, having the whole domestic nest before him. Within he saw Veronica, his mother, standing with her apron on, a strong, healthy woman, in the bloom of the autumn of life, with her quiet, penetrating, but deferential woman's eye fixed upon the court fiscal, who was sitting calmly there fastening the broad bowl of a pipe upon its twisted handle. His father, fully powdered and in his Sunday coat, walking restlessly about the room, now in terrible fear of this great embodied law book sitting near him, who was as bold to all the world, even in the presence of princes, as Lucas was himself timid; and now anxious lest the *corpus juris* should take it ill that Walt did not appear. At the window, next to the apple tree upon which Vult was perched, sat Goldine, a beautiful, but slightly deformed, young Jewess, looking down upon the ball of red sheep's wool yarn, from which she was knitting a cardinal's stocking.* Veronica sustained this extremely poor, but delicate-natured orphan, because Gottwalt loved and praised her, and called her a precious little jewel, that would be lost without careful setting.

"The servant has been sent for, the simpleton,"

---

* A Jewess knitting a cardinal's stocking, — an instance of Jean Paul's delicate irony.

said Lucas, as the fiscal, yet angry, reluctantly told them that Walt had not taken the trouble to point out to him his own fields, to say nothing of those of the departed Van der Kable, but had sent a bond-peasant of the latter to show them, while he had uncivilly wandered away; and Vult knew from this that of the fortunate testament the fiscal had not yet said a word.

At this moment Walt came in, dressed in a blouse, bowed hastily and awkwardly to the fiscal, while tears of joy ran from his clear blue eye, and fell upon his glowing cheeks.

"What has happened?" asked the mother anxiously. "Oh my dear mother," he answered her softly, "indeed nothing; I am ready this moment to be examined."

"And are you crying at that?" asked Lucas.

Walt now raised his voice and his mild eye.

"Father, I have to-day seen a great man!"

"So, and have you suffered the great fellow to thrash you? Good!"

"Ah, God!" cried Walt, and turned to the sympathizing Goldine to relate the circumstance to her, and thus to the listening fiscal. He had above, upon the pine grove, found a carriage waiting, and not far from it, upon a woody hill, an aged man, almost blind, who looked round to try to see the beautiful spot as the sun went down. Gottwalt knew immediately, from his likeness to the engravings, that he was a great German author, whose German name shall here be translated into that of the Grecian Plato.*

"I took off my hat," Walt continued, warmly, "and looked at him until from admiration and love I could only weep. Should he have been angry with me, I would at least have spoken with his servants, and asked them much about him; but he was so entirely courteous, and spoke to me with the sweetest voice. Yes, he asked me of my history, and of my parents. I wished that my life had been longer, that I might have confided it to him; but I made the relation brief, that I might hear more from himself. Words like honey-bees flew from his flower lips, they penetrated my heart as with the shaft of love, and then filled the puncture with honey. Ah! I felt immediately how he loved God and little children. I wished I could see him when he prays secretly, and when he must weep at any great joy. I will go on, said Walt, presently," for he was now unable to speak from emotion; but as he looked around and perceived no sympathy in his relation, he immediately resumed, turning to Goldine. "He said," continued Walt, "the *best things!* 'God,' he said, 'gives in nature, as in an oracle, the answer before the question is asked.' And further he said, Goldine, 'that what to us appears like the sulphur of hell and of punishment, is changed at length into the mere yellow farina of a future flower.' One very

---

* Herder.

good sentence I have wholly forgotten, because I turned my eyes too steadily and earnestly upon his face. There was the world around full of magic mirrors, and above all the sun. I was happy, and felt no sorrow but that for his poor eyes. Dear Goldine, I was so excited that I made a verse upon the spot. 'Double stars appear in heaven like one; but thou, greatest of all, thou comprisest a whole heaven of stars in thyself alone.'

"He took my hand within his own, so white and soft, and said that I must show him our village; and then I felt courage to repeat the verse I had made with entire confidence. See, I said, how beautifully everything seems reversed, for the sun seems to follow the sunflower. 'That,' said he, 'God only does; as he follows man, he turns to them more than they to him.' He joked pleasantly with me about my poetry and a certain warmth I had shown. 'Sensibility,' he said, 'is like the stars, that can lead one only when the sky is clear. *Reason* is the magnetic needle that guides the ship when they are wrapt in darkness.' That was all I heard, so much was I disappointed as he turned to his servants and carriage, for now he must leave me. Then he looked so kindly at me, as though he would console me for his loss, that I seemed to hear the sounds of a flute from the evening sky."

"I blew upon my flute," said Vult, in a low tone, but deeply interested, "as the sun went down."

"And," asked old Lucas, who hitherto had kept

silence on account of the respectable, official name of Plato, and who every moment expected his son would produce a considerable sum that the great man had thrust into his hand, — "and did he go away without giving you a penny?"

"Oh, father! how that?" exclaimed Walt. "You know Walt's delicate nature," interposed Veronica.

"I know nothing of this scribbler," said the Pfalzgraf, "but it seems to me that instead of such empty histories, that lead to nothing, we had better begin the examination that I must go through before I create anybody a notary."

"Here I am, ready," said Walt, stepping up to him in his blouse from the side of Goldine, whose hand, merely from her sympathy in his happiness, he had thus openly and unconsciously taken.

No. 7. *Violet-stone.*

CHAPTER VIII.

THE NOTARY EXAMINATION.

"WHAT is the name of the candidate?" asked Knoll. But let us describe the scene. First, there sat the Pfalzgraf Knoll, with his pipe before him, apart from the others, like a firmly knit, bony, but living revolutionary tribunal. Lucas supporting his head upon two elbows that were placed like an Egyptian caryatides upon the table, and silently scanning every question; his pale, gray eye, and his lean, bloodless face brought into strong relief by the white powder upon his dark complexion, all which gave him the appearance of an immovable instrument planted against fate itself. Veronica stood near her son, with her hands folded on her breast, praying inwardly, and her clear, quiet, female eyes, so rarely brought into the foolish work-shops of men, following both examiners and examined with the keenest scrutiny. Then Vult, with his whispered curses, as he sat among the unripe apples, and near him every reader of this book, who may look through the window into the apartment. All are in great expectation from the result of the examination. Knoll was the most excited, for he knew from certain if not from the secret articles of the will, that the possible ignorance of the candidate might put him back many months from the enjoyment of the estate.

"What is your name, Mr. Candidate?" he began.

"Peter Gottwalt," answered the usually timid Walt, extremely surprised at the question; but speaking out with boldness and decision. After such moments as those we have mentioned, like the moments of a first love, all men are nearer and dearer to us, although less important than at other times. He thought more of Plato than of Knoll himself, and was dreaming of the hour when he could talk long and unreservedly with Goldine about him. "Peter Gottwalt," he had said; "Harnish must be added," said his father. "And the parents, and the dwelling," added Knoll. Walt could to these make the most satisfactory answers.

"Is Mr. Harnish born in wedlock?" asked Knoll.

Walt blushed to the temples, and was silent. "There is the baptismal register," said the justice. Knoll replied that it was only according to order, and asked, further, "How old?" "As old as my brother Vult," said Walt. "Four-and-twenty, namely," added the father. "Of what religion? where had he studied?" etc., received satisfactory answers. "What authors has Mr. Harnish read upon contracts? How many persons must there be to form a jury in a regular action? How many essential documents belong to a regular lawsuit?" The notary repeated those that were essentially requisite, but omitted one unimportant and inconvenient addition. "No, sir, thirteen are requisite, according to Baier's Valkmann on the Law," said the Pfalzgraf, violently. "Have you not studied the Emperor Maximilian's directions to notaries established in the year 1512 at Cologne? It ought to be, not only often, but justly read and interpreted." "It could not have been copied more accurately and faithfully than by me, Herr Court-fiscal," interposed the father.

"What are *lytæ?*" asked Knoll. "*Lytæ* or *litones*, or *Leute* (people)," Walt readily answered, while Knoll smoked quietly upon this puzzling question, "were with the old Saxons *knechte* (servants), but who yet possessed a third part of property, and could therefore make contracts." "A citation," said Knoll. "*Moeser*," answered Vult.

"Very well," said the fiscal after a pause; and smoked his pipe from a corner of his shapeless mouth, which looked like a wound that had been made in his face and imperfectly healed. "Very well! but *lytæ* are very different from *litonibus*. *Lytæ* were the young jurists, who, in the time of Justinian, after four years of study of the Pandects were absolved from learning any more; yours was an answer from ignorance." Gottwalt said, very simply, that truly he did not know that. "Well then, very probably you will not know what is knitted into the stocking that the Emperor draws on at his coronation in Frankfort?"

"*The clock*, Gottwalt," whispered Goldine softly to him from behind.

"Naturally," continued Knoll, "Herr Tychsen has translated it into German, from the Arabian text, in the following manner: 'An ornamented royal garter.'" Upon this translation, and the translation of a stocking into a garter, the Jewish maiden burst into an unconstrained laugh, while the father and son assented reverently.

As soon as Walt had passed timidly and modestly through the snarled net of the examination, the Pfalzgraf went on to the *nomination.* Without taking his pipe from his mouth, and without rising from his chair, he recited by heart, to the astonishment of all, the notary-oath, and Walt, with a voice tremulous with emotion, repeated it after him; while his father took reverently his cap from his head, and Goldine paused in her knitting to listen. The first oath that a man takes makes him serious, for perjury has ever been considered the sin against the holy spirit, because it is committed with the utmost reflection and audacity, as though from the throne of the moral law.

The notary was now finished, even to the last limb, the Achilles heel. Pen, ink and paper were handed him by Knoll, who said, "Hereby I invest you." The golden ring was put on, and immediately drawn again from his finger. At last the Pfalzgraf drew a little round cap, called a Barott, from his pocket, and placed it upon the head of the notary. It was without a single fold, as, added Knoll, must be the business of a notary.

Goldine called out that he must turn round, that she might see his cap. He turned and displayed to her and to Vult a pair of large blue, candid eyes, under a brow highly arched; a simple but inspired countenance, that seemed formed less from the influences of the outward world than from the promptings of the inward; — these regular features and a delicate mouth, resting upon a rustic torso. He appeared so ridiculous to Goldine that she laughed and cried at the same moment; but to Vult in the apple-tree, to whom it all seemed a touching comedy, he looked in his blouse like a *meister sanger* just come from Nuremburg. His notary signet, and his diploma to practise law in Haslau, were delivered to him; and thus Knoll, in this glass-blowing hut, had blown with his pipe a perfectly finished notary; or, to adopt another metaphor, he had brought out from his heated oven, upon a baker's shovel, a perfectly baked and sworn public officer.

Walt now approached his father, and pressing his hand he said, in a touching voice, "Truly, father, you shall see what I can do—" He paused from emotion and modesty, and his father answered, "Consider especially, Peter, that you have sworn upon the Testament, to God and the Emperor, to remind all persons making their last wills not to forget hospitals, and other needy persons, as well as public roads; now you know how bad are all the roads and highways to our village, and among needy persons you are yourself the first to be helped."

"No," said the son, "I will be the last." Veronica now secretly handed to the father a square folded paper containing some money, first, from delicacy, that she might conceal his strange selfishness, and, secondly, replenish the purse, if there was not enough therein. Lucas pressed it politely into the long, bony, open hand of the court-fiscal, with the words, "*On account*; it is the bargain * money of our cow," he said, "and something over; the price of the beast herself will pay the expenses of our notary in his journey to the city. To-morrow he will ride in on the horse to the butcher's who bought her of us. He is miserably poor, but all beginnings are poor and difficult. At the opening of the hunt the hound limps. I have seen among the learned many sore hunger-pains, for they in the beginning must live upon nothing. Be only carefully vigilant, Peter, for as soon as a man has learnt something brave in this world ——"

"A notary," interrupted Knoll in a cheerful voice, thrusting the money into his pocket, and holding his pipe up to the light, "is indeed nothing wonderful. In this empire they are very numerous; namely, *notarii*, says the Diet of 1500, article 14th. I myself in my office can create only notaries, but no instrument." "Like many pfalzgrafs, and many fathers also," said Goldine softly, "they can create

* *Schwanzegeld*, literally, the tail money;—that which, in buying or selling, is abated, or given in, over and above the real price.

a poet, but never a poem." "Nevertheless," he continued, "there is often in Haslau a will to be made, a criminal investigation, sometimes a *vidimus*, sometimes, but rarely, a *donatio inter vivos* to be made. In case now the young man becomes an advocate ——"

"*That* my Peter must be," interrupted Lucas. "In case," continued Knoll, "that he can begin aright; that is, undertake with alacrity in the beginning, doubtful and equivocal causes, such as great advocates, it is well known, throw up; and if he at last consult them, and wind, and bend, and turn ——"

"Yes," said his father, "he can then bring water to the mill that his father turns; he may from time to time be able to bring me in a considerable sum of money."

"Oh, my parents! if I could ever do that for you," said Walt in a low voice, and his whole face was illuminated with eager wishes.

"Ach Gott, you must stand by me," said Lucas angrily, "for who else? Not thy vagabond brother, Vult, the whistler."

The latter, who heard this from his retreat in the tree, swore ever to remain concealed from such a father.

"In case," coutinued Knoll, angry at being interrupted so often, "in case the young beginner is no imaginative fool, but a man that lives and weaves in the juridical meshes of the web, like his sensible father here, who probably understands more of law than ——"

Lucas could hold out no longer. "Mr. Court-fiscal," he said, "Peter has not half his father's mind. They should have made me a judge. God! I had gifts from my giant memory and sedentary life. He is no justice, who is not at the same time a civilian, a financier, a criminalist, a feudalist, a canonist, a publicist, as far as he can be all these. I had long since laid down my office, (for what do I get by it but a salary of three bushels of corn, and one cask of beer, with much delay and vexation,) were there in the whole village a man fit to take it from me! Where then are the country justices, who have, like myself, the four justice regulations in the house, namely, the ancient Gothic, the Electoral, the Wurtemburg, and the Haarhaarische; and do I not venture in every book lottery, and draw the most sensible and discreet things; among others, Julii Bernhard von Rohr's complete rights of housekeepers, in which the most useful regulations respecting farms; for buying and selling and leasing, especially the arable lands and gardens, and other economical matters, are all treated according to sound sense, for the Roman and German laws have treated the possession of farms in the same manner, or have administered the laws relating to them in the same way. The second edition of this work, Leipsic, 1738, is edited by Martini, bookseller; but there are only two volumes."

"I have them myself," said Knoll.

"Here, indeed," continued the father, "a justice cannot go like a blacksmith, with his pockets close by his hands in his leathern apron; he must have them in his pantaloons. God bless you! Herr Court-fiscal, where there are trusts to make, taxes, quarterings, things without end to record, verbally or written, bridges to make over brooks, gypsies to hunt out of the country, streets and fines to take care of, in villages where there are vagabonds, pestilence, or excess, — is not the justice always the first to be called upon in such places? these things are as praiseworthy as to be the governor of a province, or one of the nobility. Das Wetter! a justice cannot, like a pulpit hour-glass, run only once a week; he must run, to the ruin of his own housekeeping, day after day, and night after night, into all holes, into all fields and woods, into all the houses, and afterwards to the city, where he must first report verbally, and then in writing, what he has noted in his pocket-book. Now I challenge any farmer or peasant, even the poorest inhabitant of the village, to step forth and say, 'Lucas, you have flaws in your business, here or there, you have been remiss in your duty.' Oh! the horrible slander! Do you not see, that I go six fathoms deep in debt, were not the notary in future ——"

"Be quiet, justice," interposed Veronica calmly, now for the first time speaking, and turning towards the fiscal, whose debtor her husband was; "Herr Fiscal, he only says this for the sake of saying something. Do you not wish some refreshment? afterwards I have a request to make."

Lucas was very willingly silent, for in his marriage duet he had already been accustomed to have the left hand of the Frau reach far over his right, and strike the higher notes, thereby increasing the harmony.

"A *schnaps* is very well before supper," answered Knoll, much to the astonishment of Walt to hear such postillion's slang from a courtier out of the city.

The mother retired and brought back in one hand the needed refreshment, and in the other a thick manuscript book. Walt, blushing deeply, took it from her hand. Goldine's eye, for the first time, looked boldly up, and shone through its liquid light. "Thou must read to Herr Knoll from thy song-book," said his mother, "the learned gentleman can tell us if thy poetry is good for anything. Herr Candidate Shomaker will praise it excessively."

"And I praise it indeed no less," said Goldine.

At this moment the schoolmaster himself entered the room, bowed only to the court fiscal, and saluted the others with a strange light in his eyes. He saw from appearances, that the report of the will had not yet been received in this apartment.

"Very late," said Lucas, "the excellent act of creating is already over."

The candidate asserted circumstantially that he had left the city precisely at the vesper hour. "I assert also," said he, looking steadily at the justice, for he could not look steadily at such a renowned gentleman as Knoll, — "I assert that for a large quarter of an hour five geese, in the court below, with wings outspread, and warlike bills, have prevented me from entering."

"No, there were six," said the sarcastic Jewess.

"Six, were there? one had been enough, as I have read in ancient history, to destroy a man, and by a courageous bite make him wholly mad and hydrophobial for life. *Ah ca,*" and he turned to Walt, he could not command more French, "your poetry?"

"What is it?" asked Knoll, drinking.

"Herr Graf," said the schoolmaster, and led the Pfalz aside; "Herr Graf, it is, in fact, a new discovery of the young candidate's, my pupil, sir! He makes poems after a free metre entirely his own, consisting of one verse only, free from rhyme, which he prolongs at his own pleasure, and calls a Streck-vers;* and he has faith in their success. What he calls Streck-verse I call polymetres."

Vult in the apple branches from impatience cursed them all; but Walt placed himself with the manuscript in his hand, so that the light shone upon his

---

* The word Streck-vers is not to be found in the dictionary. A learned German informs me that the Streck-vers bears more resemblance to Chateaubriand's translation of Milton than to any other form of composition. They are the spontaneous expression of a poetical nature, without the effort for concentrative effect.

nobly arched brow and Grecian profile, while he turned slowly over all the leaves, and looked inconceivably long for the entrance into this temple of the muses. The candidate thrust one hand into the pocket of his vest, the other into that of his hose, stepped to the window above which Vult was sitting— and — spat ——

Hesitatingly, and with an unsteady voice, the poet began.

No. 8. *Arsenic.*

CHAPTER IX.

STRECK-VERSE.

"I KNOW not how it is," Walt said, "but I find no true poem. I must go on in course."

THE REFLECTION OF VESUVIUS IN THE SEA.

"'Behold! how the flames beneath the water rush among the stars; how the burning streams roll heavily from the mountain to the deep, consuming fair gardens in their course. But, uninjured, we, upon the water glide over the cool flames, and our image smiles at us from the burning waves.' Thus spoke the seamen, and looked anxiously towards the raging mountain. Behold! thus bears the muse, lightly reflected in her immortal mirror, the heavy sorrows of earth; the unfortunate look therein, and smile at their pain."

CHILDREN.

"The smallest are nearest God, as the smallest planets are nearest the sun."

"Why does the strange fellow weep, when he thought it all out himself?" cried Lucas.

"Because he is blest," said Goldine, "without knowing the cause. He wept merely from emotion, without being conscious of either joy or sorrow." He read on: —

DEATH IN THE MIDST OF THE EARTHQUAKE.

"A youth stood near his beloved, who was slumbering under the myrtle hedge; the earth slept also, and the quiet sky rested above her. The birds were silent; the zephyrs slumbered in the curls of her hair, and moved not the smallest ringlet. But the sea arose in its might, and the waves came rushing on like the herds.* 'Aphrodite! prayed the youth, thou art near; thy sea moves powerfully, and the earth is fearful. Goddess! listen to my prayer! Unite the lover eternally with the beloved!' An invisible net seemed to bind them to the sacred ground, the myrtle hedge bent over them, the earth trembled, and its gates sprang open! Beneath, in Elysium, the beloved awoke, and the enraptured youth stood near her, for the Goddess had heard his prayer."

Vult, from pure delight, was powerfully agitated at this reading. His soul, shut to common influences, stood wide open for the entrance of the muses. "Dear little Gottwalt," he cried, "to thee alone I will be known. Yes, to thee will I open my whole soul. Ach Gott! how will the gentle inspired simpleton be astonished when I confide everything to him."

"I should presume," said the schoolmaster, "that

* It is well known that before an earthquake the air is motionless and the sea much agitated.

he had not studied the authors of the anthology under my direction without benefit."

As Knoll made no answer, the father ventured to say "read on." Walt, in a little lower voice, read—

TO THE NEAREST SUN.

"Suns, beyond suns repose in the remotest blue of heaven; their foreign beams have been on the wing for thousands of years to reach our little earth, and yet we see them not. Oh thou beneficent sun! thou art so near to us, that the infant scarcely lifts his feeble eye to thee, but thou sun of suns, beams upon it with thy lovely light!"

THE KEY OF THE COFFIN.

"'Oh fairest and dearest of children, closely art thou imprisoned in thy deep, dark dwelling. The key of thy lone chamber shall remain eternally in my hand, and none shall invade thy rest.' The weeping mother turned her eyes to the eternally shining stars, and she heard the voice of her child. 'Mother! throw away the key, I am here! I am not beneath the earth.'"

No. 9. *Flowers of Brimstone.*

CHAPTER X.

THE BATTLE OF THE PROSAISTS.

"OH Heavens! were it only morning, brotherlein!" cried Vult. "I have had enough," said Knoll, who during the reading had sent from his pipe regular clouds of smoke, one after the other, without showing the least emotion.

"For my part," said Lucas, "I cannot rightly understand these things; and the verses, it appears to me, want their true tails." "But there are pious and melancholy things well expressed therein," said his mother.

Gottwalt was immersed, both head and ears, in the gilded morning clouds of the poet's art, and the distant form of Plato seemed to him the sun that shone upon them.

Shomaker looked sharply at the Pfalzgraf, and waited for his sentence. He always believed he should sin if he ventured hastily to decide. Never had he the surgical courage to whip the children of his school; he tormented himself with the possibility of fractures or wounds, but he punished them less corporally, by making horrible faces at them from the next room.

"My opinion," said Knoll, as he drew down his angry black eyebrows, "is shortly this; verses of this kind are merely a waste of time. I do not despise a verse if it is Latin, or if it rhymes; I made them myself, as a young simpleton, a chitty-face, and I flatter myself something very different from these. Yes, as *comes palatinus*, I create poets with my own hand,* consequently I cannot entirely despise them. Capitalists, stock and landholders, that have nothing else to do, and enough to live upon, may, if they please, make verses, and read them too, as many as they like; but a sensible man, a man of the law, who has his fortune to make in the best way he can,—he, I say, should despise them; especially verses without rhyme or metre, such as I could make by thousands in the hour, if it were necessary."

Vult, who sat quietly in his tree, enjoyed the thought, that he should find fitting time and place to reward the Pfalzgraf for this sentence. And yet he could scarcely restrain his anger and impatience when he saw Knoll and the schoolmaster sitting there so long at their ease, without making known the glad news of the will. Could he have seen and written, he would have sent a stone, with no gentle doves-post into the window.

"Do you hear," said Lucas, "they are not yet

---

* The Emperor, at that time giving the title of *court poets* to some distinguished authors, and it being the duty of the court fiscal to execute the diplomas.

printed, and, as I perceive, not even well written out, and as he carelessly turned over the leaves of the manuscript, he made an attempt to consume it in the lamp; but the poet standing aside, and hitherto sunk in his own fancies, seized his hand, and with a powerful grasp, saved it from the flames.

"But may he not, in his spare hours, make use of his talent?" asked Shomaker timidly, to whom merely the title of court fiscal was the twin sound to hobgoblin. The word *court*, or *the king's*, if it belonged only to the court drummer, was to him a sound that made him shudder; how much more when the word fiscal was added, a word that threatened hanging or imprisonment for life to every one upon his path, or at his door step.*

"In my spare hours," answered Knoll, "I read every public or private business transaction. I collected every fact upon every occasion, and this perhaps has made me what I am. Excessive wateriness is the character of these pieces, and at last this defect will pervade the business style of Mr. Harnish, and poison it irretrievably, and is justly considered the worst defect in a lawyer. A justice must oppose it then as inept ——"

"It was natural and pardonable," began Shomaker; "ignorant as I am of law, I thought poetry might be united with it, but it is now quite probable

* Fiscals, at this time, being charged generally with cases of criminal justice.

that Mr. Harnish, devoting himself to his new profession, will give up poetry forever. Is it not so, Mr. Notary?"

At this decision the mild and gentle Walt was excited to rebellion, and his indignation burst forth at the desertion of the teacher, who had formerly excited and approved him. He did not understand that courtiership, which, like a barber's razor, cut forwards and backwards. Shomaker was not capable in the presence of a servant of the crown of taking part with his pupil; he feared he should thus be guilty of rebellion, if he did as he ought to do, in the presence of the fiscal.

Walt, with the agility of a lion, sprang towards the candidate, and seizing his shoulders with both hands he poured from his long tortured breast a strain of indignant eloquence, so powerful, that the schoolmaster thought himself struck by his death blow. "By God!" he said, "I shall be a good lawyer, faithful and industrious in business, if it were only on account of my poor parents; but, Herr Candidate, may a thunderbolt pierce my heart, may the Eternal palsy my right hand, if I ever give up my poetry or desert the divine art of the poet." He looked wildly around and said firmly, but with a low voice, "*I shall continue to make verses.*"

All in the room were silent from astonishment. Shomaker was half dead. Knoll alone showed an iron and an angry smile. Vult upon his apple tree cried out, *right*, *right*, and groped blindly for some unripe apples to throw at the stupid session within. Walt went slowly, as a conqueror, from the room, and Goldine followed him, murmuring, "You were right, — *they*, the profane!"

Contrary to Vult's expectation, he placed himself under the apple tree, and raised devoutly towards the blessed stars his inspired countenance, upon which all his poems, and all the dreams of his life might have been counted. The flute player had nearly fallen upon the injured breast of his brother. He would willingly have been that poor bird, which, rising like the lark above the dead sea, and drawn down either by the poisonous waves, or struck by a too ardent sunbeam, falling, died upon the spot; but Goldine's presence forbade so beautiful a disclosure. She tenderly took Walt's hand in hers; but without heeding her, he looked steadily where only the clear stars were seen, and the troubled earth hidden. "Herr Gottwalt," she said timidly, "think no more of these prosaic simpletons. You have to-day made them yield to you. I will scatter pepper in the tobacco of the justice, and tobacco in the pepper of the candidate."

"No! no! dear Goldine," he said, with a gentle, sorrowful voice, "I have to-day been too violent; I was not worthy that the Godlike Plato should have embraced me. Was it then possible! Oh God! it should have been my last joyful evening at home. My dear parents earn with severe labor the money to make me a notary. The poor candidate has given me instruction from my earliest years; God has blessed me to-day with the Heaven that I found upon the heart of Plato, and I have acted like a Satan from Hell! Oh God! oh God! But my old faith, Goldine, always comes back; a heavy misfortune always follows every true, deep feeling of blessedness."

"That is exactly what I expected from you," said Goldine, angrily. "They place you upon the cross, but you would get one nailed hand loose, to press that of your tormentors. Have *you*, then, or those tormentors, turned this day's vintage of hope into an acid harvest of vinegar?"

"I am certain of no injustice," he answered, "except that which I have myself exercised towards others. Ah! there is always more error in hatred than in love! If there exist a nature that is the antithesis of mine, and there must be such, we might easily meet, and I am as much the antithesis of that nature, as that is of mine, and I have no more right to complain than the opposite, that we cannot accord."

Goldine, as well as Vult, although they remained extremely displeased, could not object to this manner of thinking.

Veronica now called gently to Walt, and his father cried angrily, "Run! Peter! hasten, *we are in the will*, and cited to appear before the court the thirteenth of this month."

No. 10. *Rotten Wood*

CHAPTER VI.

CHAOS OF HAPPINESS.

The Pfalzgraf covered his astonishment at the violence of Walt with the remark, that such a *sans facon* did not deserve a place in an important testament, to the opening of which he had come to invite him, and whose conditions he thought would not agree very well with poetry. This was the striking wheel, and the damper thus removed from the schoolmaster's intelligence-bursting soul, all the bells immediately sounded out. Shomaker knew and told the most agreeable articles of the will, while the fiscal mentioned only the disagreeable. The candidate always acted thus generously after an offence, until his forgiveness had been sought and granted. Lucas, as already mentioned, merely for the sake of saying something, cried out angrily for Walt to come in.

Blushing with a delicate and conscious shame, Walt appeared. All except Knoll were deep in the will, and he remained unnoticed. Since the reading of the verses, Knoll had been seized with a violent hatred to the poet; for music, while it charms nightingales to sing, excites dogs to howl. The circumstance that such a poor poetical lawyer should be more fortunate than himself, fretted him so much, that the perception, from his selfishness and knowledge of the world that Kable could not have selected an heir so likely and willing to forfeit the whole inheritance, had scarcely power to console him.

Walt listened, touched and pleased at the continued repetition of the words and conditions of the will; but when about the ears of Lucas, fluttered the sounds of eleven thousand guineas in the South Sea Company, two tenants, together with their fields in the village of Elterlein, his face was flushed as if a sudden warm zephyr from the south had played upon it, and made it bloom again; he cried out *eleven thousand?* threw his cap, which he had in his hand, far over the heads of all, and his beer glass, that scarcely escaped the head of Shomaker, in fragments against the door of the room. "Justice!" cried Veronica, "what is the matter with you?" "My friend," said the fiscal, somewhat displeased, "your son has yet some pretty hard nuts to crack; afterwards, he may possibly be the heir."

With entire confidence Walt approached the disinherited fiscal, and drew his hard, hairy hand into his own. "Believe me," he said, "thou messenger of joy, to us an Evangelist, believe me! I will do *all* to deserve the inheritance, *all* that is demanded will I do; for these, he added, (looking like an angel upon them,) who have done so much for me." (What would you with me, said Knoll, withdrawing his hand.) "Perhaps if my brother yet live, for him also.

Are not then the conditions very easy? and the last so heavenly! that of becoming a pastor. The good Van der Kable! Why then has he been so good to us? I have a lively recollection of him, but I thought he loved me not; yet he made me read my *Streck-verse* to him. Can we then ever think too well of people?" Vult laughed in his tree, and said "*scarcely!*"

Blushing with shame, Walt approached Shomaker and said, "Perhaps I have to thank my poetic talent for this inheritance, and certainly I have to thank the teacher, for the art of the poet, who will, I hope, forgive the former moment of anger." "Let it be forgotten, and call me no longer Herr! Joy must now reign. But your brother, of whom you just now thought, he yet lives and flourishes! A facetious gentleman, by the name of Van der Harnish, assured me of it, and beguiled me into an unpermitted communication about your family, for which, as I do not deny you my pardon, you will grant me yours."

Gottwalt cried out in an ecstasy of delight, "My brother yet lives!" "A gentleman from the distant Elterlein, in the Saxon mountains, met me in the city," said Shomaker. "Oh God! he will certainly be here to-day or to-morrow, dear parents!" exclaimed Walt. "Very well," said the Justice, "but I shall certainly mow off his legs with the scythe beneath the house door, and pelt him with wild apples, the vagabond!" Gottwalt, without noticing the violence of his father, approached Goldine, who was weeping. "I know why, excellent girl," he said, and then more softly, "it is, because thy friends are happy!" "Yes heaven, knows it," she answered, and looked kindly at him.

His mother, who had been silent under the announcement of Vult's being alive, now said she had often been deceived by such prophecies of the return of her good son, and immediately drew nearer to the men to try to soften the displeased fiscal, and asked him in a friendly manner to explain the intricate and difficult clauses of the will. But the Pfalzgraf, still displeased, rose hastily, and asked rather imperiously for the costs of the *citation* which he had undertaken for the servant of the magistrate. He had been cut off from his part of the inheritance by Flachs, who had wept for the house, and he now destroyed the hope of the delighted family that he would stay for supper. He preferred taking his supper with the landlord of the inn, who had long been indebted to his father, and he ate and drank there as often as he came to Elterlein to hold a court, by way of having the debt paid.

As soon as he was gone, Veronica ascended her feminine pulpit, and pronounced her usual sermon of investigation to the men. "They must be prepared," she said, "to expeet that the fiscal would immediately demand the capital he had lent them. Their joy at the will must have made him, who was one of the disappointed heirs, extremely angry. Will he, or shall I, draw the interest for the present?" she asked.

"He," answered Lucas. Shomaker now told them that Flachs, the morning preacher, by a few fortunate tears, had already got possession of the Van der Kable house in the Hundstrass. The justice declared the house was just as much as stolen from his son, for anybody, he said, can shed a few tears. Gottwalt declared that it almost consoled him for his own good fortune to hear that another poor heir had also something.

"*Thou* hast as yet nothing," said Veronica. "I am only a woman, but I have heard something about this will from visitors out of the city, and whisperings about the conditions of the inheritance; but I said nothing to my husband. *Thou*, Walt, hast no knowledge of the world, and no talent for business; ten years may easily pass by before you have anything, or are yourself anything. And how then, justice?"

"I will pledge myself," said Shomaker, "for the Herr Notary's success. Poets, it is well known, are as cunning as foxes, and have wind for everything. There was Grotius, the linguist, an ambassador; Dante, the poet, a statesman; and Voltaire, both poet and statesman." Vult laughed, not at the schoolmaster, but at the good-hearted Walt, who modestly replied to all this. "I have, perhaps, dear mother, learnt more worldly wisdom from books than you imagine. But let us think how it will be after two years. Good God! let us at least paint to ourselves the splendid time, when after our trial we shall all live here free and happy. I shall neither need, nor wish for anything. I shall be too blest to dwell on those ancient holy mountains, the pulpit, and the mountain of the muses.

"I will allow you, then," said Lucas, "to write poetry the whole day long. You are as much of a simpleton in this as your father is in law." "But at present," said Walt, "I shall be very attentive to the business of a notary, as it is my first duty prescribed by the will; pleading may well be put off for the present."

"Do you see," cried his mother, "he will be again at his wearisome verses; he has sworn not to forego them. I have not forgotten your oath, Walt."

"*Donner and Teufel*, so would I too," cried Lucas, for he wished to be gay. "Must we then, as you do, make a pin's head out of every steeple knob?" Lucas at this moment would hear of no evil. He drew smartly the married man's bow string—*silence*. Veronica was instantly silent, although she resolved to renew the subject somewhat later.

They went to the table as they stood, Walt in his blouse, although it was the hay harvest, for he must spare his little nankin coat. Goldine's wine of joy was watered with many tears, on account of the tomorrow's separation. Walt was infinitely happy at the delight of his father, who, when he had digested the news a little, became milder, and with knife and fork in hand expatiated upon the yet winged dove of the inheritance, and said to his son, for the first time in his life, "Thou art a blessing to me."

Vult had waited all this time upon the tree, but now as his mother began to collect from Shomaker the scattered information he had received from the flute player about her warm motherly heart, he descended. He feared the bitterness of the blame he might hear, would outweigh the sweetness of his own praises. He was happy enough on account of his brother, whose innocence and poetry had so closely enwrapped his heart, that he would willingly have seen the night swallowed by the yet glowing evening sky, that with the morning, he might take the Poet to his breast.

No. 11. *Common Wood.*

CHAPTER XI.

A CAVALRY PIECE.

Early in the blue of the dewy morning Walt stood at the house door equipped for his journey, and for riding. As universal heir to Kable, he could afford to spend a little, and instead of his blouse, he had on his good spring and summer coat of yellow nankin, a round whitish brown hat upon his head, a riding whip in his hand, and filial tears in his eyes. The justice cried, halt! rushed back, and returned immediately with the Emperor Maximilian's directory for notaries in his hand, which he thrust into the pocket of the yellow nankin. Opposite, before the inn, stood the erect, slender student, Vult, in his green travelling hat, and the host, who was the antichrist of the family, and moreover a Lefter.

All the village knew that it was the universal heir's first ride, and had collected about the spot. Veronica, who had all the morning been giving him directions for his life in the city, and at the opening of the will, now led the horse by its long bridle from the stall. Walt must mount. Much has been written and spoken in the world, of horses and of riding.

More than one Elterleiner has attempted to execute a tolerable picture of horses, but has given rather a rough, wooden, and colored sketch, than a delicate combination upon the canvass.

As this is the only cavalry piece of any importance, that I shall paint and hang up in the course of this work, I shall spend some labor upon it, and try to give it with truth, and the colors of life. In the Apocalypse there stood an old pale white horse, until the butcher, death, mounted, and rode out into time! The poetic spring of Walt's horse, when he bore his own flesh, instead of that of his rider, lies far behind him in the land of memory. Life he had borne, and men, those riding tortures of wounded horse nature, too long. Had heaven been pleased to present to the animals that are for the use of man a voice of pain, that men, whose hearts have their seat in the ear, might pity them! The keeper of every animal is the tormentor of that animal; for instance, the hunter of his horse, the wagoner of his dogs, and the officer, to every one except his soldiers, is a true lamb, gentle and tender hearted.

Walt, a combination of the most delicate nerves of our nature, who had the day before in the stall examined the rowel of the spurs, the saddle and the curb-bit, and who for all the world would not have laid his finger on one of the scars of the poor horse, not to mention the whip or the spur irons, *his* white horse enters this morning upon the stage, and Walt must mount. The day before, he had placed the horse before him in every possible position. In imagination, he had mounted him from the left side, and broken himself and the horse into every emergency. He had tried to imitate the skill of the Prussian dragoons, who mount as well from the right as the left. If some persons, among whom were Vult and the tavern-keeper, laughed at his attempt, they only showed they were ignorant that all cavalry must know how to mount with the right stirrup, because the left may be shot away. Walt kept his eye firmly fixed upon the left stirrup, tears darkened his sight, — "I could much easier mount a throne," he said, "than a saddle," — yet he held fast to the left side; but now came the new problem, how he should unite his own left with the left of the horse, so that both faces should turn forwards.

At last, on the saddle, Walt had to be his own quarter-master, to sit there erect, and saddle firm, to spread out (his finger in the rein) his coat-skirts over the back of the horse, and with his foot in the stirrup, turn round, to take leave, and — to start! To the last condition, the quiet beast would not willingly consent. Walt's gentle cracking of the riding-whip was to him like the tickling of a horse-hair, and a couple of motherly slaps on the neck from Veronica, he mistook for caresses. At last, the justice snatched a hay-fork, and with the iron handle gave him, upon the shoulder, a smart *accolade*, sufficient to send his son from his own village, like a knight, into the learned, as well as the beautiful world of chivalry. This was a hint to the animal, that he must go to the brook; here he stood tasting of the mirror that reflected his rider, while all the village laughed. The horse perceived his mistake in remaining there any longer, and bore Walt from the brook back to the stable-door, the equanimity of the rider only being disturbed.

"Wait a moment," said the justice, laughing, and running into the house, he returned with a rifle bullet; "put this into the ear," he said, "with this he will not fail to go, for the beast must feel the lead." Scarcely was the horse turned from the stable-door, with the shot in his ear, than he rushed through the street, past all the eyes of the village. Thus Walt escaped the good wishes of all, and especially of the candidate, Shomaker, who bowed like an inverted comma, as he rushed by on the horse.

"He is away," said Lucas, and went out to the haymakers. His mother quietly wiped her eyes with her apron, and asked the great farm-servant, "why he waited there, and stared?" Goldine had covered only one tearful eye with her handkerchief, that she might look upon Walt with the other. "May he be happy!" she said, then she went slowly up to his empty study.

Vult hastened after his brother; but as he passed before the May-tree of the village, and saw near the window the beautiful eyed Goldine, and in the little domestic garden his solitary mother, bowed down, and plucking, with tear-dropping eyes, the kidney beans and garlic, the warm, mild blood of his brother seemed suddenly to overflow his heart. He leaned against the May-tree, and blew upon his flute a church-choral, so that both the mother's and Goldine's eyes overflowed with soothing tears, and their hearts were elevated; for with intense tenderness had Vult appreciated their feelings, and elevated their noble minds.

It was a pity that Walt, flying with the horse over the smooth meadows, between the green hills, shimmering in the sunlight of the splendid harvest-day, knew not that his brother touched with his music hearts so dear to him in the village he had left behind. At the first hill he threw himself upon the neck of the horse, and drew from his ear the oppressive bullet. After he had succeeded, the poor animal stepped on even more gravely than a man behind a corpse; at the hills only, he hesitated, but on the plain he went like a smooth, silver stream, that moves only imperceptibly on. In this repose, established upon the saddle by the quiet horse, Walt enjoyed the wide, rejoicing day. To a perpetual foot-plodder, the elevated seat upon the saddle seemed to place all the hills and the meadows beneath him, and he felt like the sovereign of a country thus brilliantly lighted. At the foot of a new hill, there appeared a procession of wagons with seven drivers, that he would willingly have passed quickly, so as not to be disturbed from his dreams by their notice; but at the foot of this hill, the ridden Blondin asserted his right to enjoy nature, which to him, even more than to the riding Blond, consisted in grass, and stood firmly still. Walt at first made powerful efforts to move him either forwards or back; but when he found he could make no impression, he suffered the beast to feed, and turned himself quietly round in the saddle to enjoy with peaceful observation the wide spread prospect behind him, and allow the drivers to proceed so far, that he should not again come under their observation.

But there must be an end of all things. The equestrian at the foot of the hill, after having turned his face forwards, wished himself heartily at the top, for he saw the slender student following, who had also witnessed his attempts to mount the horse. Walt would not again, on account of the incredible difficulty of removing the bullet, quicken the fixed mercury with the living quicksilver in the ear; he therefore alighted from the horse, and attaching himself to the reins, wound himself together with the horse to the top of the hill: here fresh troubles awaited him. He saw behind a long procession of Catholic pilgrims creeping upwards, and beneath, in the village, the mischievous drivers drinking and watering their horses. The hope that had bloomed for him was in vain; he must overtake them, whether he would or not. A new hope arose through the nag, *Allegro ma non troppo*, to spring past them, and he went at a quick pace down the hill into the village; but once there, the horse turned, without the least hesitation, into the village inn. He knew the host. Every alehouse was his daughter, every inn his mother church. "Good, good," said the notary, "I had myself the same thought," and he ordered a lounger to give the horse something to eat.

Now came up the slender green hat. Vult's heart swelled with love to his brother, when he saw him lift his hat from the heated, snow-white, but beautifully arched brow, and the morning wind wave the curls upon his childlike face, tender with early bloom; and observed his unpretending eye, that looked so meekly yet so lovingly at all, even at the seven wagoners. Vult could not help joking upon the subject of the horse. "This horse," he said, looking at his brother with his dark flashing eye, and stroking its mane, "goes better than he looks. He went like Pegasus through the village."

"Ah, the poor beast!" said Walt compassionately, and with this tone disarmed his brother. The travellers collected about the inn, and drank in the free air; the pilgrims went singing through the village; animals neighed and crowed with delight; the cool northwest wind blew refreshingly through the fruit gardens, and induced all healthy minds to venture out into the free, open, inspired life of nature, and to enjoy the blessings of the beneficent God.

"A divine day," said Vult; "pardon me, mein Herr!"

Walt looked at him bashfully, but said with great

warmth, " Oh, yes, mein Herr! all nature seems to be celebrating a hearty jubilee, and from the blue heights above a hunting song, as from Alpine horns, sounds gently down."

The drivers now began to put the bits in their horses mouths. Walt paid quickly, and without taking the change mounted in haste, anxious to get on before them all. But it is an established principle with horses as with planets, only in approaching the neighborhood of the sun, that is, an inn, to go quickly; but when approaching their aphelion, to move slowly. Walt's horse placed his fore feet, like those of the Nuremburg play things, firmly in the varnished board of the earth, and established there his anchor-hold. Walt, with his green vest and whitish-brown hat, might as well have placed his saddle upon a mountain and spurred it forwards. Some of the gentlest of the drivers whipped the hind quarters of the *quietest*, he raised them, but kept his fore feet firm. Walt had now listened long enough to that compassionate nature which induced him to spare the beast, and without further hesitation he placed the shot in his ear.

He flew,—he rushed impetuously behind the flock of pilgrims, who timidly spread themselves apart, till at last, at the very extremity, he came upon a deaf female singer, who understood neither the clattering of the hoofs nor the warning voice of the rider; his knee, in the quick passage, was violently thrust against the shoulder of the pilgrim, and threw her down. She arose quickly enough to curse him heartily, supported by all her confessional brethren. When he had escaped the curses, he was able to bring with his finger and thumb this problem between good and evil from the ear of the horse, vowing never again to make use of such an horn of Oberon.

All would now have gone well, for he managed the beast as they do an harmonica, namely, slowly, so that the greatest criminal could have sat upon him, even the state itself, could there be any other tower for that, than the tower of Babel. All would have gone well, if he had not turned round upon his *statua equestris et curulis*, and seen a host with and without carriages quickly following,—pilgrims full of curses, the seven philosophers full of jokes, and at last the neat slender student. He determined therefore to diverge from the highway to the meadows, where there was a sheepfold, and where, partly from unsconsciousness of his ridiculous appearance, partly with blushing consciousness of losing reputation, and with the offer of money and kind words, aided by the bright eyes of gentle youth, he obtained permission from the shepherdess, that the horse should eat as long as it seemed necessary (for he knew nothing of the appetite of a horse) for his enemies to have so decided a start, that with mathematical accuracy he might rely upon not meeting them again, even should they stop for two hours at the next inn.

Thus saved and newly blest, he sat down in the cool air behind the shepherd's hut, shaded by a dark green linden tree, while his eyes drank deeply of the splendor of the green hills, the deep night of the dark blue ether, in which the snow-white silvery clouds were floating. His fancy, after the old custom, climbed the garden wall of the future, and looked into the paradise which was full of beautiful blushing flowers, while showers of white blossoms fell around him. After one or two flights to heaven he made three impromptu *Streck-verse*. Upon death; a children's ball; the sunflower and night-blooming violet. He could not indeed induce himself to leave the cool linden, even after the horse had had hay enough (he had fed for two hours), and resolved to journey no further than to the next so-called ale-house, a short mile this side of the city.

At one o'clock his enemies had halted there for their mid-day refreshment; and at the same ale-house his brother Vult rested, waiting for him, as he knew that the high road and the horse would lead Walt through the hamlet. Vult had to wait a long time; he therefore turned his thoughts to the nearest object, which, for instance, was the host, a Moravian, and his sign, upon which he had painted his own inn, with its sign; and upon that sign, another inn with the same sign.

At length, about six o'clock, as he looked out from his window, he heard the host call out, "Ho, fellow! is he going the upper way? is he going to pass?"

The inn stood upon a hill clothed with birch trees. Walt had come up the side by the Hernhutt burying-ground, through the pales of which the horse had plucked some husks, while the master suffered his dreaming eye to wander through this garden, sown with those who had been its gardeners.

Although he could not see the person through the birch trees to whom the rough bass voice belonged, he approached very slowly. Men of such delicate nerves and tender emotions as Gottwalt, are most easily wounded by roughness of voice ; yet he drew the pilfering racer's mouth from the pales, and continued with wet bit to the door of the stable. From thence he asked the serious host, who was standing bare-headed in the door of his house, whether he could lodge here with his horse ? At this question a heaven of stars opened in the breast of Vult, and continued there to shine.

The host also grew cheerful and sunny ; how had it happened that a passenger on horseback, so early in the evening and so near the city, had asked for leave to repose there ?

As he observed that the rider described a many, or at least a three-angled figure over the saddle as he alighted with his right leg from the horse, and that he bore his limbs heavily, as though a natural saddle were upon them, into the house, without looking further after the horse, or his state, the villain knew very well whom he had to deal with, and he laughed, not indeed with his lips, but with his eyes, at the guest, wondering how he could think it possible that the oats which he should charge the next morning in the reckoning would ever be placed before the white horse.

"Now comes," said Vult figuratively, as with a beating heart he ran down the steps to meet his brother, "a wholly new chapter."

No. 12. *False winding stairs.*

CHAPTER XIII.

KNOWING AND NOT KNOWING.

In the room for common guests below, Walt, after the manner of novices in travelling, that the host might not think he meant to spare expense, demanded a private room, and that a solitary supper might be speedily served.

Vult now entered with the easy, confidential, good-humored manner of a man of the world, and said he rejoiced that they had met for the night at the same place. "If your horse is to be had," he said, "I have a commission to purchase him for a battle horse, for I believe he will stand fire!" "He is not mine," said Walt. "He feeds bravely," said the host, who invited Walt to follow him to his chamber. As he unlocked it, they saw that the western wall was not so easily closed, for it lay a story below in apparent ruins; indeed a double ruin, for the new wall lay also near by in stone and mortar. "Besides," added the host, with pious calmness, as the guests looked a little astonished, "besides, in the whole house this is the only empty room. It is summer time, and the weather is warm."

"Good," said Walt firmly, and endeavored to

order, if it were only a broom to clear out the premises. The host went humbly to execute the orders.

"Is not our host a true sharper?" said Vult. "Indeed, mein Herr," answered the other, "I like this better. It is more beautiful. What a splendid reach of fields and villages meets the eye! Then the glow of the evening sky, and the light of the moon; even in bed we can have it to ourselves the whole night."

This consent to his destiny, this falling in with all the inconveniences of the inn, did not arise merely from that original sunny temper which led Walt to present to his mind only the gayest and pleasantest events, and to turn away from the emptiness of men, and the void of life; but partly also from that divine enthusiasm, that ecstasy of poetry, with which travellers, who were never before on a journey, especially such as Walt, close a day that has been filled with new views and new dreams. The prosaic fields of life are to them, as in Italy, bordered with myrtles, and the bare and empty poplars hung with clusters of the vine; Vult praised him for that wild-goat like faculty by which he could leap from summit to summit over the abysses of life.

"We should," replied Walt, "hold life like a trained falcon upon the hand, ready to let it soar into the ether, and again ready when necessary to recall it to the earth."

"Mars, Saturn, and the moon as it is well known," said Vult, "disturb our earth in its course, but that world within, very properly called the heart, should never be shaken in its course, or turned aside except by Pallas; the beneficent Ceres, or the celestial Venus! With your leave, mein Herr, we will unite our frugal suppers, and I will eat with you before this breach in the wall where the young moon will be reflected in the soup, and the evening glow will gild the roast."

Walt cheerfully assented. We prefer to make romantic acquaintances in the evening, rather than in the morning; but Walt, like every youth upon a journey, aspired to make many friends, especially of the respectable class, among which he reckoned the lively humorist of the green travelling hat.

The host entered with the broom, and swept from the apartment its rubbish and litter, while from his left hand finger hung a broad wooden-framed slate. He pointed to it, and said they must both record their names thereon, as here in the country, as in Gotha, every village host was obliged to present the names of those who had lodged with him at night to the magistrate in the city the next morning.

"Oh! we know you, host," said Vult, and seized the slate. "You are as curious to know what sort of a bird you have caught, as any governing court in Germany, that causes the certificates of all those who pass in at its gates to be seized, as it has no better Index *Autorum*." Vult wrote upon the slate with the pencil attached to it, the date, with this inscription, "Peter Gottwalt Harnish, publicly sworn notary and Tabellio on his way to Haslau." Walt afterwards took the slate to protocol his name and character. Astonished, he saw it there already, and looked alternately at the green hat, and at the host, who wailed till Vult again took the slate, and returned it to him, saying to Walt, so quickly that he could not catch the words, afterwards friend! *ce n'est qu'un petit tour que je joue a notre hôte.*"

He answered *oui;* but through the cloud of his exitement the most brilliant sparks were struck out, all presaging the most brilliant adventures; he was at this moment so filled with romantic expectations from the sports of destiny, that he would not have been surprised to meet with the most splendid fortune. It would not have exceeded his aspirations, although cherishing all the reverence of the son of a country justice for the higher ranks, if the daughter of a prince had fallen upon his heart, or the princely hat of her father upon his head.

We know so little what men dream, when awake, still less how they dream when asleep; we know so little of their greatest fears, that we will be silent about their greatest hopes. The slate was to Walt the chart of a comet that prophesied, God knows how, a new blazing star, that should shoot its path through the hitherto uniform Heaven of his life!

"Sir host," said Vult mildly, for he played the imperious part, as his brother did the more gentle, without pride, "*serve here*, a rich supper, and bring us a couple of flasks of the best genuine ***Kratzer*** that your shelves hold." *

Walt proposed a walk to the neighboring burying-ground of the Moravians while they prepared the supper. "I will bring out my flute," said Vult, "and blow a little over the graves of the buried Hernhutters in the evening sunset. Do you love the flute?"

"How very good you are to a stranger," said Walt warmly, for the whole conduct of the flute-player had disclosed, notwithstanding his haughtiness of eye and mouth, a deep inward love, truth, and justice. "Indeed I love it," he continued, "the flute is the true magical rod that changes all it touches in the inward world; an enchanter's wand at which the secret depths of the soul open."

"The inward world *is* the *true* world," said Vult; "the moonlight that shines into our hearts."

"Ah," said Walt, "the flute is still dearer to me," and he related how through music he had lost a beloved brother, and that he and his parents had hitherto borne such sorrow, that it would have been less painful to know that a dear relative was in the grave, than in happy hours to ask themselves, "with what dark and cold hour may now the wanderer be contending on his board in the wild sea of the world?"

"But if, as you say, your brother is a man of

---

* Sour German wine called a *scratcher*.

musical power, he can ride on the top of the wave in the great sea of the world."

"I mean," answered Walt, "that we formerly thought of him with sorrow — but no longer; and it would not be strange if every flute sounded to us like the voice of our night-wanderer, who can only thus speak to us." Vult caught involuntarily his hand, but gave it quickly back. "Enough," he said; "a thousand things affect me too deeply. Heavens! the whole landscape is hung with purple and gold, and full of perfume." His glowing soul could scarcely withhold for another half hour the fraternal embrace. The unrestrained confidence of his brother, both to-day and yesterday, had kindled a new flame, where every breeze upon his journey had blown upon one love coal after the other, and now the fire in his breast flamed up without the smallest opposition. Both walked in the lonely evening silently. As they entered the God's field, the rays of the setting sun shot horizontally over its surface. Had Vult gone ten miles around to seek a pedestal upon which to place the group of reconciliation of the twin brothers, he could scarcely have found a better than the Moravian garden of the dead, with its regular beds, where gardeners from America, Asia and Barbary were sowed, each following the other with that last beautiful swan-song of life, "*Gone home!*" How beautifully here was the bony spectre of death clothed in the living garment of youth, and the last pale sleep shrouded in wreaths and flowers. Around every quiet bed in which the true heart was planted, lived faithful trees, and the whole of loving nature looked with her young face upon them.

Vult, who had now become very serious, rejoiced that he probably had not to play the flute in the presence of a connoisseur, for, unaccustomed to such agitation, he had scarcely retained breath for the effort. He placed himself at some distance from his brother, reclining opposite the sun, and near a cherry tree, around which a honeysuckle was entwined, and blew, instead of the most difficult passages, only simple *ariosos*, with interspersed imitations of an echo, such as he believed would excite in the uninstructed ear of his brother the quickest curiosity, wonder and joy. It had this effect. Gottwalt, with a long branch of cherry blossoms in his hand, went backwards and forwards, from east to west, with slower and slower steps, far more blessed than ever before in his arid life ; for he looked upon the departing rose-color of the love-eyed sun, over the broad, green, burnished country, where pointed towers rose above the fruit gardens ; and then down upon the regular, white houses of the mother village of the silent, sleeping colonists of the garden ; and where the zephyrs seemed to awake the melodies of the perfumed landscape, and to open the leaves of the flowers. If he turned his excited glance towards the east, and looked at the undulating hill and valley, with country houses, and at the entrance of leafy woods traced upon the distant hills, upon which undulations the sky appeared to sink down, the tones of the flute seemed to play upon the rosy light of the heights, and to mellow the notes of the birds, that, like messengers of Aurora, fluttered around. Then there awoke upon the dark, sleeping thunder-cloud a living gleam of lightning; a zephyr from the east again bore the flute tones to the setting sun, and echo, like a lovely child, repeated the soft sound from a rose-colored evening cloud. The song of the lark disturbed not its harmony as it rose in the pauses of the flute.

Walt now entered an alley of fruit trees, whose giant shadows trembled in the evening light; heavily the sun swam upon its glowing sea, then sank beneath, and the illuminated summits of the hills gleamed a moment in the blue vault, and the echo died away like the splendor.

Vult turned, the flute still at his lips, looking for his brother, and saw him standing behind him, the quiet tears in his blue eyes, and blushing with this effect of his emotion, and the reflection of the crimson wings of the evening, while from the breast of the flute player the fountain of impatient love overflowed. Music reveals to men a past, and a future, that they never experience. Walt ascribed this emotion to the sounds alone, but still pressed with trembling love the creative hand. Vult looked at him piercingly as he said, "Ah, I was thinking of my brother, how could I at such a moment help longing for him."

Vult threw his flute aside, seized and held him off, for Walt would have embraced him, and said, with a piercing, burning look, "Gottwalt! do you not know me? Am *I* not your brother?"

"*Thou!* Ah, sweet heaven! And *thou* art my brother Vult!" and Walt fell upon his neck. They wept long. It thundered softly in the east. "Hear the voice of God," said Walt. His brother did not answer. Without another word, they went slowly, hand in hand, from the graveyard.

No. 13. *Berlin marble with shining spots.*

CHAPTER XIV.

THE ENCHANTING EVENING.—PROJECTED WIND-MILL.

To those who looked at the brothers from the door of the inn, as they strolled in circles in the fresh mowed fields, with long branches of cherry blossoms in their hands, they might have been taken for comedians, rehearsing to each other the parts of Orestes and Pylades; but they were exchanging, as they did the cherry blossoms, the history of the past; each, his own confessions. The exchange was too unequal. The flute player assured his brother, that *his* romantic adventures, artistically played through the whole breadth of Europe, interwoven with the strangest love passages, and heightened by his musical talent, might, if they had chosen to follow his footsteps, have been a rich fund for the novelists and romancers of the time; but now he had other things to say to him, and especially to ask about his *own* life. Somewhat of this brevity might have been induced by the thought, that there were chapters in his history, which would lessen the heartfelt confidence with which the pure minded, inexperienced brother had clung to him; he therefore merely remarked, "that people in travelling were, as at home, unrestrained and careless."

Walt's romance of life would have shrunk into that of the university romance that he played at home upon the settle, reading romances, and his *Acta eruditorum*, in the course between the hall and his own little study in the fourth story, had it not been for the Van der Kable will; but by this help, Walt's history became important.

He would have surprised his brother with all the particulars of this fortunate event, but the latter told him he knew all; that he had been sitting upon the apple tree at the examination, and had witnessed his quarrel with Shomaker.

Walt blushed painfully that Vult should have heard his outburst of anger as well as his verses. "Perhaps," he said with some confusion, "you came with the Herr Van der Harnish, with whom the candidate had spoken of him?" "Yes, indeed," said Vult, "for I am myself that nobleman."

Walt was much astonished, and asked, "who then had made him noble?"

"I myself, in behalf of the Emperor," he answered; "for of course it is only a deputy title of nobility."

Walt shook his head, "and not unlawful," continued Vult; "it is certainly permitted according to *Wiarda*, who says, without hesitation, that Von may be placed before the birthplace, or before the name of the ancestor from which one descends. I might as well have baptized myself Herr von Elterlein, as Herr von Harnish. Am I called gnadiger Herr?

I know I am listening to a Viennese, who addresses every citizen who looks like a gentleman thus; and I willingly leave them such an innocent custom."

"But how could you endure yesterday to see your parents, and to witness, at the supper table, the sorrow of our mother at your unhappy fate, without rushing down and falling on the care-worn heart?"

"I did not sit long enough upon the tree. Walt!" he said, suddenly springing before him, "look at me! To one of thy extensive reading, it need not be told how people formerly came home from their honorable wanderings through Europe, as rotten, worn, and shot-pierced, as a flag from a battle. But it would be immediately understood, if a flag-bearer of this kind were born in an old baronial house, where the picture-gallery of his ancestors, like Hogarth's tail-pieces, is closed with himself; if this young Count were before thee, risen from the dead, and his limbs clubbed together, like a Paris breakfast, from half the old world; his hair from the side walks of Vienna, his voice from the conservatory at Rome, his nose from Naples, where many a statue has a new one; his brain and many other things from the propaganda of death; in short, (for my figures are rather confused,) in short, he finds nothing upon the churchyard near him, but that into which he, as well as the bodies in the Church of the Innocents in Paris are wholly changed—*Fat.* But now look at me; at the blush of youth, the strength of manhood, the bronze of travelling, the flashing eye, the full life!

I need? what thou needest! Something to live upon. Walt! I have no money!"

"So much the better," said Walt, as indifferently as if he knew well the main wheel, the moving principle of all virtuosos; that they must be either too full or too empty, and only through these alternations could they move. "I have no more, but shall we not both have the inheritance?" He would have said things yet more generous, but Vult interrupted him. "I wished only to signify, friend, that I will *never*, through all eternity, stand in the presence of my mother as a prodigal son and vagabond, much less before my father! Could I enter the house with a long purse of gold; by Heaven! I would soon present myself. I assure you I often intended it. I once took extra post horses, to be able to bring them, in my own person, as fast as horses could fly, a considerable sum won by playing; but alas! I spent it all in the expenses of such a rapid journey, and had, half way, to turn back. Believe me, good brother, as often as I tried again, with the hope of succeeding, the money has melted away also."*

"Always money," said Walt. "Parents cling to their child, not to his gifts. How could you thus depart and leave our mother to that long, fretting sorrow, from which you have relieved me?"

---

* So oft ich auch nachher ging, und flötete, das Geld ging auch flöten.

"Enough," he answered; "might there not something be written of a Herr von Harnish (by a creditable man from Amsterdam or the Hague), that excellent young man, their son, whom he valued so much, and that this son had now means upon which to live? Ah! I could myself ride to Elterlein, relate Vult's history, and carry his letters to myself, to my father. My mother, I believe, would know me; or she would soften me too much, for I love her — as a child loves his mother —— Parting! didst thou say? I shall go with thee, brother!"

These words fell upon the ear of Walt like concealed music, that suddenly breaks out as upon a birth-day. He could scarcely forbear to express his joy, while Vult went on to explain his remaining in the city. First, and principally to be near him, like the unsuspicious singing bird, formed rather to fly above him in the free air, than to work beneath in a mine; while, under his *noble incognito*, he could watch the seven villains (the heirs); "for," said he, "I do not place much confidence in your own victory."

"You are, it is true," said Walt, rather embarrassed, "a travelled man, and a man of the world; I must have read and seen too little if I had not at once remarked it; but I hope, keeping my parents always in view, who have so long, chained at the oar of the slave-ship of debt, led a miserable life, and with all my faculties completely awake, I shall be able to fulfil the conditions of the will. I trust I shall myself gain the power to strike that chain asunder, and see them at last landed upon the shore of a fertile island, where, under the free heaven we may all embrace each other. On the contrary, I have hitherto felt only pity for the poor heirs themselves, and nothing reconciles me to the expectation of succeeding, but the thought, that if I fail they will not be the gainers, and my parents alone the sufferers."

"The second reason," interrupted Vult, "why I shall remain in Haslau, has nothing to do with the first. It merely relates to a splendid wind-mill, that will be driven by the blue ether, by which both of us (thou, in the mean time, fulfilling the conditions of the will) can grind as much bread as we need. Indeed, I know not whether there can be anything so agreeable or useful for either of us, as this ethereal mill, which I will project; the shearing mill, the ribbon mill of Bonne, the *Molæ asinariæ*, or asses mill of the Romans, cannot be compared with mine."

Walt was in the highest expectation, and entreated him to explain. "Above," he answered, "and with a glass of *Kratzer*."

They hastened up the hill to the inn, where they placed themselves quickly at the table, upon which their supper was laid out. The wine was placed upon a bench in the open air. Through the open wall of the apartment the last rays of the evening light were reflected upon the white table-cloth of their supper.

Vult immediately began upon the model of his future wind-mill, but with praises of Walt's yesterday's verses. He expressed his astonishment, that with such overflow of feeling, Walt could command such steadiness and repose in his poetry; like a Bavarian water carrier, who, with a tub of water, or of hippocrene upon her head, could venture to run a race, and not shake over a drop. Then he asked, "How, as a jurist, he had attained this poetical imagination?"

Walt drank the *Kratzer* with great pleasure, and said, doubtingly, that if indeed there were anything poetical in him, were it only the first incipient down upon the poet's wing, it came from his eternal aspiration while in Leipsic, to rest upon no lower point; but in every hour that the law left free, to climb the high Olympus of the muses, the only divine repose for his heart; and that no one had ever encouraged him, except Goldine and the candidate. "But, good Vult, upon this subject do not joke; our mother early called thee the quizzer;—is thy judgment serious?"

"I will hang myself, Tabellio," said Vult, "if I do not admire thee, and thy verses, from the power of a full, earnest, artist's soul! Would you hear more?"

"Why then am I so superstitious," interrupted Walt, and drank; "yesterday I met Plato, to-day thee! exactly my own superstition, that no good nor bad accident ever comes alone. You must yesterday have heard all my verses!" Walt was walking up and down the room, but stopped every moment to smile at the host's little boy, that he might not be frightened, who in the court beneath was throwing up potato-balls into the room above.

Vult began, without answering him, to describe the model of his air-mill, totally unconcerned, as every experienced traveller is, about any accidental fifth ear. "Dearest brother ànd twin laborer! there are some Germans, (for they write in it) such are those who make verses like yours. There are others, who do not wholly comprehend the language, but review it, and especially excellent jokes in the same. They wish to place a line of their own under the standard line of beauty, and acknowledge no poet but one who has a public office to support him, a thing just as bad as to have two diseases at the same time.* According to Lightfoot, no one was allowed to pass through the Jewish temple merely as a passage to another place; thus, a thoroughfare through the temple of the muses should be impossible. You should not pass over Parnassus merely to rush down into a rich and luxurious valley. — But let me begin again differently; let us not get angry; drink! now Walt! I have, during my musical travels, given to the press a satirical work in manuscript; The Greenland Lawsuits. 2 Vols. Published by Voss & Son, in Berlin."† "I am completely astonished,"

* Some passages are here omitted concerning the German cotemporary Reviews.

† One of Jean Paul's earliest works.

said Walt, reverently. "But I should mislead you without any purpose, if I were to try to make you believe that the publication of these volumes had made me known in the smallest degree!"

"However, we must be just," he continued, "and I dare not pass over the fact, that it is with books like salted meats, that, according to Hexham, when moderately and properly salted will keep a long time, but with too much salt they spoil immediately. Walt, I made my book too good, consequently too bad."

"You overflow with conceits," said Walt, "when speaking sportively; have you then as many windings and heads as the Lernean serpent?"

"I am not without wit," answered Vult, with a coxcombical expression, trying in vain to make his brother laugh; "but you interrupt me. What can I do with my wit, I alone? Nothing; but with thee, much; — namely, a work, a book. A pair of twins, their own opposites, must together produce a book that would be unique! an excellent double romance! Within its pages I will laugh, you shall weep, or soar! You shall be the evangelist; I the animal behind him; each supporting the other. All parties will be satisfied; man and wife, master and servant, I and thou. (Host, more *Kratzer!* but the genuine.)"

"Now what sayest thou to this project and millstream by which we shall grind out and make splendid celestial bread for our customers, as well as daily bread for ourselves? What sayest thou to a mill turned by Pegasus?"

But Walt could say nothing; he merely embraced the project maker, and was silent. Nothing excites men more, especially reading men, than the first thought of appearing in print. Old, forgotten aspirations, deep wishes of his heart, started at once full grown and perfect into the mind of Walt, and threw out their luxuriant blossoms; as in a southern climate the northern shrub or brier grows up to a Palm-tree's height, so Walt saw himself celebrated and inspired for long weeks upon the poetical tripod. In his ecstasy he doubted of nothing but the possibility of accomplishing such a thing, and asked, "how two men could write together, and where they would find a romantic plot?"

"Plots, Walt? I have upon my travels lived a thousand and one, and heard of many more. All these shall be taken collectively, and well mutilated and disguised. How can twin authors dip into the same ink bottle, dost thou ask? Beaumont and Fletcher, utter strangers, or enemies, stitched together on a common tailor's board comedies and tragedies, for whose seams and stitches critics to this day pick and feel. With the Spanish poets a child has often nine fathers, that is, a comedy has nine authors. And, of the first book of Moses thou mayest have lately read, that is, if you have read Professor Eichhorn's Commentaries, that three authors take part in the history of the flood, beside the fourth in Heaven. In every epic work there are chapters, in which men must laugh at digressions that interrupt the life of the hero. These I think the brother who blows the flute can make and furnish; but of course there must be perfect equality, as in a Republic. Each must have as much servitude and night-watching as the other. If this be done with discretion, we may bring forth a work, a Leda's egg, that shall only differ from the Homer of Wolff in this, that in the Iliad so many Homerists have written, that perhaps even Homer himself may have taken a part."

"Enough, enough!" cried Walt, "let us now rather go out and observe the beautiful evening about us." Indeed, without, life shone in every eye. The guests, who had already supped, drank their beer in the open air, all ranks standing and sitting together; the *authors in the tièrs-état*. The bat, like the tropical bird of beautiful eastern lands, skimmed above their heads, announcing fair weather on the morrow; and on the rose hedges crept the sparkles of the glow-worm. The distant village clocks, and the lowing of the herds upon the hills, sounded like a lovely echo from ancient time. They needed not, although so late, not even in the thickets a light, for by the reflection of the western sky they saw distinctly the heads of the reapers above the high summer grain. The twilight spread far and broad from the west, with the slender silver crown of the moon upon its head, while at the back of the house crept on unseen, the great deep night from the north. Even at midnight, there was a tender glow in the west, like the color of the apple blossom, and the lightning, faintly flashing from the east, played upon its delicate red. The surrounding birch trees shed their perfume upon the heads of the brothers, and the haycocks their fragrance from the meadow. Many stars peered out in the twilight, and lent wings to their souls.

Vult forgave his brother that he was so restless with joy. He, poor devil, had so many things in his head, and among them the *Kratzer*. This terrible wine was a true vineyard poison for Vult, and, like memory, carried him back to his twentieth, his eighteenth, and at last to his fifteenth year. We often meet people who will swim back to their earliest years, even to the fountain's head. The abbot in his morning's visitation sermon says, *be ye like little children*, and in the evening, when he and his monks return to the cloister, they stammer and prattle like children.

"Why do you look at me so, dear Vult?" asked Walt. "I am thinking of past times," he said, "when we used to beat each other. The battle pieces hang like family pictures in my memory. I was angry at such times that I was stronger and more passionate than you, but you, with your courage and the elastic quickness of all your limbs, often had me down. Ah, Walt, those innocent childish pleasures will never come again!"

But Walt saw and heard nothing except the radiant car of Apollo, as he fancied it rolled towards him, and upon which he already saw the colossal figures of their future romance. He was already composing great sections of the book, and would have repeated them to his wondering brother; he would at length have listened, but Walt continued to insist upon a title for their book. Vult proposed *Flegeljahre*, but Walt said decidedly he could not consent to a title at the same time so wild, strange, and indeterminate.

"*Good*," said Vult, "thus may the double nature of the work, as by a new favorite author, be indicated upon the title page. *Hoppel-popple, or the Heart*, *this* must be the title."

Both mingled again with the company. Walt took his glass, and turning unperceived by the others to Vult, said softly, "Happiness to our parents, and to the poor Goldine. They are doubtless at this moment sitting without a light, and talking of us." The flute-player took out his instrument and played to the laborers assembled there some common waltzes. The late host began a slow dance with the sleepy boys, many of the guests moved their legs in involuntary measure. Walt shed joyful tears, and looked into the faint, western light. "I might, indeed," he whispered in his brother's ear, "treat these collected wagoners with beer?"

"Probably," answered Vult, "feeling their honor injured by such a proposal, they would throw you to the bottom of the hill. Heavens! they are Crœsuses to us, and look down upon us!" Vult suddenly called upon the host, instead of dancing, to serve *them*; but Walt, in his poetical enchantment, could neither eat nor drink. "For my part," said Vult, "I respect all that belongs to the stomach, that balloon of the human centaur. The *Real* is the Sancho Pansa of the *Ideal;* I often go so far as to make noble souls, that is, female souls, ridiculous, when in my imagination I represent them to myself as eating, etc." Walt suppressed his displeasure at this speech, when suddenly, with distant thunder, a summer cloud floated over leaf and grass, and the golden evening light looked through the tear-dropping night. All nature became a perfect flower, that breathed fragrance, and the freshly bathed nightingale drew a long stream of melody through the night. "Do we now miss the trees of the Park, or of Asia, or the attendançe of servants, or services of plate and crystal glass, upon which often play false colors?" asked Vult. "Truly not," said his brother, "behold nature places the most precious gem upon the marriage ring of our union." He meant the lightning. He would again have spoken of their double romance, and of collecting the materials, and said that behind the sheepfold he had to-day composed three *Streckverse.*

But the flutist soon wearied of the same subject, and after exciting emotion, needed the refreshment of a joke. He therefore asked Walt why he came on horseback? "I and my father, before we heard of the inheritance, thought that thus I should be better known in the city," said Walt, "for at the gates, you well know, only horsemen are mentioned in the Intelligence sheet." This made Vult renew his joke about Walt's riding; he said, "Your horse goes as, according to Winkelman, the great old Greeks always went, slowly and surely. He has not the fault of watches, to go quicker, the older they are. But perhaps he is not much older than you are, Walt, though a horse should always be younger than his rider, as the wife should be younger than her husband. He is a beautiful Roman monumental stone, with the inscription, *Sta viator*, for every one who sits upon him."

"Ah, dear brother," said Walt, gently, but blushing with emotion, and scarcely understanding Vult's humor, "say no more of *that*. How could I help it."

"Ah, ha! hot gray head!" cried Vult, and reaching his hand across the table, he stroked the fine curls from the white brow of Walt. "Read me, then, the verses that you made behind the sheepfold." He read the following.

THE OPEN EYE OF THE DEAD.

"Look not thus at me, cold, fixed, unmeaning eye! Thou belongest to the dead! Yes, to the departed! Veil that eye, oh ye friends! *he is not dead, but sleepeth!*"

"And wert thou so melancholy this beautiful day?" asked Vult. "I was as happy as I am now," said Walt. Vult pressed his hand, "that pleases me; thus is the true Poet; go on!"

THE SUN-FLOWER AND THE NIGHT-VIOLET.

"The gorgeous sun-flower boasted, 'In the day

I am the favorite of Apollo, I expand in his presence. He wanders around the globe, and I, his favorite flower, follow in his path.' The night approached, the violet whispered, 'In the lowest thicket I conceal myself, and bloom only in the short night. The mild sister of Apollo shines for an instant upon me, and I am observed. Then am I plucked to die upon a human breast!'"

"*The night-violet* must remain the last flower in this day's wreath," said Vult with emotion; for art played as easily upon him as he jested with nature; and embracing his brother, he retired.

Walt's night was sown with wide beds of violets, as there came to his pillow through the open wall the perfume of the refreshed landscape, and the clear morning song of the lark. As often as he opened his eye, it fell upon the thickly starred western sky, where the late constellations went down, one after the other, as announcers of a beautiful approaching morning.

No. 14. *Model of an Accoucher's chair.*

CHAPTER XV.

THE CITY.—FURNISHED LODGINGS.

WALT arose the next morning with his head full of the morning glory, and was seeking his brother, when he saw his father, who had left home at one o'clock, upon his long legs, and pale with walking, striding through the court of the inn. He called to him, and Walt was obliged to defend himself through the broken wall against the reprimand of his father for being there. After this Walt entreated him to mount the horse, while he would run on foot by his side. Lucas accepted the offer without thanks, and longing for his brother, who durst not show himself, Walt left the stage where their innocent and joyous comedy of the previous evening had been played.

Upon the horizontal road, from which no water-drop could roll, the horse moved blamelessly along, at an equal step with the humble pedestrian, so that the father, from the pulpit of the saddle, could send down innumerable rules of life and jurisprudence. But how could Walt listen to them? He saw only within and without the bright morning fields of youthful life, or the landscapes on both sides of the road; or, more distant, the shaded flower-garden of love, and the high, the cloudless mount of the muses, and at last the towers and columns of smoke from the outspread city.

Lucas told his son to mount, and ride through the city gate to the butcher's with the horse ; then to his new lodgings, and about ten o'clock to repair to the sign of the *Soft Crab*, where he would meet him, and immediately go with him to the magistrate.

Walt mounted, and flew like a cherub through heaven. The weather was so enchanting that the rows of white houses shone in the clear day. In this dewy garden of the morning even his poor beast was poetical, and as he came hungry from the stable of the Moravian, he trotted on, unurged towards his own. Walt sang aloud in sympathy with his horse, as he looked down from the Etna of the saddle upon a widespread life, full of the *fata morgana*, and saw the inverted city and ships hanging mirrored in the air.

At the gate they asked Walt "From whence?" "From Haslau," he answered hastily; and then, recollecting, improved his error by saying, "to Haslau." The horse, like a sage as he was, now assumed the direction, and brought him safely through the populous streets to his stall, where Walt in haste, but full of thanks, dismounted, in order to be able directly to seek out his *furnished lodgings*. But he willingly paused to listen to the full, animated cries of the city, as well as to look at the narrow streets, like the alleys of a pleasure-camp, although he was pleased that he could not find the court agent,

Newpeter in them. Thus he gained time to disinter the holy city of childhood, to put the pieces together, and to carry away the rubbish; so that at last the same streets came out in the sunlight;—as ornamented, as broad, and as full of palaces, and of ladies, as they were, when as a child he had once passed through them. Now, as at that time, he was amazed at the eternal noise of rushing carriages, the lofty houses with their ornamental statues, and the flitting gala and opera dresses of many of the passers by. He could scarcely believe that there was in the city, a Wednesday, a Saturday, and such plain, rural gala days; but he thought the whole week must be a series of seven days of festival. And very bitter was it to him to believe, for he must indeed observe it, that such common people as smiths, shoemakers and tailors, and even other toiling members of the state, that belong indeed to the villages, dwelt and went about among the finest people. He was astonished also at every working-day dress, for he himself, although in the middle of the week, had come with his Sunday coat of nankin. He filled every great house with splendidly dressed lords and ladies, invited by the hospitable host, and looked up expecting to see them at every balcony and window. He threw sharp glances upon every gilded carriage, upon every red shawl, upon every *friseur*, who found occupation for every day of the week in preparing others for the feast. He looked at every head of sallad, that was being washed in the running fountains in the morning, instead, as at Elterlein, only on Saturday evenings.

At length he came to the lackered door with the gilt title leaf upon it, "Merchandise, by Peter Newpeter & Co.," and went in through the shop door. Here he waited in the lower store, till the clerks, springing here and there, had served every one who had entered before him. At last a friendly apprentice asked, What would he have? "Nothing," he answered, as gently as possible. "I came for my furnished apartment, and wish to present myself to the Herr court agent." The boy directed him to the glass door of the office. There sat the agent, with more silk in his morning gown than the justice's wife had in her whole Sunday suit; and after finishing a letter, he turned a round, and red face upon the tenant.

The notary probably thought, with his riding spurs and his riding whip in his hand, he should present an imposing appearance; but to the agent, who had business with the greatest people all the week, and was their creditor through the year, threescore of travelling notaries were of no great importance. He called out sharply to an office boy, to show the way to the gentleman. The boy called again, from the upper step, to a very beautiful, slender, but ill-natured young maiden, to show the gentleman with the spurs to the fourth story. The stairs were broad and polished, the banisters were garlands of wrought iron, all well lighted. The entrances to the apartments, as he ascended, appeared beautifully gilded, and upon all the thresholds lay large variegated carpets. On the way, Walt sought to cheer the silent maiden for her trouble, by praising the neatness of the apartments, and to reward her for her care by gently requesting to know her name. She answered, shortly, "*Flora!*" and with this name alone the beautiful, but obstinate little girl must go down to posterity.

The *chambre garnie* was opened, and indeed for few persons had it been any other than a *chambre ardente.* Many persons who had slept in the Red House in Frankfort, or in the Palais Royal, would not have been overpleased with this room, crowded with the most ancient, cast-off furniture, hidden here after being excluded from the splendid apartments. But a poet, a man perpetually inspired, and in the heavenly months of youth, always looks upon the hardships of life as a connoisseur looks upon the severe cartoons of Raphael, merely through a softening, poetical glass; and in every fisher's, every dog's, and every peasant's hut, opens a window and cries, "Is it not beautiful—without?" One, who in the Escurial, which is built like a gridiron, would have found its warmth; in Carlsruhe, which is like a fan, its coolness; in Meinungen, that is like a harp, or in the shell-fish, that is like a pipe, would always find only sweet tones. I mean, that a man like the notary, with a head full of wide views over the whole summer flora of his future life, estimates lightly the amount of honey already in his hive, and at every entrance deposits a small layer, gathered from a thousand flowers; we should not be much surprised if such a man, disregarding the furniture, rushed instantly to the window, and tearing it open, cried out, in the presence of Flora, "What a heavenly prospect! Beneath, the park; here, a part of the market place; there, the two church towers; and above, the mountains; — truly, it is beautiful!" Besides, he wished, through these signs of his own satisfaction, to give a little joy to the poor girl.

He now threw off his little nankin coat, and in shirt sleeves began to put his things in order; so that, when he returned from his disagreeable appearance before the mayor, he might be completely at home, and have nothing to do but go on with his Elysium, his poetry, and perhaps do something for the out-sketched double romance. The rubbish of time, the dregs of past fashions, that the agent had suffered to accumulate in his chamber, he took for delicate indications of the especial regard the merchant would manifest for him. He bore one half of twelve green chairs, covered with cloth, and stuffed with cow-hair, into his bedroom (else, from the abundance of seats, he could not have stood in his room), and added them to an old umbrella of wax cloth, and a fire screen, ornamented with a female profile. From a *commode*, a small house within a house, he drew with both hands one story after the other, that it might be ready for the deposite of his baggage, that had been brought to town. Upon his tea table of tin, both cold and hot would have been drunken *cold*, for it would have cooled both. Walt was astonished at the superfluity in which he should in future revel. But there was yet one Paphos there (he knew not indeed what it was), a sort of book-safe, with glass doors; but as the glasses and locks were gone, its use was incomprehensible. However, he deposited his books upon the upper shelves, and his notary business upon the lower. A defaced, blue painted table, pasted over with a variety of cut pictures of hunting, flower, and other subjects, at which he could sit and compose, when he did not prefer his work-table with deer's feet, on which there was an ink fountain of lackered metal, and upon which he laid his fine paper for poetry, and his coarse for business. These, are perhaps the most important articles pertaining to his apartment, if we leave out trifles, such as empty counter boxes, a ladies' work table, a dark basalt Caligula, that from want of gravity could no longer stand, a small cupboard, etc.

After he had once more looked round upon his cell and its order, and once again from the window upon the white gravel-walks beneath, and the dark, full-leaved, umbrageous trees of the park, he prepared to go to his father, and rejoiced, as he descended the broad stairs, that he possessed a poor nest in such a costly house. On the steps he was arrested by a light-blue envelope for the lady of the court agent; it was perfumed like a garden, so that he immediately rose upon a cloud of perfume to the elegant writing cabinets of the most lovely queens, duchesses, and countesses. However, he held it his duty to go through the store, and honestly deliver the envelope with the words, "that it was for Madam." When his back was turned, the whole collective clerks and boys laughed outright.

He met his father at the appointed place, who introduced him to the assembled guests of the Crab as the universal heir. Walt blushed, to stand on this account, an object of remark, and hurried on their appearance before the mayor. Bashful and timid he entered the council-room, where, contrary to his nature, he stood as the elevated bridge of the instrument, upon which the strings of other men's hopes were stretched. He cast down his eyes before the accessory heirs, who had come to confound their breadstealer. The proud Newpeter only, failed, and also the church-rath Glanze, who was much too celebrated a preacher, both in the pulpit and at the writing desk, to go three steps to see an undistinguished man, from whom he demanded not only to be sought with the greatest eagerness, but also the greatest admiration.

The principal executor, who was the mayor Kuhnold, at the first glance was made the secret friend of the youth, who with such painful blushes was placed alone, at the covered table of fortune, before so many ravenous and repining spectators. Lucas, on the contrary, only watched everything with sharpened attention.

The will was again read. At the end of the third clause, Kuhnold pointed to the morning preacher Flachs, to whom the house had been justly assigned. Walt quickly cast upon him eyes full of congratulations and good wishes. When he heard the fourth clause, in which his dead benefactor addressed himself personally, the tears that he was ashamed to shed *there* would have fallen, if the alternate praise and blame had not made him blush. The laurel crown, and the tenderness with which Kable had placed it upon his brows, excited in him a warmer love, than the horn of plenty that he had shaken over his future life. The succeeding clauses, which foretold only advantages to the seven heirs, took away the breath of the justice Lucas, while they enabled his son to breathe more freely. At the ninth clause, which, upon his unsullied swan's breast, could suspect or forbid the shame spot of female seduction, his whole face was one entire crimson flame. How could, he thought, a friend of man, upon his death bed, write so coarsely?

After the reading, Knoll required that, according to the eleventh clause of the will, Harnish must take an oath of him, to borrow nothing upon the prospect of the inheritance. Kuhnold said he had already promised the same thing. "I can take the oath," said Walt, "to me it is the same thing; a word is as binding to me as an *oath*." But the honest Kuhnold would not suffer it.

It was protocolled that Walt had chosen the notary

business as the first condition of the fulfilment of the will. His father desired a copy, to have one taken for his son to study daily, as his old and new testament, the rule and guide of his life. Pasvogel looked at, and studied the heir, not without satisfaction, and did not conceal from him his longing for the possession of *those poems*, which the testament had cursorily mentioned. The police inspector, Harprecht, took him by the hand, and said, "we must often see each other. You will be no enemy of mine, and shall always be the friend of the heir. We must b used to each other, and then we can as little d without each other, as without the old post before ou window, which, as Le Bayer says, we can never se removed without emotion. We will give each oth pet names, for love always speaks with diminutives.

Walt looked him in the eye, but Harprecht kept his unchanged, and steady.

Without the least form of leave taking Lucas parted from his deeply touched son, to visit the Kable inheritance, the garden and wood without the gate of the city, and to look, as long as it would take the clerk to copy the will, at the lost house in the Hundstrasse.

Gottwalt again breathed the breath of spring when he left the council chamber, that narrow, damp, winter conservatory, where he had been as much withered and oppressed, as if sad and melancholy flowers had been left there through the ice of the winter. He had for the first time witnessed the hot, ravenous hunger of the worldly heart, and seen himself hated, and also entangled in the meshes of avarice. The inheritance which from a distance had filled his fancy like a mountain full of varied prospects, now fell upon and oppressed him, excluding itself from his view! His brother, and the proposed Romance, that in his narrow world had held out the promise of the infinite, had become to him as to the prisoner, who sees without the bars of his cell blooming branches waving, and butterflies darting forever before him, and strives in vain to reach them.

The agreeable intoxication that every one feels for the whole of the first day in a new city, had been dissipated in the council-house; at the *table d'hôte*, where he dined, nothing came over his tongue, except something smoked like itself. No warm brother sound, to which he could speak or answer. He knew not where to find Vult, and on the fairest day of his life he remained at home, that if Vult came he might not fail to find him. In his solitude he prepared a small insertion for the Haslau war and peace Messenger, wherein he advertised who he was, and where he might be found as a notary. Also a short anonymous *Streckvers* for the poets' corner, entitled,

THE STRANGER.

"Rough and dark is often the veil of the soul, while within, so pure and transparent. Like the grey crust upon ice, that, when severed, reveals within a pure blue light, like the transparent ether. Thus remain veiled to the stranger, but be not concealed from thyself."

I take this opportunity to remark, that it is no advantage to the poet, that his *Streckvers* cannot be printed as one long line; and it were much to be wished, that it would not give the work a ridiculous appearance, if there could flow from it long paper streams of wings, such as the child places on his mimic ship, for sails. But I fear even that, would not save it from shipwreck.

After this, Walt purchased in the shop three insignificant visiting cards; for he thought it his duty to present to the two daughters of the house, and to the lady herself, his name upon them. As he hastily offered his insertion at the neighboring printing-office, his eye fell with affright upon the latest weekly sheet, where yet stood, in wet letters,

" *The Flute Concert.* — I must continue to delay, as a rapidly increasing complaint of the eyes forbids me to read the musical notes. Van der Harnish."

What a heavy sorrow Walt bore from the printing-office to his own room! Upon the spring of his whole future summer a deep snow had fallen; that his happy brother had thus speedily lost his joy-giving eyes! for his part, he could lose his own with weeping. He walked idly up and down his room, and thought only of him. The sun rested already exactly upon the western hills, and filled his chamber with golden particles; but the beloved one was not there, whom yesterday at this very hour he first again received. At length he wept like a child, from a violent home-sickness and regret, that he could not in the morning have said to Vult, "good morning, and farewell!"

The door opened, and the full dressed flutist entered. "Oh, my brother!" cried Walt, with a painful joy.

"Donner! hush! speak low! there are people behind! Call me *you*,"* whispered Vult. Flora entered after him. "To-morrow-morning, Herr Notary, I wish that contract to be engrossed," he said aloud. "*Tu parles Français, Monsieur?*" "*Miserablement*," answered Walt, "or not at all." "The reason, Monsieur, that I came so late, is, that I sought out and hired my own lodging, and, secondly, called upon one or two strangers; for, whoever would make many acquaintances in a city, must do so the first days after he arrives; it is only then, that one concerns himself about him. When they have seen him often, he is like an old herring, that has been too long in an open cask, upon the market."

"Good," said Walt; "but my whole heaven fell from me when I read in the newspaper of your eye-complaint;" and he drew softly to, the door of the sleeping-chamber where Flora was preparing the bed. "It is well so," said Vult, shaking his head,

* Brothers call each other *thou*.

and he thrust the door open. "It was done for the sake of modesty and beauty," answered Walt, at the head-shaking. — * * *

"The German artistical public never bite more deeply than in wounds and anomalies," said Vult. "I mean merely this; that, for instance, a painter is very well recommended, and paid by the public, who paints, perhaps, something with his left foot, or a horn-player, who blows the horn with his nose, or a harper, who seizes the harp with his teeth, or a poet who makes verses, but only in his sleep; and in the same way, a performer on the *flauto traverso*, who sometimes plays well, may enjoy the second advantage of Dulan, and be totally blind. I once gave to á bassoon player and a bass violist, who travelled together, the advice, that to make their fortune, one should engage to play the bass viol upon the bassoon, and the other the bassoon upon the viol."

Flora departed, and Vult asked his brother what he meant by his Latin, on closing the door. Gottwalt embraced his brother, and then said he was so made, that he was ashamed and tormented when he saw beauty like that of Flora's in a servile condition. Beauty, in humble life, was to his mind like an Italian Madonna in the midst of Dutch low-life pictures. "Or," said Vult, "like that Corregio in Sweden, that they have nailed upon the royal stables instead of a shutter. But tell me something about the testament."

Walt told him *all*, except that he forgot to say anything of the third clause.* "Since the stroke of the vane of that poetical wind-mill, placed on the height by the builder, the *will*," he said, "has become of little importance to me."

"I don't like *that*," said the other. "I have been the whole afternoon arranging my glasses and reflectors, in order to observe from a distance the gentlemen accessory heirs; and seeing them thus, most of them deserve the gallows cord in this world, for the umbilical of the next. Thou wilt, indeed, through them have a difficult task to gain the inheritance." Walt looked very earnestly at his brother. "For," continued the other gaily, "if one only thinks of the agreeable *no* and *adieu*, when the beautiful Flora comes and asks for orders, with the *Belvidere* of her beautiful face, and, as witnesses, the seven ill stars, the disinherited heirs, to steal the inheritance, who, perhaps, merely on account of the ninth clause, have placed Flora here, merely to deprive thee of"——

"Brother!" interrupted the angry and shame-crimsoned youth, who hoped he was speaking ironically, "is this the language of a man of the world like thyself?"

"O, pure, stoical friend," said Vult, "poetry is like a pair of skates, with which, upon the pure, smooth, crystallized floor of the *ideal* you may easily skim, but miserable are they to thump about upon the common streets."

---

* The loss of the house.

He broke off, and asked him why he had found him so melancholy? Walt, who was now ashamed to acknowledge his home-sickness, merely said, "that as yesterday had been so charming, he found, that like all pleasures, it had ended in disappointment; and the news of his threatened blindness, which he had met in the newspaper, and could not yet quite understand, had grieved him."

Vult now made known his plan, which was this; healthy and sound as were his eyes, he intended to represent himself in the newspaper upon every market day, with failing sight, and, at last, as stone blind, and, as a blind man, to give a concert, which would attract as many spectators as hearers. "I see," said Vult, "you are mounting the pulpit-stairs, but don't preach. Men deserve to be deceived. Towards you I am pure and open, and prize your love of mankind, far above mankind itself." "Oh, how can a man dare to be so proud, as to look upon himself as the only one to whom the full truth is imparted," said the other. "A man," answered Vult, "must have some chosen one, to whom, when he has involved all others in vapor and fog, he can open his breastplate, and the breast itself, and say, *look in!* That one art thou, merely because thou hast, according to thy opportunities, some knowledge of the world, and art, moreover, an innocent, firm fellow; a pure poet! in that, my brother! Ah, my *twin* brother; and — so let it pass."

Walt knew well how to place himself in the position of another ; he saw, upon the beautiful form of the beloved brother, those freckles and scars, produced by a wandering life, and believed, that a life passed in the shade, like his own, would certainly have protected him from his many-colored, moral nettle-stings.

Till deep into the night, the brothers united peacefully their efforts to bring their double romance into some decided outline ; and before morning, the whole historical quarter of the celestial hemisphere arose so clearly above the horizon, that Walt would the next day need nothing but chair, pen and paper, to begin it. He saw, with delight, the morning sun of Sunday arising, while Vult thought only of the evening of that day, when, as he said, " like a blind finch, he could pipe."

No. 15. *A gigantic shell.*

CHAPTER XVI.

SUNDAY OF A POET.

Walt rose in his bed as the summits of the western hills, and the church-tower were reddened with the beams of the early July sun, and repeated his morning prayer, in which he thanked God for his future life. The world was yet undisturbed; upon the mountains vanished silently the mists of night, and anticipations of rapture, like birds of Paradise, arose softly upon the Sunday morning. Walt would have been afraid to express his nameless joy before any other than God. He arose and began to write the Double-Romance. It is well known that among all chapters, none are written so blessedly, and perhaps read so willingly, as the first and the last, as though they were a Sabbath morning and Sabbath evening blessing. Especially was he refreshed that he durst now, without any sting of conscience, go wandering upon Parnassus to sport *there* with one of the muses; for he hoped that he had yesterday worked in his own appropriate juridical business, when he had listened to, and maturely considered the testament.

The evening before it had been determined, that, through one long volume, the hero of the romance should desire and search for a friend only, not even for a heroine. Thus, for the two hours that he wrote, his hero suffered as many years in the book, he himself feeling with him, the infinite longing. This desire for friendship, that double flute of life, arose from his own solitary breast, for his precious brother could as little understand and spare him a friend, as his father.

He often sprang up, looked at the golden, perfumed morning, opened his window, and blessed the whole happy world, from the poor girl, drawing water at the fountain, to the joyful swallow in the blue sky. Thus the mountain air of our *own* poetry, draws all beings nearer to the heart of the poet; and, raised as he is above common life, the greatness in his own breast reconciles him with the littleness of others. The poetry of others, on the contrary, elevates the reader only, but does not lift the world and its affairs to a level with him.

By degrees the Sunday sounds, the cries of the swallows, the church-bells, and the backward and forward walk of the clerks in their Sunday coats, in all the corridors of the house, made it difficult for him to sit longer. He longed for one after another of the living beams of the sun, of which, in his western apartment, he could see only the reflection and the light. Not long after, when the sun-illumined nature, together with that of the writing-table, had held alternately their magnetic staff above him, the former gained the victory, and he bore his breast full of the air, and his head full of landscapes (for Aurora's golden clouds played upon him even in the streets), into the gay, noisy market-place, and to that quarter where the princely military guard was stationed, with flute and drum. The tower of the Church of St. Nicholas, tuned in another key, sent forth a wind music that destroyed all harmony. Then there were magical sounds of joy coming from a distance, and moving his inmost being to follow. These he found were without the gate, and came from a flying corps or choir of *Currende* boys, who were fuguing and singing in the suburb. Splendidly, in front of the gate, waved the variegated full-leaved Van der Kable garden, which, if he began and continued his career aright, he would at last inherit. From conscious shame, as there were people sitting therein, he would not enter, but turned aside, and ascended to the neighboring Van der Kable wood upon the hill.

He looked with rapture upon the dew and sunshine; towards heaven, and over the earth. Imperceptibly he sank into his anticipatory dreams, that are so different from the narrow after-dreams of reality; — reality plants a thorny hedge around the former, while the sporting-ground of the *possible* is ever free and open. Upon this latter arena he proceeded to erect the great, sublime image of a friend, and to chisel it (which he dared not do in the romance) exactly as he desired it for himself.

"My eternally beloved friend, whom I shall certainly some time or other meet, he said to himself, is a divine, a beautiful youth, and, moreover, noble; either the heir to a throne, or a count; of course, he must be nobly and delicately formed, and, according to his rank, perfectly accomplished. His face partakes both of the Roman and Grecian, but his classical profile is chiselled from German marble. He is not only the most courageous, but also the mildest spirit; and in his breast, armed with iron to protect others, he bears a heart of yielding tenderness. So true, so unspotted, so strong in love; yet, like a mountain-ridge, of adamantine power; exact, with a true philosophical genius; a soldier, or at least a diplomatist, and, more astonishing still, poetry and music move him even to tears."

Once, in a garden at the hour of summer twilight, Walt had listened to a poem upon the friendship of past ages; of that Grecian phalanx, that even till death, fought and loved; of the German league, of men united for defence and protection, and the longing for friendship seized like a pain upon his heart, and he dreamed of a friend that loved as he did.

The dream was rent asunder by a tall, beautiful youth, in a scarlet uniform, seated upon an English horse, that flew over the high road to the city gate. A well-dressed beggar, ran, hat in hand, now after him, now before him, to attract his attention. The youth turned the horse about, the beggar turned also; the youth searched his pocket, while the proud dance of the war-horse continued so long, that Walt could apparently remark the melancholy upon the face of the rider, like moonlight upon spring blossoms, with a proud profile, and eyes that seemed to present a victory over life. The youth threw his watch into the hat of the beggar, who bore it by the chain, while he endeavored to follow the rider with his thanks.

It was beyond the power of Walt to remain another moment from the city, into which the youth had entered, who appeared to his imagination the Godlike, *the friend*, whom he had just now, in his day-dream, adorned with all the gifts of all the Gods. "*Friends* shall we easily be," he said to himself, strengthened in his romance by the prospect of the inheritance, and trusting in his own love-gushing heart; "friends should we certainly be, if we could only once meet."

He would have gone to his brother, to cool the thirst of his heart upon his breast; but Vult had requested him, on account of spies, until after the blind concert, to receive his visits, rather than come to his lodgings.

In the midst of this holy, sacrificial fire, the court agent, Newpeter, called him into his dark office before dinner, to protest a bill of exchange — like the May fly, which, coming from a long, delightful excursion, suffers the delicate wing to hang for awhile under its little case; however, Walt did the business with true pleasure, for it was his first act as a notary; and what was of more importance to him, his first act of gratitude to the agent. No time was to him so long and burthensome, as the first quarter, when a man sheltered, or boarded, or served him, merely because so much service and trouble was advanced without the smallest return from him. He protested well, but was obliged to ask of the smiling merchant the day of the month, and was indeed scarcely himself. For, when a man first descends in his poetical air-balloon, which he has suffered to rise with the eagle into pure ether, and suddenly touches the earth, he still hangs beneath, suspended upon the silken globe, and looks confusedly around.

Thus went the Sunday morning. The afternoon appeared to begin differently. Walt had retired from the gay *table d'hôte*, where, with his powder and his nankin he had sat in the midst of satin, Manchester cambric, curled locks, swords, rings, and plumes, to his shadowy apartment in full Sunday costume; for he could not throw it off, as it consisted only in the powder with which on Sundays he was sprinkled. While, looking as white, perhaps he enjoyed the Sunday as well as the prince, who called Sunday dressing-day. Even the beggar remains always open to the pride of decoration; for, does fortune waft him a rag with which he can mend his greatest rents, he looks new-born and elated around, for he can still excel poorer beggars than himself.

But now, Walt's happy resolve of living poetically the whole afternoon, with his head and his romance, was beyond his power. Merely on account of this Sunday ornament, he found it difficult to keep his resolution, to live poetically. A powdered head works with difficulty. The present author is an example of this; for if there were placed before him, at this moment, as a trial, a royal mantle, coronation stockings, gilt spurs, or the hat of a crown prince, he would be obliged, thus decorated, to lay aside his pen, without having brought the description of this afternoon to a close. Except, perhaps, for the departed Buffon, there has been no inspiration in splendid ornaments; of him, Mde. Necker informs us, that he must first put on his gala dress before he could invest his thoughts in any dress, and when he was himself arranged, he arranged his nouns and adjectives.

Not only the powder, but the heart also, with Walt, had been disturbed. The beams of the afternoon sun glided one after the other into his chamber, and drew him irresistibly to the free outward world. He felt that Sunday *Heimweh* (homesickness), which is more heavy and far better known to the poor than to the rich. How often in Leipsic, on beautiful Sundays, had he borne this vesper melancholy through the deserted streets, and far out into the country! Only when the sun, and the pleasure-loving world had gone home, could he be relieved from his melancholy. I have known poor, tormented chamber and nursery maids, who could laugh and dance six and a-half days in the week, on Sunday afternoon be unable to eat; on that day, their heart and their weary life were too heavy; then they dwelt so long upon the memory of their obscure, humble home, till they found therein some little dark place, even an old neglected grave of father or mother, and there they sat themselves down, and wept till the mistress came home again.

Countesses, princesses, West-Indiennes, baronesses! ye, who, like true women, rule the slaves of your beauty more severely than the slaves of your service, be not imperious to the latter on Sunday afternoon. The people in your service are often poor country people, to whom the Sunday, which does not exist for them in cities, in the great world, or upon great journeys, was, in their childhood's time, when they were happy, a blessed day of rest. Willingly do they stand by thee, on thy festivals, empty and thirsty; upon thy marriage and funeral feasts, without any wishes of their own, they hold the plate and the dress; but on Sunday, the festival of the people, of humanity itself; the day upon which, with them, turn all the hopes of the week, and the poor believe that some few of the joys of the wide earth are guaranteed to them; that on this day, the joys of childhood, of that time when they really had some part in this covenant of grace and peace, must return again. That blessed time, when they had no school hours, their best apparel, resting parents, playing children, the evening roast, green meadows, and a walk within them, where the social freedom of the fresh heart adorned the whole fresh world. Dear ladies! if then, on Sundays, these, thy menials, wade less deeply into labor, that Lethe of the past and the present; if their dark life invests them more painfully, and, sighing over the unfruitfulness of the present, they recall the merry sounds of their pure childhood, which to every man promises an Eden — then chide not, nor punish their tears; but let the longing, homesick soul, wander without thy castle-gates, till the going down of the sun.

While Walt yet sighed, Vult stormed hastily in, with the mid-day wine in his head, a black silk band over one eye, his collar open, his hair flowing, and asked, why he sat moping at home, and how much of the romance he had written in the morning? Walt gave it to him. He ran it through, and said, "Thou art the very devil, Gotterchen, and an angel in writing. Go on thus. I have also," he continued in a colder voice, drawing the manuscript from his pocket, "I have also worked upon our *Hoppel-popple*, or the Heart. I have expatiated as much as will be necessary for a first chapter. I would repeat it to you, *this Comet*, for such I shall call these digressions, if, oh heavens! you only knew and relished me better; but for this reason I cannot read it. In these comets I do not spare young writers who differ from you, and, in their romances, use poor friendship as the handle of a previous love; as superfluous, as the almanac, or a catalogue of reigning heads before an anthology of beautiful extracts. The sickly hero appears in the first sheets, as though, from all the foldings of his heart apparently, he sighed for a friend, an eternity of friendship! Is the work in letters? He pours out his longings to his correspondent; yes, he languishes for a new world — a world of perfection! But scarcely does he see a young maiden, (while the reader is looking for a friend,) than both love and friendship are secured; although the friend appears now and then, even to the final sheet, where, on account of the faithlessness of the maiden, the friend is also abandoned, and the hero finds no heart, no virtue, nothing great upon the earth. Here, brother, I spit fire at the writing public. Villains! I say in the Comet, villains! be at least honorable, and then, do what you will, for your distinction between a friend and a lover, is only that between a hedge-hog and a hedge-dog."

Here Vult looked long at the paper, and then at Walt. "But is there?" said the latter. "Such my Comet asks," answered Vult, "for, according to Buckstein, there are no real hedge-hogs.* But of what use is it to your romantic authors," Vult continued, apparently reading, but adding a little more satire than he could find in the manuscript, "of what use is it to turn your earth-born pages towards heaven; they of themselves turn back; they are like the glasses placed over plants, the earthly side only is covered with dew; or like the electrical cat, one must draw a spark from the tail, before one can be drawn from the head.

"*Love*, distractedly, in your novel, for that is in the power of every animal, as of every maiden; and

* Buckstein's Natural History of Germany.

although the latter, for this reason, looks upon herself as a noble, a poetess, or a recluse, of friendship, a thing as rare among them as among animals, they know nothing. For you have never been able to learn from John Müller's Letters, nor from the Old Testament, nor from the ancients, what constitutes a holy friendship, and its divine divergence from love; that for which it is longing and striving; not the thirst of one half soul for another half soul, with which it may unite in marriage to form a whole; but the desire of a *whole* for a *whole;* a brother for a brother; a God, for a universe, not in order to create, and then to love, but to love and then create."

"Thus the Comet goes on," said Vult, and could not forbear to press the hand of his brother, whose chapter on friendship, like pure, warm, natural blood, had flowed into his heart.

Walt was delighted, but could not forbear to ask, if friendship might not succeed love — love of the same person; or even marriage; and thus the warmest and truest lover, might become the warmest and truest friend? And whether love, in itself, had not created much more romantic poetry than friendship; and whether, at last, it might not pass over to friendship for, and descend to love of one's children? He thought, also, that Vult was too severe with his ready illustrations. Yet longer would Gottwalt have delayed and objected; but Vult, distressed by his former emotion, and disappointed at the limited praise he had received from his brother, closed his ear against all justification of humanity, and said, that he saw only too plainly, that Walt, in the future novel, by over-sugaring of all good qualities, would turn them to acidity. "Your mild qualities will gain by being opposed to my sharp ones; for, exactly behind the sharp finger-nail lie the tenderest and most susceptible nerves. But," he continued, "to speak of something agreeable, of these seven heir-thieves, for whom, on your account I give myself some trouble, I must sometimes sit with you and speak of them."

"First of something *more* agreeable," said Walt, and described to his brother the divinely beautiful youth that he had seen, like a God of thunder upon an eagle, hovering between Aurora and Iris, and passing under the blue heaven as under a triumphal arch. "Ah, I thought to-day, after I had written the chapter on friendship, could I but touch his hand! Ah! do you know him?"

"Not as a God of thunder," said Vult coldly, and took his stick and hat. "But do not sit and grow mouldy in your stork's nest; walk out, as I do, to Rosenthal, where you will see all the Haslau *beau monde*. Perhaps we shall hunt up the said thunder God — possibly it is the Count Klothar. — No, friend! I go intentionally without thee. If we meet there, do not appear as though you knew me, in case, from my blindness, I should pass near you; for it is imperative that I must make myself blind. — I mean the public. Adio!"

No. 16. *Melted metal.*

CHAPTER XVII.

ROSENTHAL; OR THE VALLEY OF ROSES.

Three minutes afterwards, without having perceived Vult's ill-temper, Walt stepped gladly out upon the green path that led to the Haslau Rosenthal, which differs from the beautiful Leipsic Rosenthal, in this, that it possesses roses, as well as a valley, and is, therefore, more like the *Phantasie* in Bayreuth, which is only superior to it in its confectionary arabesques, and flowers that ornament the artistical paths. Walt could scarcely get from the city, as he found half of it on the way, and his soul was light with the thought of this participation of the pleasures of others. Upon the right and left were fields and waving meadows, rejoicing in the summer. He heard from the city the sound of the afternoon church bells, and thought within himself, how the church-goers would long for the green warm earth, and while they sat sighing upon their cold stone benches, would think of the beautiful broad sun stripes, and hope, that after church, they might rush quickly into the country.

The unbroken stream of human beings continued through the enclosed path to Rosenthal, and through the vista of the trees. Walt saw the splendid picture of a July Sunday; its small tables, each under its overshadowing tree. "How beautiful," thought Walt, "is this picture," as he observed the running to and fro of the waiters; the spreading of tents; retreating to green leafy shades; laying off of shawls; drawing of corks, choosing tables; and saw the plumed hat, stooping between the children in the grass; and the musicians behind, who would certainly begin immediately to play; the warm, blooming maiden brows, that shone like garden roses through their white veils; the work-baskets they held, the golden crosses and other jewels on their necks; and the gaiety and hope with which more people kept streaming in. "Oh! you dear people," he said, "may you truly enjoy the hour."

He placed himself at a solitary table, that he might not disturb any party, and while overflowing with the sweetness of his own happy spirit, he rejoiced in the thought, that now, indeed, almost in the whole of Europe, Sunday and gala-day were the same thing; desiring nothing, but that new heads might appear; for he looked at every one to see if it belonged to his military youth, for whom all the flower-leaves of his soul were expanded.

A clergyman passed by, before whom, as he sat, he took off his hat; he thought, that as priests in the country are accustomed, merely by the color of their dress, to move every hat in reverence, he would be pained, if, in the city, *one* remained firm when he passed. The minister looked sharply at him, but found he did not know him.

At this moment two knights, Vult and Flitt, cantered round, of which the one had little to live upon, the other, nothing. The Alsatian danced about gay and richly dressed (although his "*te deum laudamus*" consisted in "*laus deo*") among his acquaintances, that is, among every one present, for he was beloved of everybody whom he did not *owe*. He supported gaily a cursory attention, drawn upon him as one of the men who would, perhaps, inherit a portion of the Kable estate, a portion which he had already mortgaged among his creditors, and multiplied as often as the relics of a saint; because his Marseilles ship, upon which he had as often pledged a dividend, remained too long at sea.

Walt was surprised, while he observed with pleasure, that this gay dancer, who greeted all the women, took their fans, parasols and bracelets, and raised to his eyes with his own fingers, the medallions and watches suspended from their white necks, posted himself exactly before the table of the three plainest, to whom he was as attentive as to the most beautiful of their associates. These were the three Newpeter ladies, to whom Walt had yesterday sent his three visiting cards. In a short time, the Alsatian, by continued circulation, had made known to the whole of Rosenthal, that the silent Nankin sitting there, was the heir of old Van der Kable. Walt, too attentive to others, and thinking too little of himself, continued his benevolent dreams, never suspecting the side-glances of displeasure, that were turned upon him. At length Flitt stepped towards him, and made himself known. Among all the seven heirs, the gay beggar appeared the least embittered towards Walt, and this so won the hearty love of the latter, especially when he saw him the first to carry round the plate for the musicians, that Walt would willingly have thrown in a great piece of the inheritance as a reward.

Walt was particularly curious to know how his brother bore himself in this delicate and refined manner of life. It consisted in this, that nothing in the world appeared strange or new to him ; he troubled himself about nothing, and his outward manner was as though he sat warm, and at his ease, at home. "Does not such a manner," thought Walt, "indicate contempt or severity ? To appear as if there *were* no first hour of an acquaintance, but to enter boldly and confidently, as if it were the second or the tenth ? "

Vult now drew near the most beautiful of the ladies with the coldest and most composed face, and while he complained that his eyes were every day worse, he looked at them apparently like Myops, or as if his face hung pale and impassible, like a shapeless mist from a mountain point. Walt, who believed that he had seen in Rudolph's garden, in Leipsic, what refined manners and polite men were, and with what *empressement* the young clerks served the enchanting daughters of their employers, was much struck by

Vult's repose of manner, and manly self-command, which seemed to him a true refinement, and he resolved to alter his definition of fine manners, as it stood in the romance. He condensed it into the following words. "Personal dignity consists in the smallest possible motion, a half step, an imperceptible bow, a gentle motion of the elbow instead of stretching out the hand. In this way, I shall, in future, recognise the true man of the world."

At last, even the notary gained courage, and full, as he thought, of the true art of life and knowledge of the world, he rose boldly and began to walk about. He could thus occasionally catch, aside, a word from his brother, and perhaps discover the military favorite of the morning. The music, which, by its inferiority, only enhanced the loveliness of the songs of the birds, bore him harmlessly over many cliffs. But what a Flora of rich people was there. He enjoyed the quiet happiness, that he had often wished for, to be able to lift his hat to more than one acquaintance, even to Newpeter & Company, who scarcely thanked him; and he could not refrain from drawing a comparison between his present delightful situation in the Haslau Rosenthal, and the poor anonymous position which he formerly held in that of Leipsic, where, beside the few that he could not exactly pay, no cat knew him. How often, in that time, when he was unknown, could he have been tempted to perform some extraordinary feat, to dance upon one leg, or utter an inflammatory speech before heaven and earth, merely that he might draw to him those who would sympathize with him. Thus do men thirst; the young run after men and books, merely because they are men, while in after life they will scarcely stir for either great men or great books.

Walt remarked, with much satisfaction, that Vult, notwithstanding his cold repose and dignity of manner, evinced much courteousness in his conversation, and showed so much experience and so much acquired knowledge of the picture cabinets of Europe, of artists, celebrated people and public places, that he was really enchanting; in this it was true, he was not a little aided by his flashing black eyes, and also in the coldness which imposes, and like water, in freezing, is always elevated. An old court lady, of the little reigning house of Haslau, would scarcely part with him, and distinguished gentlemen held him in conversation. But he had the fault to love nothing so much as disenchanting, except perhaps, enchanting; especially, like an electrical body, to draw others to him merely to thrust them off again. Walt was more astonished at Vult's fancy for women, by the women themselves; for he could, even in passing, very well understand what Vult had said, that in their life, as with their fans, they turned the richly painted side towards others, and concealed that which was empty; and that the truly poetical, but treacherous art of man to interest women, was to anticipate the spiritual past of those they wish to please, that is, their past dreams and what else the heart has desired, which, like that little mute placed in the horn of the woods, makes its music sound like a distant echo.

"You play upon the flute?" said the lady of the court agent, addressing Vult. He drew the mouth and the middle pieces from his pocket and showed them. Both the homely daughters and some beautiful strangers besought him for one piece only. He merely placed the pieces again in his pocket, and referred them to the notice of his concert. "You give lessons?" asked the agent. "Only by letter," he answered, "for I am sometimes here, sometimes there. Not long since I placed the following advertisement in the newspaper. 'The subscriber informs all those who apply to him in post-paid letters (and he writes no others), that he will engage to give them instruction upon the splendid *Flûte traversière*, of whose merits it is unnecessary here to say more. He will, on every post-day, inform them by letter how to place the fingers, to seize the holes, to read the notes, and to keep the tune. Faults which they impart, he will in the next letter obliterate.' My name was subscribed."

The Haslauers could not but laugh, although they apparently believed him. The Lady Newpeter asked her daughters for tea. The tea-chest had been forgotten. Flitt said, gaily, he would mount and ride to the city for the chest, and return in five minutes, unless his horse, that is, his borrowed horse, should fall; (for Flitt's entrance into all houses was also the freedom of the stables;) he would also bring, he said, the Herr van der Harnish an approved pair of spectacles.

Vult treated the man and the offer, as Walt thought, somewhat too proudly.

Flitt really came cantering back, after seven minutes' absence, without the spectacles, for he had only promised them, but with the mahogany tea-chest, whose looking-glass cover displayed the duplicate of the tea-cadies.

Suddenly, as a man with a rich scarlet livery and a round hat stepped forth from the so-called poets' path, Vult rushed upon the promenading Walt, pretending, like a near-sighted person, not to know him, and asked, with many compliments, "if he was conscious that red liveried person was the Count Klothar?" When the notary shook his head, he excused himself on account of his increasing blindness, and said aloud, "Pardon an imperfect sight. I took you for the Herr Waldherrn Pamsen, from Hamburg, my intimate friend," and left him with the consciousness of an embarrassment, whose source Walt sought, not in his own simplicity, but in his want of travelling, which is said to take all that is wooden from men, as transplanting takes the woody particles from cabbages.

At this moment, the knight of the morning really appeared in conversation with a stranger, stepping from the thickest part of the grove. He was dressed in a blue frock coat, but with a plumed hat and order-stars upon his breast. The flute-player had only to cast a cold glance at the excited countenance of Walt, to know that the man of the morning had again appeared to the warm heart of his brother, and to perceive that Walt knew it was from irony, he had substituted the red livery for the blue coat. Walt drew nearer to him; and this Apollo of his imagination appeared better, nobler, and more blooming than before. Involuntarily he raised his hat. The distinguished youth bowed silently, looked inquiringly at him, and then placed himself at one of the nearest tables, without demanding anything of the alert red-coat. Walt walked backwards and forwards, for he hoped to receive a word or two from the full horn of conversation, that the beautiful youth poured out to his *follower*.

"If," began the youth, (the wind wafted the word *books* out of hearing,) "do not make one good or bad, they at least make one better or worse." The voice coming, apparently, from the inmost heart, entered the inmost heart of Walt. "How touching," he thought, "is this voice; worthy of the melancholy expression of the face!" The other gentleman answered, "the art of the poet leads its possessor to no decided human character." (The conversation had apparently arisen from the subject of poetry.)

"I do not deny it," said the blue-coated youth calmly, and without the least gesture, and Walt passed more frequently, that he might hear him, "but am of opinion, that every science entered into voluntarily — theology, jurisprudence, heraldry — not only exhibits a wholly new and established trait in men, but really produces it. So much the better. The state makes men only one-sided, and consequently, of only one character. The poet, therefore, should strive to place all the sciences, that is, all-sidedness in himself, for, in the state, he alone has the power to look at all the one-sided individuals under a new point of view, when, soaring above all, he can overlook and unite all."

"I am not sure of that," said the stranger.

"I will give an example," interposed the count; "in the whole mineralogical, atomistical, or dead kingdom of crystallization, the straight line, the sharp corner, the angle, rules; on the contrary, in the kingdom of plants, ascending from them to man, the spiral, the cylindrical, the line of beauty rules. The state, sir, like the science of mineralogy, wills that its arsenic, its salts, its diamonds, and its lately discovered metals, should shoot out into smooth tables, prisms, into parallelograms, so that they may be easily walled together. On the contrary, living, organizing power, which is therefore isolating, wills not that the whole being should be of one piece. It lives in itself, and draws its sustenance from the whole world. Such is art. It seeks the fullest, most perfect development, and an independent form, and is to be imagined only as God formerly was represented, as a circle or apple of the eye; all-seeing."

Walt now compelled himself not to listen as he walked. He felt delicate misgivings, that he thus secretly carried away the noble youth's opinions; and although they were openly and loudly expressed, he leaned conscientiously against a tree, and looked the blue coat in the face, to indicate that he was listening to his conversation; but the youth disliked this, and immediately left the table.

Walt followed at some distance. Fortunately, the count passed through a strange motley group of men, who were collected around a work of art. It was a ship, about the height of a boy, upon the shoulder of a poor fellow, with which he hoped to come to land; and by this little ship-loom, weave and hold together the thread of his hungry life. As Walt observed the youth place himself near the sailing-apparatus of the poor fellow, he pressed also nearer. The captain sang his old song, of the parts of the vessel, the masts, the spars, the sails, the ropes, and the rigging. "This must be dog-wearisome, to repeat every day the same thing," said the gentleman to the count. "Such is the result with everything," the other answered, in the tone of a teacher. "In everything that is repeated daily, there must be three periods; in the first it is new, then old and wearisome; the third is neither—it is habit."

Vult now approached. The notary gave him to understand, by a wink, the news of the *Found*. "But, captain," said the count to the owner of the ship, "the braces of the foresail should run from these great ropes to the Schinkel blocks, six or seven feet deeper through the block, and then under the deck.

Where is then your fore-tackle, the sheet-ropes of the sails of the fore-mast, the guy-ropes? &c. &c."

* * * * * *

Here the count, to indemnify the shipper, who concealed his own ignorance under admiration for the knowledge of a stranger, presented him a freight of money, such as his provision ship, and bread wagon had yet never brought from either Indies; neither from that of the noble, nor from the citizen coast.

Walt, in his new astonishment at such nautical information, united with such philosophical views, could with difficulty suffer the proud youth to pass by him without, as he could not press him to his breast, pressing him to his side, so that the blue-coat looked earnestly at him. Vult had vanished. But now the youth, with his servants, mounted and flew away upon their beautiful horses. Walt remained behind, like one enraptured, in the valley of Jehoshaphat, a secret, silent Bacchant of the heart. "This is exactly the man" he said, "that I warmly desire; so young, so blooming, so noble, so proud; probably an Englishman, as he bears philosophy, ship-building and poetry, like three crowns upon his head. Dear youth! How would you be beloved, if you would only permit it!"

The declining sun now shook its roses into the valley. The musicians were silent, refreshing themselves with the silver collected on the plates. People began to go home. Walt walked hastily around four tables, where the most beautiful ladies had sat, more for the pleasure of touching something that had been near them. He now went home, a single drop in the running stream of people, but a drop that reflected the clear rose-color of the evening sun without, and the light of genius within.

"Soon," he said to himself, as he saw the three city towers, upon which the evening golden sunshine was melted, "soon I shall learn from my Vult, who and what he is, then God perhaps will present him to me."

How interesting to him were all the young men on the way, merely on account of the blue-coated one. "Why," said he to himself, "should we love only children, and not youths, for are not these as innocent as children?" He was enchanted with Sunday, because every one, through his clean dress or his ornaments, felt himself poetical.

Gentlemen, heated with their walk, carried their hats in their hands, and spoke in a loud voice. The dogs ran joyfully, without sharp orders, from their masters. A number of children had harnessed themselves as horses, to a child's coach, full of children passengers, and all were gay and well dressed. A soldier, with his weapon upon his shoulder, led his little son home by the hand. Another led his hound by a red silk handkerchief. Many people went hand in hand, and Walt could not understand how any of the passengers could divide such finger-pairs, such love-knots, by passing straight on, instead of deviating from the path; for himself, he always went round. He rejoiced, especially, that every poor housemaid seemed to partake of the spirit of the age; that her scarf was as wide, and as Grecian in its shape as that of her mistress, so that there remained but little difference between her's and that of the most fashionable. Close to the city gate the school-children were playing about, and a respectably dressed maiden gave to the grim-looking sentinel a wreath of flowers for his weapon. Thus the whole world appeared to Walt so deeply bathed in the evening glow, that the clouds seemed to scatter roses upon the earth.

No. 17. *Rose-wood.*

CHAPTER XVIII.

THE SULLEN SPIRIT.

It needed not a diplomatic understanding, to guess that Walt would not remain at home this Sunday evening, but, however late, would go directly to the house of the theatrical tailor, where his brother lived, to learn more about the blue-coated youth. The latter received him below, and hastened down the street, which became, on festival nights, the hall, or corso of the people, and proposed a walk. Walt acceded with delight. To walk up and down under the stars, with the multitude on Sunday night, made him imagine, he said, what Italy must be, where, as now, one was never obliged to lift the hat, and might go on and continue to dream undisturbed. He was eager to speak, but Vult desired him to be silent till they reached other and more silent streets, and on no account to say *du.* "Just as you wish," said Walt. In the twilight, it was unremarked, that like a flower with dew, his heart was unconsciously overflowing with love, and he could not avoid greeting, silently, with his hand, the passers by, for he did not know, as he said, that he should ever greet them again. He even ventured, in the most shaded places, to look up where the most respectable ladies were leaning on the balconies, and to imagine himself among the guests, and standing as a *betrothed* by the side of one of the beautiful maidens, and with almost insupportable happiness, looking down upon the passers by.

At length, in a narrow street, he unfolded to the flute-player his splendid historical romance of the afternoon, which, as Vult found out during their walk, consisted in meeting the blue frock. "One might have sworn," said Vult, "that you came from Gladheim * rather than from Rosenthal, and had brought with you either Freya or Siofna ; or at least have married a Goddess, and brought a couple of pockets full of worlds as her dowry. Yet it is worth boasting, if a man can appear in a gala-dress of happiness, so little worn and tarnished (I can count the threads in mine), except when a man thinks not, that the enchanted hall of pleasure is the ante-room to the robber's castle." But Walt described the blue coated youth as the elevation upon which this day's vintage had ripened, and asked his name and residence. His brother answered, indifferently, that he presumed it was the Count Klothar, a rich, proud, extraordinary philosopher, who played the Briton indeed, but was else, well enough.

Walt was not pleased with the tone of his brother, and repeated the rich conversation and rare knowledge

* The valley of joy in Walhalla.

of Klothar. Vult answered; "in this, I see the too evident vanity of pride." "I can't endure," said Walt, "that men, who are undoubtedly great, should be humble!" "And I," answered Vult, "cannot bear, that English pride, or Irish, or Scotch, which indeed takes a very favorable aspect in books, should step out into reality, and boast itself. In romances we are pleased with strange exhibitions of love, with sentimentality, even with affectation, but in life it is all intolerable."

"No, no!" said Walt, "I like it only as I like your own pride! If we examine the subject, it is not the pride that makes us angry, but the want of foundation for pride; and for this reason, humility often displeases us as much. Our hatred of pride is not from envy of greater advantages than we ourselves enjoy, for we acknowledge the really great; it is the false, that is *imposed* upon us that we hate, and our hatred is not from self-love, but from hatred of injustice." "You philosophize like a count," said Vult, "but here dwells the count." Walt looked with inexpressible joy at the lighted front of a garden villa, whose glittering windows from the rear of the building were towards the street. It was approached by a broad vestibule of rows of noble trees. At this view, Walt suffered his thirsting soul to pour out to his brother all its poetry and all its hopes of love. The flute-player merely answered, (it was the way in which he expressed his anger,) "indeed — in certain points — however — just so — oh heaven!" all, added to other casual remarks, indicated that Klothar was not far removed from what, in common language, is called *an egotist.*

Walt held himself pledged by his avowed friendship, to defend the unknown count against this charge, and supported this defence by appealing to his noble physiognomy, and asserting that it was thus darkly shadowed, because he was looking in vain for the sun that would awake from its consecrated ashes, the ancient phœnix of the altar of friendship; and no heart could close against a love purely disinterested. "At least," said Vult, "before you present yourself to his groom of the chambers, put on a star and a prince's hat, or bind a blue garter beneath your knee; then, but not without, you may make your court. I myself, though I descend from such a noble, hoary ancestry, that his own is extinguished in my presence, I had to yield to his precedence, when with him! And how do you intend to make your friendship known to him? Merely cherishing it in your own heart will not avail." "From to-morrow," said Walt, innocently, "I shall seek to approach him, that he may read in my face the love that dwells in my heart, and will be written *there*, Vult."

"Van der Harnish! for heaven's sake why do you say Vult! You build then upon your conversation, upon its eloquent power?" "Yes, indeed," said Walt, "what else has a man to build upon, to whom so rarely, deeds are possible?"

The flute-player was astonished to find in this

modest being, who idolized the higher ranks, a quiet, firm confidence in his power to conquer them. The thing was this. The notary, for many long years, ever since he read the Life of Petrarch, had looked upon himself as a second Petrarch, not merely from his resemblance to him, in the power of creating small poems, but because the Italian was sent by his father to Montpellier to study law, which latter he abandoned for poetry; but the principal resemblance consisted in this, that the elder Petrarch was an able statesman. Walt believed, from the conversations he had many times held with Goldine and his mother, that he might, without presumption or vanity, reckon upon the same resemblance to the Italian, if he could only be brought into the right position. At this very moment, there is, perhaps, hardly a youth in Jena, Weimar or Berlin, that passes over the market-place, who does not believe, that like a shrine, the sanctuary of a saint, or a mummy-case, he bears secretly about within him, a spiritual giant, and that when the shrine or the mummy-case could be opened, the said giant would be found within, alive and vigorous. Yes, the writer of this sentence was, in early life, five or six great men in quick succession, as he imitated them exactly. But when we come to years, that is, to understanding what is really great, we find ourselves to be — nobody.

"Let us walk together up and down here," said Walt, who, enraptured with his own fancies, perceived nothing in Vult's replies, but his usual affectation.

"In bed rather; we may disturb Klothar, who already lies in his; for I hear, that to-morrow very early, he will begin a journey of some days," said Vult, as if he wished through these means to make Walt show all the treasure of his love.

"Sleep peacefully, beloved!" said Walt, and left willingly the place, and then his displeased brother. He returned full of joy and peace to his home. In the quiet streets, the stars alone looked down. As he passed the market-place, he saw through the opening of a northern street the glow of the midnight sky, as it was reflected and played upon the water of the fountain. In the clear blue, little clouds, as though belated in the day, hurried towards the west, and perhaps, bore along the genii who had showered their rich gifts upon the human day. Walt, as he entered his solitary apartment, could not suppress his gratitude, nor his tears as he gave thanks.

Very early the next morning, he received a letter from Vult, and also a sealed enclosure, inscribed, "for the proper time." The letter read thus: —

"Friend, I demand nothing of you but a short invisibility, until my blind flute concert is given, for which I have reasons, that you must yourself understand. We can write to each other very often. Should my blindness increase as it has hitherto, I shall play on the fourteenth, like a stone-blind Dülon, merely that the musical public may not be obliged to slip from one week's newspaper to another. I pray you execute no *instrument* without previously writing to me. I hope you will spare the family honor when you seat yourself upon the weaving-bench, to weave that well known ribbon-web of friendship, and that you will reckon upon me, that if it is necessary, I am ready to do all in my power to promote this friendship.

"Place your seal next mine upon the enclosure, and send it back. At the proper hour it will be broken for you. Adio! VAN D. H.

"P. S. It is necessary, on account of my blindness, to write to me with inch long letters, like these!"

Walt wrote as he requested, but from his love of truth, he would not refer to his brother's blindness. He agreed to all that Vult required, but complained of their separation after so short a union. Afterwards he promised to impart to him every step of his success with the count, and every pleasure that he shared with him. Walt recognised in this invisibility of his brother, only a careful worldly folly, or cheat, that would build itself up against the smallest accident; but nature too often, in spite of all precaution, betrays our wisest plans to the world, and to our enemies. The sealed packet might as well have been given unsealed, as Walt rejoiced in an opportunity to exercise true faith towards himself and others. The sealed letter read thus: —

"It is uncertain, dear brother, whether you will ever read this letter, and thus I can write without disguise.

It has tormented me deeply, through the whole night, that no one knows whether, after the breaking of this seal, we shall address each other as brothers. In any case, thou, not satisfied with the friendship of thy brother, as he is with thine, art already seeking a fresher and newer. It is not worth mentioning, that, wholly on your account, I remain in this stupid city of Haslau, and wage war with the infernal angels, and devils, and sharpers, that torment me; but that a man, who has already upon his travelling carriage, half worn out, martyred and broken his heart, should bring one back, and dare to trust to an exchange with thine — thine, which, though inexpressibly pure and warm, is also completely open to all the world. Yes, the compass-plate to the whole universe. Now a count arises, and mounts its throne, as if *he* were a brother; while I must sit upon a low bench, or upon a child's stool. Oh, brother! *this* burns deeply into my heart. This going in gangs, this countrymanship of love with all comers; surrounding the heart with other hearts, so as to make an Archipelago of friendship! Oh, friend, this is not to my taste. I must know, and hold close to me, all that I love!

"Should I, indeed, extend over you the sultry poison-tree under which I have slept this night, I could trust your kind, gentle, sacrificing nature; but I would eat all its fruit, rather than be thus humiliated. It displeases me already, that, to you, I have blamed the count so much. See for yourself! choose for yourself. Let your own susceptibility impel you to, or from him. I would, myself, lend you every bird's wing, every rope-ladder, every winding-stair, to lead you to the exalted count, with whom I am so angry. But then, when you are completely enchanted, or wholly disenchanted, I would loose the seal from the following description of this gentleman.

"It cannot be endured! The vanity of pride and of egotism, are the burning and freezing points of his ellipse. The vanity of a young stripling does not displease me; for I notice him not at all, or I look upon him as a picture-cabinet, where his own person is alone reflected. A glass for his own peacock's feathers. I willingly give to every male coxcomb, who would establish himself as an elegant, in a fashionable journal, a wide berth. Ah, such fools trouble me little, or not at all, who openly, who freely and without disguise, declare their vanity; but he who denies or disguises it; he who inserts the peacock's tail behind the wings of the eagle; who goes dressed in black on Sunday, only because the wearer of false jewels goes in white; one, who gravely combs his bald head; who weaves, nightly, like the spider, the web in which he catches the buzzing fly of flattery, swallows, and again stretches his net; one, who willingly unites the pretensions of philosophers and fools, is naturally, and, therefore, voluntarily, egotistic. Yes, I say, egotistic!

"Brother! if a man requires much of other men, I am willing to consent to it, provided he is willing to give as much in return; and in any collision of his own interests with another, acts generously. On the contrary, a genuine, unscrupulous self-seeker, who demands, without shame, the love that he rejects; who would grind the whole world in a cochineal mill to color his vest or his cheek red; one, who looks upon himself as the heart of the universe, the veins of which serve only to impel or repel his blood; and for whom the Creator, the devil, and the angels, are only stewards and silent servants; the rotunda of the earth and the present century, the serving establishment of his pitiful self! Walt! it is well known, that such an one I could strike dead, and bury him in cold blood. The passions are at least bold, generous, although destroying lions—egotism is a quiet, deep-biting, ever-sucking, venomous bug. Man has two chambers in his heart; the one for himself, the other for a friend; but the latter had far better be empty, than filled with that which is false. The egotist, like the insect and the worm, has only one chamber in his heart. You, I believe, lend the right to women, and the left to men, and contrive to dwell as well as you can yourself in the pericardium. Of this count I will say nothing else, but that he, a Protestant philosopher, insists upon dragging by every art, a lovely but Catholic bride, strikingly like yourself in her love to everything that breathes, by every violence from her own faith to his, merely from a proud, egotistical intolerance of her unassuming belief, which, in marriage, would censure his own as false! And would you be the bosom friend of this man?

"It pains me, even to the bottom of my heart, while I write so coolly, that you, so much gentler in your feelings, and self-sacrificing, will endure so much, before the opening of this testament — of this letter. Before that time, you will have suffered so much from two villains, of whom I am the second; for my sullen temper will be the cause of severe trials to you; that is, if my invisibility, my furious and unreasonable temper affects you deeply. It is best known to God and myself, that to you I shall be the very devil, for I know my nature. Ah, upon every fresh sheet of life, the impression of the title-page is reprinted.

"My whole evil is this sullen spirit, this *esprit de dèpit d'amour*, that one of the wickedest fairies must, at my birth, have blown into my nostrils. A worse spirit of the tormenting order could not have arisen from all the realms of spirits or demons. Its usual effect is to turn the tenderest love to hatred, as if we loved only to hate and torment the most precious of hearts; to seek to give it pain, to crush its every tenderness, to condemn and rule it like a despot! And wherefore? that I may at last take it half dead to my breast, weep over it, and cry out 'Oh, I am a hell-hound!' Thus have I acted with strangers; thus with dear friends; thus with the most fondly beloved. Three thousand two hundred times did I thus torment and reconcile myself with a beloved being, during the short honey-moon of our love, and, like a prince, celebrated the union of our souls, by the murderous explosion of my artillery; or looked upon the sweetest, most amiable dew of love, till it became snow! Under such circumstances, I swore solemnly, that only a God or a devil could marry. If the person you love is not absent, (for absence goes far to increase love, or absent, which is better, through death, for love, and the will of the beloved, are first made one through death,) the leaden-winged years, after the first few fleeting moments, are like life near a chimney-fire, where one half burns while the other freezes; or like ice in water, melting above in the fair sun, beneath, in the flowing waves. Then — God knows the misery!

"I cannot too often repeat, let every one protect himself from a sullen, egotistical spirit, for there can be none worse! I am obliged to travel from old acquaintance to new, that I may not quarrel, but continue to *love*. Heaven knows how I may torment thee! But as I said before, this is written in the best humor. May the leaf, when opened, prove my protecting fig and olive leaf.* Q. H."

* The reader will recollect that this letter was not to be opened by Walt, till some future time.

No. 18. *Echinit.*

CHAPTER XIX.

SUMMER-TIME. — KLOTHAR HUNT.

The notary now began in earnest the business of a notary. He became the universal contract-maker of the novelty-loving city. The executors of the will kept in their possession the description of debts, the protocols for contraband dealers, leases about shop-cellars, contracts for repairing city clocks, and the like, all which he prepared in so short a time, that an old limping notary knew not what to say, but that he hoped to heaven that his brothers in office would follow his advice, and when the seven heirs tried him by the secret articles of the will, they would punish him severely for every notary mistake or crime; and for this they would daily pray.

Walt found nothing incomprehensible in all this, but that he, or rather his seal, should be so important as to ratify the weightiest affairs. He could indeed have believed it, had he been a married man, or even a citizen of Haslau, instead of a merely unconnected youth. He wrote to his brother, that in the midst of his notary instruments, he was continually weaving upon their romance; and that he found time, while one copy of a deed was drying, to continue his poetry, like D'Aguesseau, who asserted, that he had composed many of his works in the interval between the words *qu'on serve*, and those, *qu'il était servi*. Vult wrote back prayers and commands, in heaven's name, to remain collected and firm, never to let the date of an hour, nor the smallest accessory of a contract to be forgotten; never to let his imagination wander, nor to abbreviate with sign or *notis*, although the name of notary had been taken from this; that he himself had learnt, that every stroke of his pen was watched; and only on this account, that he might detect errors, the court-fiscal continued to send him a host of customers.

His father Lucas, once wrote him in the same manner, after having visited him for the same purpose every third day; and asked, among other questions, if there had been anything written upon the rights of dogs, of bees, of wasps, of hens, of ravens? and what had been the precedents in the rights of bees, if one bee destroyed another, or even a couple; and adjuring him, never, in his instruments, to erase a letter, nor to make use of two kinds of ink.

His son sent a polite and grave answer, with a card, in which he inserted a *max d'or*, as an honorable acknowledgment of the counsel. He had made an exchange at great discount with Newpeter, in order to send gold, that phœnix and Messiah of country people, to his parents. He obliged the old errand-woman, solemnly to assure him of the very quarter of an hour of her arrival; first, that he might enjoy, in a blissful dream, the happiness of his parents, and secondly, that he might know the exact quarter of an hour when the whole family would be assembled in Elterlein, Shomaker called from the school, and the gold scales from the parsonage, to decide upon the exact value of the money. How much sweeter is it to send by a messenger, than to give into the hand; to send to a distant friend, than to give to one, who, perhaps, would open the envelope and thank you!

His soul's sister, Goldine, also received a letter by the errand-woman. He began the letter by saying, that in view of his present position and his future hopes, he did not exaggerate, by declaring, that he looked upon himself as a favorite of fortune, a child of destiny; but with the Grecian's fear of Nemesis, that his first flight had been too happy, his first palm already full of fruit; that his evenings were gilded by its star, and upon his mornings, rose the morning-star of hope. Afterwards, he went on to paint his summer life as follows.

" The summer now reigns alone. Ach Gott! what a season! So entirely is beauty diffused around, that I cannot always tell whether I wander in the fields, or remain in the city. If I go without the gates, I rejoice that the beggar will not freeze, that the post-rider can sit, with pleasure, all night upon his horse, that the shepherd can sleep in the open air. Men need not dark and sultry houses, for every spreading shrub is an apartment, where we have the presence of industrious bees, and of the most splendid butterflies. The pupils of the gymnasium can sit in the open air, in gardens and upon hill-tops, and find their words in the dictionary. The laws against hunting forbid all shooting, and the innocent life in bushes and furrows, and in trees, can securely enjoy the privileges of existence. Travellers arrive upon all sorts of open carriages, the saddles of the horses adorned with green branches, and the drivers with roses between their lips. The shadows of clouds course along the fields, intersected only by the shadows of happy birds; the apprentices wander idly with their bundles, and scarcely need to seek work. Even in rainy weather we remain in the air, and inhale the fragrant refreshment, that injures neither the shepherd nor herdsman. At night we sit in the shadow, where we can look upon the lingering day-light of the northern horizon, and upon the sweet, warm stars of heaven. If I look for a second away, I find my precious blue, the blue of the corn-flower and flax-blossom, and of the infinite heaven, in which I would bathe as in a river. As we return home, we find fresher joy. The street is a veritable nursery, where the little ones, even after their supper, although their covering is slight, may be left in the open air, and not, as in winter, hunted to the bed-clothes. We sup as in broad day-light, and hardly know from whence the light comes. The windows stand open, day and night, in our sleeping apartments, without danger to the sleepers, and aged women sit and sew by them, without injury from cold. Flowers are scattered everywhere, near my inkstand, upon my business orders; they lie upon the sessions and the shop-tables. The children in the streets are noisy; we hear the rolling of their hoops upon the pavement. People go about the city in the night, talk loud, and look at the shooting stars; even the princesses walk before supper in the park. The foreign musicians, who go home at midnight, continue to play in the streets, and the dwellers in near houses lean from their windows to hear. The mail comes later; the post-horn and the neighing of the horses, awake those that sleep, and the whole starry heaven opens to them. Ach Gott! what a life of joy upon this little earth! and yet this is Germany only; how then must it be in Italy, Goldine! Beside these pleasures, I have the most inspiring prospect, that this harvest-dance of time, that I describe in such dull prose, because I know your love and indulgence, will hereafter be enameled with the brilliant colors of poetry.

"Friend, I am writing a romance! Enough, enough! Goldine! dare I to pour this joy into your sympathizing heart? Ah! I cannot conceal these splendid sun-beams with earth-born clouds! Adio Carissima."

Here Walt sprang up, suffering the deed to which he had appropriated the day to lie unoccupied, for, while drawing it, he heard Klothar had restored heaven again to his neighborhood, and he hastened to the garden of the count. While writing, Walt was the master of his phantasy, but in real life, only the servant. If, therefore, it playfully showered its flowers and fruit alternately upon his head and in his bosom, he irresistibly followed with his earnest heart, to pluck them from the highest branches. He hoped for a precious meeting in Klothar's park. The windows of the villa were open, but no head appeared within them. The gardener, who took him for an amateur of flowers, went to meet him with a garland, hoping that he would read this gardener's flower language, and reward him with a couple of *groschen*. Walt politely declined the blooming present, but took it at last with the most grateful expression of thanks to the gardener, who as no groschen accompanied, threw over them the web of his own dark expression.

Walt roved blissfully through the whole place; into the nests of dark thickets; to the inscriptions upon rocks and walls; to the turfed seats for prospects, and every where expected a flower-wreath to fall upon his head, or a summer-bird on his breast. He felt a lively joy wherever he looked, as the garden-bed from which would spring for his future friend, some flower or fruit of this fleeting spring of life. "Here, upon this bank," said Walt, "the noble youth may have looked long at the evening glow of the western sky. In the twilight of these thickening branches he may have woven out the dreams of his heart; upon this hill, his soul full of emotion, he may have thought of God. Here, by this statue, oh here, (if he is so blessed) he will take the soft hand of his betrothed; and when he prays, it will be, surely, in this majestic grove."

"The English garden is truly divine," he said at the gate to the silent gardener. "In the evening, friend, I shall certainly return." Indeed, at the evening hour he again entered the garden door. There was music in the villa. He concealed himself and his wishes in one of the beautiful grottos of the park. From the rock behind him, gushed a fountain overhung with trees. Before him, the smooth stream spread its mirror through the meadow lands. A gentle western breeze wooed the rose-colored sunbeams from the flowers, to rest upon the hills. A statue of a Vestal, with the hands concealed in the drapery, stood, with bent head, near him. The music from the villa seemed to hang in the fountain, and sparkle like stars in the rushing water. As Walt knew not what instrument Klothar played, he gave him every one in succession, for all breathed out the elevated and deep thoughts that he had himself lent to the soul of this youth. Many times, under the influence of these sounds, he made a sketch of his inexpressible happiness, if the youth himself should enter the grotto, and say, "Gottwalt! Why do you remain here alone? Come to me, for I am thy friend." He tried a *Streckvers* upon Jonathan, for thus he called Klothar in the Haslau newspaper; but he succeeded ill, as his emotions were too vivid to hold the pencil steadily. Two others that he sent to the *Wochenblatte* were called, and really were, much better.

"THE RAINBOW UPON A WATERFALL."

"Ah! how steadily hovers the bow of peace upon the angry rushing water! Thus, as the stream of time swells and rushes on, God in heaven rules the waves with his bow of peace."

"LOVE, A SPHYNX."

"The unknown, peaceful form, draws thee to it, and smiles upon thee with its lovely virgin face. But dost thou understand it not, it draws upon thee its talons."

The gardener approached, and as he wished to close the gates, requested him to depart. Walt thanked him, and went willingly; but to his great astonishment, he passed in the street of the theatre, a torch-lighted carriage with six horses, in which sat Klothar and another person, so that he found he should have sought him in vain in his garden. He walked backwards and forwards before Vult's window without seeing him; but yet the latter saw him, and was thinking of him.

A few days afterwards, Walt had the happiness to meet the count, who was walking and speaking English with an old stooping lady in one of the garden-walks, and to bow with eyes of reverence and love at his earnest beautiful face. He sought again several times to meet him, and from ignorance of the usual garden ordinance, raised his hat as often as they met. This became, at last, so displeasing to the count, that he remained under shelter. The gardener, also, who over Walt's close observation of the villa, had established his own, was confounded, and believed something suspicious lurked beneath.

Late in the evening there arrived a runner from the Polish General, Zablocki, who possessed, in Elterlein, the well-known manor castle, with an order, that punctually at eleven o'clock, Walt should present himself there, upon business of importance. "Oh, if Klothar should wish me to draw out a contract, how could I find a more honorable opportunity." But at eleven o'clock the same runner came, and countermanded the order; and that day at the *table d'hôte*, he learnt what a celestial world had been thrust aside from him.

The society at the table were unanimous in according the most heavenly disposition to Wina, the general's daughter. There are many eternities in the human heart, in this poor life of *time*. Eternal wishes, eternal hopes; perpetual pictures, perpetual sounds. The sound Wina, nay, even the similar sounds of *wine*, *wish*, etc., excited Walt's imagination like the perfume of the auricula, upon whose fragrance, as upon a cloud of incense, he had always floated into new and unknown worlds; but at this moment the earliest auricula of his consciousness expanded, and lay dewy before him. The cause was this. When, in his childhood, he lay blind with the small-pox, the Fräulein Wina, the daughter of

General Zablocki, to whom the so often named *left* of the village belonged, came with her mother to the justice's house, because she had heard at home what the little servant-girl said, " that the poor little boy was at the point of death ; " and she would herself carry him all her auriculas, for every other hand shrunk from the infection. Walt always asserted, most religiously, that he ever remembered clearly, although blind, how the sweet perfume of the auriculas penetrated and intoxicated his senses, and the painful longing he felt to touch only the finger-tip of the child, whose sweet voice lingered long and from a distance upon his ear ; and how he pressed the cool petals upon his hot lips, till they withered. This flower history was also related to him unnumbered times in his illness, and afterwards in health ; thus Wina had never faded from the twilight of his childhood, although he had since never dared to look in her face, for it would have been a sin to efface the sacred gift of memory, by looking at it in the light of day.

If respectable poets place their wings and arms together to form a sort of Minerva's shield, upon which to elevate an ideal beauty above the clouds, above the moon, to the midst of the far-off night suns, Walt himself placed the invisible, the sweet-voiced Wina, far above these, even in the darkest, deepest blue, where the most remote and brilliant suns have glowed and beamed, and their rays have never reached this earth. There, like the great central sun of Herschel, alone in its splendor, its beams returning to be absorbed in itself, ever revolving in its own light.

Gottwalt asked if the Fräulein Wina was the daughter of Zablocki; and he heard that she was also the betrothed bride of Klothar. How surprising, he thought, that a manly, strong, penetrating mind, like his friend's, should be united, and living with the tenderest love, in the atmosphere that would be to him the softening echo of his own; a hero near a holy virgin; and then, on the other side, to think of Wina as the bride of *his* friend; of this spiritual sister, this God-consecrated nun in the temple of friendship; for to an elevated mind there is no being more lovely and sacred, than the betrothed of a friend. Such dreams of joy could scarcely have been wafted to a man by any other news than the latest, "that this very day the marriage contract would be signed and sealed by the general." Walt, who from his countermanded orders, knew the contrary, now almost shuddered at the thought of the contract being postponed. I believe I could not act, he thought, in the presence of two such beings, if I found in them the love I have imagined; and if my head were pledged for it, the contract would be made with ten thousand errors.

He heard yet more. "The count," said one, "with *his* fortune, marries for beauty and accomplishments only, for he has ten times more money than the general has debts." "What then," said an unmarried comedian, who always played the old father, "the beloved is charity itself, and covers a multitude of *debts*."* "The mother, who is in Leipsic," said a consistorial secretary, "finds it easier to consent, as she, like the bridegroom, is of the Lutheran confession, but the father —— " How so?" asked the comedian. "The daughter and father are Catholics," he answered. "Will she change her religion?" asked an officer. "That we do not know," said the secretary; "but if she adheres to her own, there are many conditions to be complied with. They must be twice married; once by the Lutheran minister, and afterwards by the Catholic priest." "You consistorial people are, by heaven, true puzzlers," said the officer; "nothing can be more useless, more wearisome, than your idle rules. They disgust me! How would you stand against a field preacher?"

Walt rose from the table with the heavy, but sweet sensation of a love-wounded heart. Thus, according to medical history, are people who awake in a chamber where the pomegranate has opened its blossoms in the night, oppressed, but enchanted with its summer perfume. He would, he must, see the affianced pair. Wina, of whom he had heard yet earlier than of the count, and he could with propriety petition her to present him to the count, and then the latter, whom he had so long sought, would present him to the

* *Schulden*, the same word for sins or debts.

bride. The remark let fall at the table, that Wina was a Catholic, had pleased him much, for he had always represented a nun, and an Italian beauty under the same form ; that she was a Polander imparted to her new charms ; not that he had assigned to any *one* nation the flower-wreath of beauty, but because he had so often imagined, Ach Gott! how delightful would it be to love a Polander, or an English woman, or a Parisian, an Italian, or a Berlinian, a Grecian, a Swede ; or one from the thirteenth century, or from the age of chivalry, or from the book of Judges, or out of Noah's ark, or Eve's youngest daughter, or that poor, good maiden, who will be the last upon the earth at the last day. Such were his thoughts.

He went about the whole day in this new temper, so brave and light-hearted, as if he himself were in love ; it was to him as if he possessed all, and yet nothing. He would have led as a bridesmaid to Wina, one that he could eternally love.

He longed for his brother, not to tell him or to learn anything from him, but that he might press a human heart upon his own. A rainbow, appearing in the east, elevated him yet more. The lightly-hovering arch appeared to him the open door of an unknown paradise. It was the ancient arch of victory of the sun, through which so many bold and beautiful ages had passed, to which so many longing eyes had turned.

No. 19. *Marl-stone.*

CHAPTER XX.

PIANO-TUNING.

It is well known, that, according to the sixth clause of the will, the notary, in order to deserve the inheritance, must tune pianos one long summer's-day. Vult and his father, who could not wait, that they might know how the so-called tariff, in the secret articles of the will, would punish his mistakes, insisted upon this, as the employment in which he would be most likely to err, and thus would be shown the sincerity of the deceased testator. But Walt had always represented to both the injustice of thus holding his old deceased benefactor as a villain. Now, however, from reasons known to himself alone, he was ready to tune. These were the three-fold hopes, that, as his office of tuner must be published in the weekly newspaper, he would thus get into the most respectable houses, and should see the beautiful daughters of these houses, for daughters and pianos are not far apart; perhaps open the most costly, and place his own fingers upon the keys where the betrothed hands of Klothar and Wina had rested.

Walt hurried the business on, without asking counsel of any. He made known his intention, indeed, to the executors, or rather to Kuhnold, the mayor, who informed him, that, according to the secret tariff, he would receive on that day four *louis* from the estate, for the testator would in no case oblige him to receive pay for such a service. He added, "I would, if my duty permitted, earnestly advise you not to suffer your ear, while tuning, to be drawn to any other subject. I also, will furnish an instrument," he added, with a benevolent smile. Walt, who was always touched with any indication of love, recollected with pleasure Kuhnold's marriage, so fruitful in daughters.

The advertisement was put in the newspaper. As soon as it appeared, Vult wrote him a serious, cautionary sermon, full of instruction upon the numbers of the strings, the danger of their springing, *false tuning*, etc., beseeching him also, for one day to lay the poet wholly aside, and, instead of drawing instruments, to think only of tuning them, like an established Regensburg musician.

The evening before the day of tuning, Walt received a list of the houses. His own residence was not among them; Newpeter was too proud to avail himself of his services; neither Count Klothar's, nor Zablocki's, but otherwise, fashionable enough. As he considered it his duty to go first to the house where he had received counsel, he presented himself early in the morning as a piano-tuner, at Kuhnold, the mayor's. He found an elegant polished piano in an apartment appropriated to music, but, instead of the Mademoiselles Kuhnold, only the formerly-mentioned, limping notary, whom the fiscal Knoll had sent to witness and record the mistakes and faults Walt might commit, and report them to the seven heirs. Knoll had also insisted, in a long letter, that this tuning-day should not be deducted from Walt's time as a notary, to which Kuhnold replied, that he had himself proposed, that it should not.

The cheerfully arranged apartment, although without daughters, bore in every part, like the colored ashes of butterflies' wings, the traces of beautiful fingers, the variegated and fanciful implements of female work. The piano was already tuned, but only a note too high. A tuning-fork lay near. Upon the keys the numbers of the strings, and upon the sounding-board the corresponding numbers had been retouched with black ink. Quiet was established in the adjoining apartment. Kuhnold himself came to look on, but said not a word. He invited both notaries to breakfast. Would to God, thought Walt, that one of the daughters would appear. Instead, an old, wrinkled, manly head, with more years than hairs upon it, brought in the breakfast, and served it with as much hospitality as if he had himself been the host. Both notaries breakfasted, but the executor spoke little, while the soldiers paraded under the window of the room, with their gay uniforms, and the noisy drums and trumpets that admitted of no tuning.

The whole forenoon passed without faults, and

with the entire loss of the presence of daughters, and both notaries returned wholly displeased to dinner; the limping, that he had sat there without being able to record the smallest possible fault in the tuning; and the other, that the morning had passed, and he had not seen *anybody*. There are years in the life of both sexes, when *everybody* includes the one sex, — nobody, the other.

After this, both notaries went to the house of the bookseller Pasvogel; whose piano needed, not so much tuning, as new strings. Instead of the tuning-hammer, Walt, with the master-key, was obliged to work upon the musical keys. In the mean time, a beautiful girl of fifteen, gaily dressed, the niece of Pasvogel, led in his only son, a boy of five years old, with his little shirt only, upon his childish form, and began, from the accidental tones of the tuning-hammer, to weave a sort of dancing music for the child. The contrast of the little shirt upon the boy, with the gay dress of the young lady, was pretty enough. Suddenly, three strings broke; A, C, H.

"Merely a few letters from your name, Harnish," said Pasvogel. "You remember the musical anecdote of Bach, nothing fails but my B." "I am tuning upon B," said Walt, "and I cannot account for the breaking of three strings." The limping notary possessed enough understanding to see, that in the use of a tuning-key, three strings could not spring at once, he therefore rose, and looked gravely on.

"From the A, C, H, there may be a B, A, C, H," joked the bookseller, to divert their attention. "Accident furnishes us with puns, which no library of sciences or the fine arts would acknowledge," said Walt. The limping notary asserted that the thing was wonderful, and worthy of a protocol; and, as he scrutinized the sounding-board, and peeped behind a roll of papers, a mouse jumped out. "He has done it," he cried, and as he wrote it down, he shook his head, as though he suspected the bookseller had placed the mouse there from selfish purposes.

Walt asked, musing a little, "Shall I continue to tune? I see upon every string traces of the mouse, and they will all break;" and he laid the tuning-key aside. Pasvogel, like a violent man, would have quarrelled with him, but Walt disarmed him with the assurance that he should continue to tune till evening, and that if he found other strings, he would come to him the last.

They now went to Herr Van der Harnish, who had placed himself upon the list. He said he expected his hired piano every hour, and suffered them both to wait a long time. This would have offended the lame notary, had not the nobleman appeared so courteous and amiable, and, moreover, he could not understand why Walt looked so full of love. Walt ascribed their detention to the brother's desire for a prolonged interview, while Vult had no other object than to curtail a large piece from the tuning-day, that fretting-worm that was preying upon the inheritance. At last he suffered them to go, after he had twice asked if they were yet there, "as in his blindness he could not *hear* them."

They came next to the beautiful young widow of an ensign of artillery, who sat with her embroidery-frame (she was working the cover of a drum) close to the highly polished instrument, which she suffered him to tune, that she might, perhaps, play upon him meantime. He listened, so charmed with her conversation, that he once let the tuning-key fall upon the sounding-board, and a couple of strings were untuned. At the close of business, she produced some musical dice,* and challenged him to the trial of composition. He complied, and played his first written music. He would have continued to play, for one never plays with more satisfaction than after tuning; but the limping notary interposed with the clause of the will. The widow struck with powerful hand some proving accords, and the lap-dog leaped with four legs upon the keys, and untuned them a little. Walt would have gone over them again, but the notary restrained him with the conditions of the will. He went reluctantly. The widow was a fair blonde, of about thirty years old, consequently five or seven years younger than an unmarried lady of the same age. Walt rejoiced that the strings had led him once, at least, to the sounding-board of beauty. And, "oh heaven!"

---

* Dice, with musical notes, so that however they fall, they always present a melody.

he thought, "I can make use of this day to disguise many occurrences in my double romance."

He must now to the police inspector's, Harpretch, who, as the protocolist said, was shorn bare with a whole flock of daughters.

Harpretch received him very graciously, dusted hastily an old hack-brett,* and placed it very politely before Walt to be tuned. The daughters were not visible. Walt bowed, and said, with gentle courtesy, "no! In the sixth clause of the will, pianos alone were mentioned for this day's tuning. To-morrow he would willingly return, but on account of the many remaining houses upon his list, (and he showed it,) all possessing an equal claim upon his services, he could not comply." The notary also said, that a hack-brett could not be included under the name of piano. "But yet, sometimes," answered Harpretch, with his old gracious affability, smiling with one corner of his mouth, so as only to wrinkle one line in his countenance, "it may in strict justice be considered one. But, as together with the court-fiscal Knoll, he hired an instrument in common, for their children, he would follow him to the apartment, that he might prolong the satisfaction of his company, and bear witness to the accuracy of his tuning; and as the instrument was held in common, every tuning fault must of course be doubled, and Herr Harnish would thus gain time and spare trouble." "Indeed,"

* A dulcimer in the shape of a chopping-board.

answered Walt, "I would it were according to the will. I could ask nothing better." Harpretch pressed his hand, and said he had long wished to find such a young friend. They went together to the children's apartment. "It is just the hour," said Harpretch on the way, "for the dancing and music lessons of my daughters and Knoll's."

It will not be beneath the dignity of this history, to record, that Harpretch and Knoll kept one spinet as a dancing accompaniment for their young people, borrowed from an old musician, and that the spinet stood alternately one quarter in the house of each. Harpretch had also borrowed the French grammars from the gymnasiums, for the lessons of his daughters, and said, he was not ashamed of it.

A shorter path to the fiscal's house led through a garden of various colored flowers, where the summer had ripened the fruit before it had embrowned the leaves. Walt, who felt the friendly warmth of the vesper sun in his face, longed to be out in its evening glow. "Are you in the humor," asked Harpretch, "to make upon the spot, a poem in your new species, a style, which is so much praised. Something, for instance, like a poem upon the poet himself, as you now stand, so happily upon your distant ideal world, that you see little or nothing of the real. Walt reflected, and looking up at the sun, at length a beam from thence inspired in his heart a sort of poem. He reminded Harpretch of the astronomical opinion, that the body of the sun itself does not shine, but its light is imparted by the atmosphere that surrounds it, and recited the following.

"ILLUSIONS OF THE POET."

"Beautiful and attractive are even the dreams of the poet. They enlighten the world, that the errors of common men have darkened. Thus is the sun in heaven, dark, beneath its clouds; but splendor illumines its clouds. They impart its light and warmth to the cold worlds beneath. Without its clouds the sun is but a ball of earth."

"Pretty and pointed enough," said the inspector, with honest praise of the irony which he found in the *Streckvers*, that chance, rather than the poet had placed there. "Thus," hastily answered Walt, "can thought be created, for every human thought is an impromptu, but the formation of the verse requires time and labor. I would never consent to give such poems to the public."

They entered the noisy apartment, where, in addition to the pupils for the spinet, and the singing-master, was the little dancing-master, thus throwing both nests of the buzzing, romping company together; which consisted of thin, small-bodied, stooping, girlish figures of every age, among whom two boys were waltzing. The dancing school waited for the music school, and that waited for the tuning of the spinet. The little music-master swore the instrument was so high to-day, that it could not be used, although the police inspector had told him confidentially, to prepare it for the young Mr. Harnish, by letting down all the strings too low; and, in his zeal of preparation, he had effaced all the numbers of the notes, etc. In short, almost every thing was wanting.

Walt began. One string after the other snapped. Harpretch rolled the ball of wires from one hand to the other, and observed, as this was apparently a wearisome occupation for his young friend, he would remain to hand him the ball of wire, and to beguile the time with discourse. In the beginning, Walt accommodated his tuning to the dancing-school, for no hour of human joy was ever indifferent to him, and he sought by tuning on the octaves and quarters, and hammering on the pegs, to produce a sort of dancing jingle. But when every string, and nearly his own tympanum had broken, which indeed others as well as himself had stretched to the utmost, he sought to establish a little quiet. They were all silent; he tuned and sounded alone. Walt toiled through this calm of wind and sea, the wires only springing, instead of the dancers. This tuning, untuned his heart. The approaching night was before him, the remaining houses upon his list, full, as he believed of beautiful daughters, in his heart. He had lost all vivacity of mind; for no exertion presses so severely on the brain as that of the ear. The limping referee had recorded the seven-and-twentieth broken string, when the evening bell sounded. Walt threw the tuning hammer far into the room — "Donner and blitz! what is that? The civil and canonical day is at an end! Herr Inspector, I will pay for the strings."

The next morning the secret articles of the regulating tariff were opened by Herr Kuhnold, where it was ordered, that for every string broken in his office of tuning, he should forfeit a garden-bed in the inherited acres. According to the protocol of the limping attorney, he was thirty-two strings, or beds, poorer than the day before. Walt was alarmed on account of his father; but when he looked in the melancholy and sympathising face, of the honest mayor, he guessed that, which consoled him for all; namely, the whole extent of his yesterday's goodness; that in his own house he had made everything easy to him, and by a highly tuned instrument in which no string could be broken, and the removal of his beautiful daughters, he was relieved from a portion of the time he must have spent in other houses. This refreshing experience of warm goodness in the human heart, so indemnified him for his pecuniary losses, that he took leave of the burgomaster with a glad and grateful emotion, which the other seemed only half to understand.

No. 20. *Cedar of Lebanon.*

CHAPTER XXI.

PROSPECTS.

GOTTWALT swore as he entered his own apartment, that after such a heavy shower, such a mouse-colored rain from destiny, he would find a pretty spot of sunshine. Flora brought him the sun-beam, namely, a verbal invitation, (he was not considered worthy of a written one,) as agreeable as a letter of exchange upon happiness had been, to appear on Sunday at dinner, to *eat a little soup* in honor of Newpeter's birth-day. The Germans rely upon the opposite poles of the dinner; soup, and the concluding bread and butter; never upon the intermediate fish, hare, pork, and the like. Flora said, that on account of the Count Klothar, they would celebrate the birth-day as early as at two o'clock. Walt answered, he would certainly attend.

A second warm breeze of fortune blew upon him from the newspaper, with Vult's information to the public, "that he would rather give his concert on Sunday evening, stone blind as he now was, than continue to disappoint a revered public, by keeping them longer in painful expectation of his recovery." With the newspaper, there was a little billet to Walt, asking for the advance of a couple of *louis* to pay the necessary expenses of the concert; also for the protocol of the tuning-day; for a couple of ears for to-morrow evening's concert, and with the ears, the heart.

Walt was happy, and wished to communicate his happiness. He wrote immediately. The desired loan was doubled from that which he had yesterday received from the inheritance. Then he mentioned his precious hopes about Klothar and his hitherto unsuccessful efforts to meet him, and also his *Streckvers* upon the count. He added his dreams for the success of the to-morrow's flute concert, and his hopes of a future life of happiness with his brother, when his blindness had ceased. Finally, the loss of the thirty-two garden beds.

Man ought always to tremble in the presence of his highest happiness, as, also to believe that there is a soft, gentle dew from heaven, that ever falls upon the stony earth; and that there are calm, tranquil places, even in the cavern of the winds, where he could sink into the pure, open flower-cup of peace, as the pure and perfect pearl is found in the melancholy, stormy sea. We expect the answer will immediately follow the letter, and be an echo of our own. Vult wrote in the disposition described below.

Since the yesterday's interview, he had thought of his brother with wholly new feelings of love, and he would secretly assure him of his esteem and confidence, by requesting him to lend the *louis*. He had formed plans from lively hopes, that as soon as the

Sunday's concert should be over, he would be able to see, "and then all sealed letters between us," he said to himself, "will become daily more stupid, and when we live together like brothers, will cease altogether." He had felt, most deeply, that one fleeting winter of the heart could no more take away the summer of the heart, than a remnant of ice left on the threshold of spring, could chill the summer of nature. In this disposition he received Walt's letter; a congratulation, as it were, to a blind man who had been secluded so long; against whose seclusion Walt had never protested; upon whom he had made no poem, although upon that foolish stranger, the count, he had made two or three; upon a man whom the amiable Walt loved a thousand times more than himself, and —— In short, he wrote the following answer: —

"With this I return two of the *louis*. More are not requisite, although no man needs so much money as he who despises it. The devil take the thirty-two beds, and let the fiend sow them with tares. Such a *gamut* will lead rather to hell than heaven! Any other than you or I would have said to himself, 'by heaven! I will succeed!' Cato wrote a book of cookery. Could not a poet tune a piano if he would? But the contrary does not follow, that a cook could have written like Cato, far less like Cicero, that ancient Ciceronian Roman. Bad dreams, the *real* soul-bugs of poor sleepers, against which my poor head is not so well protected as a horse's head against flies, have preached to me many truths, which I will repeat to you, Mein Herr!

"You excite my wonder, that after you had received the marching orders from and to General Zablocki's at eleven o'clock on one day, you should have received a counter order for a counter march the next day, at exactly the same hour, without venturing to think that he had taken a whole day to change his mind! Sir! are not, then, the great, the only quicksilver of the immaterial world? Their changeableness; their rolling, shifting, slippery nature, will always remain their first resemblance; other resemblances are countless. Like quicksilver they are cold, and yet cannot be brought to firm, stoical ice; shining, without light; white, without purity; easily taking the perfect spherical form, but incapable of receiving an impression; harmless, and yet sublimated to a corrosive poison; flowing together, without the power of adhesion; good for foil to underlie mirrors; amalgamating readily with the precious metals, yet with true, electric affinity, only with quicksilver itself! Sir, thus would I name the great world, whose golden age is of quicksilver. Upon such a smooth, cold, polished globe, no honorable man can dwell. I enclose entrance tickets for the concert. *À revoir*, *Monsieur*.

VAN DER H."

Walt was as sorry at the return of the *louis* as if they had borne the stamp of Louis XVIII. He took

Vult's stamping anger, rather as dancing-steps of pleasure. But could he have divined the painful struggles of love and misanthropy, with which Vult was alternately impelled to him, or banished from him, he had found but little happiness in his present life. Ignorant as he was, he slept sweetly till the morning.

No. 21. *Wydmonder, or great mouth.*

CHAPTER XXII.

PETER NEWPETER'S BIRTH-DAY FESTIVAL.

The whole of the next morning, Walt could do nothing better, than to form plans for appearing on this day of honor, like a second Petrarch, or a village encrusted jewel, which had already, in the polishing mill of the city, received a new lustre. He reflected, that it would be the first time that he had turned in the zodiac of the most refined circle, or *Kranzchen.** "Ach Gott!" he thought, "how elegantly and brilliantly they will express themselves, and say everything, in a few chosen words. I, for my part, shall collect a great deal to put in my romance of the *Heart.*"

Walt arrayed himself, by times, in his Sunday dress, the yellow nankin, the only gilding he could afford, and placed, instead of the faded brown hat which he would carry in his hand, more powder than usual upon his brown hair. He walked, completely dressed, for a couple of hours to and fro in his chamber, and heard with great satisfaction, one carriage

---

* *Kranzchen*, term for an assembly, held by a family in the first circles in Germany.

after another thunder in. "Let them come, the invited guests," he said; "more freight and merchandise for my romance, in which people of rank will be as necessary as the ink. And then how will my Klothar shine on every page, as the ancient, true, heroic friend! God will so help me that I can to-day say something to him."

At length, at the rolling in of another carriage, he thought it was time to close the circle, and to round it with his own bow. He placed himself upon the upper step of the corridor, with his hat in his hand, and looked long for an opportunity to slip into the saloon without being remarked, and without much bowing.

The saloon was very brilliant. The gilded locks had been divested of their paper covers; the lustres had thrown off their dust and sackcloth; from the velvet chairs every stain of a black coat had been removed, and from the tessellated floor, the cotton that had preserved the carpet, and the coverings, also, from the tapestry, had been withdrawn. The East India hangings were now displayed in their full splendor. The merchant had also succeeded in ornamenting his saloon with living things, and, like a pastry, it was stuffed with such forcemeat as aigrettes, chemisettes, red noses, patent ornaments, and French clocks, so that from the church-rath Glanze, to the neat travelling agent, and the serious bookseller Pasvogel, all were obliged to mingle together.

The great merchant sought to enter no higher class

than that of creditors, whenever his noble debtors failed. A cold, quiet, impartial judge of merit, he valued the lowest citizen, if he had money, and the highest noble, if his ancient blood, running in gold and silver veins, nourished and watered the tree of commerce. Indeed, as father Hardouin considers the coins of the ancients of more historical value than their literature, so the merchant never placed the parchments of the nobles and their quarterings, so high as their money, and spoke of the first with great indifference.

Walt found himself much more tranquil in the midst of the imposing aspect of this day of honor, than he had hoped; for he soon remarked that he was not observed, and that he could make a velvet seat the weaving-stool of his dreams, as well as any other. As yet, he had seen nothing of the count, of the festival, or of the two daughters; but, at last, Klothar, the dinner-king, to his great joy, entered, blooming and beautiful, but with a frock coat and boots, as though he were prepared for a parliamentary wool-sack, rather than the agent's silken chair. "Herr Court-Agent," he said, without looking at the assembled guests, "*serve*, if you please, for I am cursedly hungry." The agent ordered the soup, and his daughters. He had long and truly valued the count, for, as he had been the collector of his rents, he best knew their value, and that of the count also, and had often asserted, that a man of such a yearly income, had a right to assert his own opinions, and that others should assent to them.

Suddenly, as the soup tureen appeared, music was heard, and with it the printed birth-day songs; the daughters entered with a long garland of flowers, with which they so adroitly enveloped their father, that he looked as if he had suddenly bloomed into fresh flowers. The clerks distributed the poems, and the instrumental music accompanied the singers. The whole company, with the copy in their hands, joined in as at a table-blessing, and even Newpeter himself, with the manuscript in his hand, looked as if he sang his own eulogium.

Vult would not have remained serious, when the man with his blooming decorations, joined in his own praises; but Gottwalt was well prepared for it. A man who thinks properly, is as serious at the thought of his birth, as of his death. We are like Chinese pictures between two long shadows, and it is no matter on which we fix our eyes, for they must soon mingle. Walt was tormented only with the low singing of Newpeter's bad voice; but when it was over, and the old man appeared embarrassed at his forgetfulness in singing his own praises, and touched with the congratulations of his friends, there was not one among the good wishes, more sincere than that which remained silent in Gottwalt's heart. It pained him to see men, even men, as he thought, who belonged to the court, upon that sacred day, when they should look over, and settle all their accounts with life, that then they should listen only to the rushing of strange waters; that a man should celebrate his new creation with the noisy repetition of the old, rather than with new resolutions; that he should seek the dry eyes of strangers, instead of solitary emotion with only those, whose cradles and graves stood nearest his own! Walt resolved to celebrate *his* next birth-day, of which some friend should remind him, in a different manner. In his humble poverty, not one had been celebrated — far otherwise; they had passed in tender, quiet, and pious reflection.

They placed themselves at the table. Walt was next that poor devil, Flitt, and on his right, the youngest clerk. It troubled him little, as the count sat opposite. The table, like a large plate in partnership, or like coined money, was round, which, like death, makes all equal. Walt, dazzled by the splendor of the dishes, and the novelty of their contents, endeavored to use his hands with dignity, and eat with true grace. To use the spoon and fork, of which he had often read, and treat the blade of his knife as a true sword of honor. He thought of his old difficulty of mounting the left side of the saddle, and determined not to begin till he saw how others did. But what drew his attention far more than their contents, was the form of the castors, the dessert spoons, the egg-breakers and ice cups, the golden fruit knives; because he could describe all these new luxuries in his *double romance.* "The rest of you may *eat,*" he said to himself, "as much as you please of the plovers' eggs, the Mainze ham and smoked salmon, if I can only learn, through my good neighbor Flitt, the *names* of the dishes, I can serve them up, ready cooked, in my new romance."

He closely observed the count, as belonging to the highest school in the art of living; who made nothing of calling for white port wine and the wing of a capon, which he divided with his teeth alone, not to speak of the pastry, which he ate with his fingers. This charming freedom in boots and a frock coat, spurred Walt on to imitate him, as well as the other gentlemen, who put in their pockets confections for their children; and he reckoned it his duty, if he would appear like a man of the world, to put in his pocket (although they were wholly indifferent to him) some little papers containing sweetmeats and mottoes.

In the mean-time, it was his perpetual wish, to say something which should be understood, if not answered, by Klothar; but he did not succeed. As a mark of respect to the count, the church-rath Glanze was placed on his left, and on his right was the lady of the agent; *he*, however, only ate. Walt reflected deeply, in how far the present example of the most refined manners should be followed; namely, that of saying no word to the lady of the house. Like one in love, however, he looked on with the optical glasses of the present, instead of the future. It was, at least, a refreshment to him, when the beautiful youth took something from his plate, or his flask, or looked around, or musingly at the sky beyond the window, as though it were a lovely face. He was bitterly angry with the church-rath, that he could sit in such a rich, fruit-bearing neighborhood, without making the least use of the privilege, when he might so easily touch Klothar's hand with his own, and draw him into conversation. Glanze, however, preferred shining himself. He was the idolized pulpit orator, sermon writer, and upon his face, as upon the Bologna coins, was stamped, *Bononia docet.* As other orators close the eyes, so he his ears under the current of the tongue; and with his author's vanity, also, the proud lips of Klothar, so that Walt could not open his own. He considered it a duty of the feast, to be politeness itself; to throw across the table, upon every face, a flower of joy, and to *speak*, at least, a little. How willingly would he have spoken out to the whole; but, alas! he sat like Moses, with a radiant face, but a heavy tongue; for he had so long sought to say something that would strike, that now every thing would appear crude and insignificant. It was impossible for him to utter such common places as came from the lips of the others. A Westphalian, who spins a fine and delicate thread, cannot learn to draw a coarser. The longer a man delays the uprising of his own luminary, so much more splendid he thinks it necessary to appear; but does the eastern sky fail him, he will not willingly appear in the west. For this cause much light is obscured.

Walt now determined to rely upon deeds. Both the daughters of Newpeter had, among all the beautiful female faces he had ever seen, the most ugly.

The notary even, who, like all poets, believed that beauty belonged to the middle ages of woman's life, and who needed only a few weeks of emotion, to sow the most desert face with the flowers of beauty, yet could not engraft one of the blossoms of his fancy upon either of the stems already there. It was too difficult. But as there was no misfortune for which he felt so much compassion, as for female ugliness, which he pitied as a life-long sorrow; he looked at the blonde (Raphaela was her name, who sat within his line of sight, on the right) with indescribable tenderness, hoping she would guess how little he felt repelled by the sharp corners of her face. Also upon the brunette, (named Engelberta,) he suffered, from time to time, a gentle, touching side-glance to fall, although on account of her extreme vivacity, he felt for her only a moderate compassion. It was some consolation to him, under his pity, to find that both maidens, by ornament and ostentation, had drawn upon themselves the envy of the ladies.

Flitt, his neighbor, rose very high in his estimation, from the sympathy which he seemed to feel, as he emulated him in attention to the extremely plain Raphaela. The poor devil wished for nothing from the beauty, but her hand, with the marriage-ring and dowry. Walt pressed Flitt's hand, under his napkin, after the third glass of wine, and said, "I, also, among many beauties, would first speak and dance with an ugly woman." "Very gallant," said the Alsatian, "but do you see what a superb form?"

This drew Walt's observation upon the forms of both of the daughters, who, if decapitated, might have been Venuses; nay, if they had only looked backwards in the glass, each might have believed herself a grace. The learned recognize no beauty but that of the physiognomy. Walt had reached his majority without knowing that he had whiskers, or that other people had fine forms, beautiful fingers, ugly fingers, etc. "Truly," said Walt, "I could, without the least sting of conscience, tell an ugly woman, that although her face was plain, I saw her beautiful form, as it were, in her face; and could so praise it, as to make the poor girl aware, and proud of it." If Flitt did not exactly understand him, he asked no questions, but merely said *ja*, rather hastily.

Walt now turned his eyes very eagerly upon Raphaela's form, that he might study and understand this new beauty. The blonde drew back from his glances, and endeavored to be very virtuously offended at the boldness of young Harnish.

"Which is the dearest to me, Sir, the blonde or the brown?" said the court-agent, excited with wine. "Undoubtedly the blonde, for she costs the *Casa* twelve groschens less every quarter. For three dollars twelve groschen, good money, I can purchase in Weimar a flask of *vinaigre de rouge*, namely, for the blonde; but, for the brown, it costs exactly four dollars, and had she perfectly black hair, I must pay four dollars twenty-two groschen. Raphel, thy health!" "*Cher père*," she interrupted, "call me Raphaela!"

"He deserves," thought Walt, disgusted by Newpeter's indelicacy, that she called him, "*scheer bar!*"* Thus he appeared to Walt.

"To-day, the poor blind baron gives his flute concert," said Raphaela quickly. "Ah! I remember yet how I wept over Dülon." "I don't yet know the man's name," said the brilliant mother, whose own name was Pulcheria. She was from Leipsic, where she had frequently sent both her daughters, as to the highest school of good manners. "This *Habenichts* is a vulgar clown, and a juggler beside," she said. Walt became agitated, and glowing with the wine he had drank, sought the quickest defence. "How a poor, petty nobleman," she continued, "can learn or teach *anything*, I cannot exactly understand; what then can he do for people who have already heard *something?*" "He is," said Walt, hastily and suddenly, "neither vulgar nor needy, nor deficient in any accomplishment, but truly a superior man." He was immediately conscious of the warmth and haste of his voice, but the assertions of the lady had chafed his gentle spirit; he wished, indeed, not to be extravagant, but only just. They listened to his sudden outburst, with a feeling of astonishment and contempt. Newpeter took up the thread. "Vulchen," he said to his wife, with wine-excited benevolence, "as he is said to be such a poor rogue, and blind

* Off, bear!

also, I will get three tickets for you women, for the benefit of the poor fellow."

"The whole city will be there," said Raphaela, "and my dearest Wina. O! thanks, *cher père*. If I hear this poor unfortunate in *adagio*, I am sure all the imprisoned tears of my heart will flow. I shall think of the blind Julius in Hesperus, and tears will water the flowers of joy."

Her father listened delightedly at her style of speaking, although he, as an old man and a father, was contented to go on with his own. Flitt was equally excited, and Walt looked again at her countenance, with the hearty wish that it might be a *little* more tolerable, or that it might be embellished by love, which, as he lived under the same roof with her, could not be thought a wholly disinterested wish. But a storm had arisen in his soul at the mention of Wina, and he was looking with an inspired eye, upon the count, her betrothed, when Raphaela produced a complete revolution at the table, by the question addressed to Glanze, "How does it happen, Herr Church-rath, that an image is reversed in the eye, when we see no object reversed?"

While the church-rath, through his extensive reading, explained slowly and wearisomely the cause, and the table wondered and admired, the count became excited. He was either satisfied with eating, or with hearing, or more than satiated with the theological half science and shallow philosophy of Glanze, of which one quarter was moral, another immoral;

one part of reason, the whole stolen; enough — he began and supported a long and heated argument, which will find a place in the next chapter, No. 23, *being a congeries of mouse-gray cats' tails.*

No. 22. *Sassafras.*

CHAPTER XXIII.

TABLE-TALK OF KLOTHAR AND GLANZE.

As Glanze had asserted, that all objects in the eye being reversed, the mind was reversed with them, consequently, we could not be aware of the circumstance.

The count opposed: "Why, then, is not the image out of the eye reversed? Why do not the blind who have been couched see objects reversed?"

Glanze answered (from Garve), "Our knowledge and experience amount in the end to nothing! therefore, humility is our only duty."

The count opposed: "I do not see, at least, why I, a beggar, should be humble towards a second beggar; and if he should be proud, that I should have any merit by being more humble than he."

It was a favorite position, taken from Glanze's printed sermons, that children, for despising age, would receive the retributive justice of being despised by their own descendants.

Klothar answered, "Consequently, the depreciated age in its youth despised others, and thus it goes on without end; or, can the punishment be received without the sin?"

Glanze remarked, how easy it was to overload the memory.

Klothar answered, "*That* is merely impossible. Is it, then, a trouble for the mind to retain anything? Should a man recall in thought, all the treasures that twenty years of life have accumulated, will his memory be more burthened than it was in his youth? And further, the peasant bears as many ideas in his memory as the learned, only of different things; of trees, fields, men; overloading the memory is, then, nothing but neglecting to cultivate the other powers!"

Glanze said, that one could, by proceeding to final ends, establish Voltaire's joke, that the nose was created to bear spectacles. Klothar replied, that it surely was, for when all the powers in the world are recognized, the power of grinding glasses must come into view.

Glanze answered, he would find it asserted in all his printed works, that in the artistical order of the world, there was an Infinite intellect.

Klothar asked, how was the above-said intellect shown? Glanze answered, in the motive, the end. The other opposed,—that in every artistical creation, that is, in organized bodies, they unfolded through unconscious powers, not through foreign creation; these again grew in unconsciousness: where, then, throughout these mechanical ends, does the lightning of mind strike in?

Glanze asserted, soon after, that a limited monarchy, like that of England, was for every one the best practical government.

Klothar answered, "Yes, for everything but freedom! Why had my ancestors alone, the right to choose their laws, and I not? Why, I beseech you, wherever I go, do I find laws already made? The *ideal* of a state should be, that even the smallest federative state should give itself free laws; should divide itself into federative villages, federative families, and at last into federative individuals, who, at any hour, could give themselves a new law-book."

Glanze asserted, that through these small states war would indeed cease.

Klothar replied, — "Exactly the contrary. War would arise more frequently in different places, in the same moment of time. In order to have war cease upon the whole earth at the same moment, it must be divided into two monstrous states. One must conquer the other, then there would be one state in universal peace, and love of country would become love of humanity."

At the dessert, Glanze felt so much impelled to express the fullness of his mind, that he thought best to inquire into the solution of the *former* belief of witchcraft.

Klothar answered, that the subject had never been thoroughly investigated.

Glanze shook his head slightly, and the other went on to say, "I do not know which of the two opinions you support, but you can cherish only *one* of two;

either everything was a deception of the age, or there was something miraculous in the thing. In both cases you err."

Glanze shook his head again, but said, that he was, as every sensible person, of the *first* opinion.

Klothar replied, "The miraculous history of witches is proved as historically as that of the Grecian oracles in Herodotus, and this is just as authentic as every other history. Herodotus divides the true from the pretended oracles. Under any circumstances, it was a glorious time, when gods linked themselves with the history of the world, and played their part therein. In this, Herodotus is as poetical as Homer. Common souls find in these historical sybils merely the work of imagination; but those who have read the trials for witchcraft find that impossible. To hold on to an imagination like this, of various and positive facts, reaching through centuries and nations, is as impossible as the belief of a whole nation, that they had had a king or a war that had never existed. Will they declare this imagination only a form or copy of an universally-existing imagination, they have to account for the original. Most of the actresses of these tragedies, were simple, destitute, old women, exactly the individuals the least susceptible to the influence of imagination, but who painted their phantasies in great, indiscriminate, but modest manner. We make only pitiful repetitions of the traditions of the neighborhood, where the lover or the devil following the lady on foot, and in a common dress, to some near mountain, where they dance, and play well-known games, receive miserable food and drink, meet their acquaintance from the village, and after the dance go quietly home with their lovers. The traditions of fables about the Bloxberg are merely for those who dwell next the mountain; and in other countries, the near hills are chosen for dancing-places. But do they pretend that all such confessions in court are fabulous creations, they forget that in the trials for sorcery they find, even after torture, two or three undoubted witnesses retracting, then confessing again, and sealing all with death; at such a time, they were too religious to die with a lie upon the tongue.

"The intoxicating drinks, and the herbs with *which*, upon the Bloxberg, they procured their enchanting dreams, are in no instance proved in the trials, and, from all known laws of physiology, they are impossible. No beverage exists, that can create such decided visions; and then, to be able to use these charms, they must have thought themselves witches."

Glanze asked, "Why then have they ceased? and why has everything become so natural and ordinary, as you yourself allowed just before? Yet I do not make these objections, Herr Graf, as if I believed that you seriously held these opinions."

"Then," said the count, "you mistake my manner of thinking. How? can we, on account of the antiquity or occasional non-appearance of an experience,

—for instance, an electrical or somnambulistic appearance,—decide against its possibility? It can be proved only from *positive* appearances, for negative are a logical contradiction. Do we know the conditions of such an appearance? Many years and generations pass over, and no great genius appears; but you will not deny the existence of genius. May there not be sabbath-day children, who alone have eyes and perceptions for spirits? If your objection is, that they were common at that time, and extraordinary at this, it holds also against all positive revelations of religion, which were only common to its first apostles. Everything spiritual accommodates itself *apparently* to the natural, as our freedom to the laws of nature."

Glanze said he should like much to know what could be said in favor of the opinion, that there *was really* something miraculous in these appearances.

Klothar answered, "In the first place, the witnesses for the first, that is, that it was a deception. These witnesses, to condemn a woman, required nothing but conditions wholly foreign to the facts. If a sudden misfortune followed; the death of a child, or the death of cattle, they drew their conclusions, and these conclusions were their only witnesses. Secondly, the whole process of enchantment turned out, perhaps, to be a cattle-poison, or slow, injurious powder, that the lover, in the form of the devil, gave to the deceived woman, together with some magic money, to gain admission to the house, which as he entered she found turned to lead. The power of the devil never gave them riches, nor protection against the burning fagots. I infer from everything, that in those days, men availed themselves of this faith in enchantments, and under this disguise, their perfidy found occasion to deceive women. Even a secret conspiracy might have concealed its meetings and purposes under the shelter of a dance of witches. Men, in all trials for witchcraft, have been devils towards women, rarely the contrary. But it remains incomprehensible, that women, who at that time shuddered at the devil, and feared him as they did hell, were not terrified at his appearance, and the infernal baptism of apostacy."

Glanze smiled, and said, that now, perhaps, they met in the same opinion.

Klothar answered, very gravely, "Hardly! an imitation will scarcely constitute or establish a particular original, though it may imitate what has gone before. An authentic history of this miraculous belief is yet to be written; or rather of the belief of miracles, from that of the oracles and spectral appearances, down to witches and sympathetic cures. No narrow-minded nor narrow-sighted experimenter could write nor undertake it; but a divine, poetic soul, who would seek not without, in material accidents, for the highest and holiest experiences of humanity, but *within*, in his own soul, and find in himself, that first of all miracles, the belief of a

God, after which nothing is miraculous. This first spiritual existence *within* us surpasses all the spiritual appearance upon the narrow theatre of humanity."

Walt could restrain himself no longer. He had not expected such splendid developments of thought from the elevated youth. "In every age," he interposed, "poetry has been earlier than prose; and the infinite must indeed narrow itself, to enter the conceptions of prosaic men. What we think, *as* of higher beings, *that* we are ourselves, even, because we think so of them."

"Where our thought ceases, there being begins," said Klothar, warmly, without attending particularly to Walt.

"We withdraw only one theatre-curtain from another, and see only the painted stage of nature," said Walt, as warmly, who, as well as Klothar, was excited by the wine, and neither answered the other. "Were there nothing *more*, nothing yet *un*explained, I should wish to live, neither *here* nor *there*. An *eternal* thirst is an impossibility, so is also an eternal assuasion of that thirst, — there must be a third state of the soul, as music is the interpreter between the present and the future. Holy and spiritual tones are created from forms, and they again create forms," * said Walt; for now, not the wish

* If glasses are filled with fine sand, and then struck in harmony, the sand will take, it is said, the form of musical notes.

for friendship, but the fullness of truth impelled him forward.

"A spiritual power forms the body; the body then impels the spirit, and the spirit, thus impelled, acts; the mightiest power on earth," said the count.

"Oh! that subterranean water of the deep second world, that the lowest miner in his cell thirsts for, and drinks, has been bored and trickled through from heights above him; this, for the true soul, forms the great flood of death, that draws him into an intermediate state," said Walt, and rose slowly from the table. He heard no more.

"Real speculations," — began the count, —

"Mr. Vogtlander," interrupted Newpeter, turning to the bookseller, and holding Klothar by the arm, "these twenty-three ells of speculation, have you booked them? now further, Mr. Philosopher."

The count heard the discord of this misapprehension, was silent, and rose quickly. The long-forgotten company rose yet more readily. The temerity and boldness of the notary, in speaking out, had most entertained them. The church-rath, Glanze, had whispered to his neighbors what they ought to think of the count's speculations, and that such things wearied him as much as they disgusted every one else.

Walt was transported to the third heaven, and carried the two others in his hands to give away. He now felt from his own emotions, that he and the count must bear the knight's chain of friendship between them; not because he had spoken to him, (Walt thought no longer of himself, nor of his wish of an audience) but because Klothar appeared to him a great, free soul, sporting upon a wide, deep sea of thought, with all his rudder-rings broken, and thrown into the waves. The course of this bold spirit appeared to him like one making wide steps, without getting onward; and Walt belonged to the small number of men who can sympathise with goodness unlike their own; as the piano can vibrate in sound with every wind and stringed instrument.* Thus are men in the precious season of *youth*, and notwithstanding all their faults, they are like the Titans. Heaven is their father, the earth but their mother; and if the father dies for them, how hard it is to be nourished by the mother!

How wholly differently companies *rise* from table! Even at courts, how much less reserved, less viper-cold and viper-smooth, than a few hours before they had sat down. How winged and singing the heart! how feather-light and feather-warm! Newpeter gaily invited the count into his park. The latter assented. Walt followed. On the way, the agent tore away the bands of flowers, and put them in his pocket. He would not, he said, *look* like a *fool!*

---

* It is well known, that, for instance, a piano tuned exactly like another wind or string instrument, sends forth, without being played, sounds that correspond with those of a violin, etc.

No. 23. *Congeries of mouse-gray cats' tails.*

CHAPTER XXIV.

THE PARK. — THE LETTER.

The count walked between his groomsmen. The one on his left (Walt) endeavored to turn the wheel which should draw out a double silken thread of conversation and love; yet in narrow places, where only two could walk, he was often obliged to pause. A boy went behind, to sweep all traces of their footsteps from the sanded walks. The agent took Klothar to the most splendid parts of the park; to the statues of children beneath the loftiest trees, the group of Hercules strangling the serpent, in the midst of flowers, with the hope to receive some words of commendation from the lips of the count: but he paid no attention. Newpeter valued these statues, especially some of the most celebrated, in proportion to the gold they had cost him, and he protected them against rainy weather with water-proof overcoats; he brought the count before a Venus, draped in oil-cloth. Klothar was silent. Newpeter made another effort, by undervaluing his own garden, and hinted that his park could not be compared to one in England, namely, Hagley; but, he added, the English have the means, — the cash!

The count did not contradict him; only Walt remarked, that, in fact, every garden, however large, — that is, every artistical limitation, — must appear small, like a child's garden, in the midst of illimitable nature, but the heart only could form a garden that might be ten times smaller than this.

The merchant asked the count why he did not turn his eyes to the trees, where much fruit was hanging. He looked up. White table-rates of emotion were there placed by Raphaela. "By heaven! my daughter can make reflections without quoting from others, and you will find them new and elevated." The count paused before the next table of emotion, the heart-leaves of a poetic flower, and Walt also read what was written on the trees, like a physician's prescription on a glass of medicine, which told in what doses, in what spoons, and at what hours beautiful nature should be taken. But Walt was pleased with every indication of feeling. They were to him the entrance, or Easter programme, to the spring festival of nature; free tickets for the seasons; secretly printed title-pages to nature's pictorial bible. The count strode silently away, but Walt, excited by the trees and the tablets, said, "Truly, we should revere poetry, even in its feeblest strivings for expression. Only the highest, the Grecian poetry, although upon the surface it is cold, like the deep shafts of the earth, is warmer the deeper we penetrate it, while other poetry is warm only upon the surface."

"My lodger, Herr Notary Harnish," said Newpeter to the count, rather displeased at Walt's boldness, as the latter looked significantly at him. "My wife calls the reservoir *du Lac d'Ermenonville.* She understands gardening, for she is from Leipsic. The *reservoir*, as I call it, is merely to surround that little island, where rest the relics of my departed father, a merchant, such as there are few, now. The statue within is of himself." In the midst of weeping birches and poplars, the old *departed* looked around upon his solitary island, like a Robinson Crusoe; although old Newpeter, hewed in stone, and the dress that he wore upon the Bourse translated into marble, with his bag-perriwig, and the petrified wrinkles in his worsted stockings and in his coat-skirts, gave no one the idea that the old merchant could ever have been undraped.

When, after a while, the count came back from *Ermenonville*, Walt made many radiating courses, to come upon his footsteps, and to walk in the same path; but the count wished to remain alone, and intentionally turned away. In the end also, the union would have been more displeasing to Walt, for the boy, with his diluting-brush and step-counter, continued behind, and numbered his footsteps while he erased them. But at this moment, he found upon his path something better, — a letter, addressed to Klothar. He looked around, to return it to the count, but he had gone back with the rest of the company to the house. Walt hastened after him, and learned that he had already ridden to his country-house. It was not a very bitter thought to Walt, that, with this letter in his hand, he should have the right to seek him to-morrow at his own house.

He hastened up to his own, with a secret feeling of joy, that he alone could remain at home, while all the other guests must depart. He looked calmly at, and read the outside of the already broken envelope; but to look within, or within anything not addressed to himself, was wholly out of his power. His instructor, Shomaker, who Vult asserted was a law-maker for hoary antiquity, had told him, that not even a printed paper should be read, if it appeared against the intention of the author; that neither the partnership, nor the facility of such an act, atoned for the sin.

A dove, with an olive branch in her beak and at her feet, hovered upon the seal. The envelope was agreeably perfumed. Walt drew the letter out, and holding it far off, folded it up a little from the bottom of the sheet, and read the name of Wina! He laid it hastily from him. "*I will give him all my auriculas,*" she had once said, in the dim, distant days of childhood; since that day, now grown over with flowers, this tone, like a concealed nightingale, had ever sung to him. But now the trembling string was touched, that had hitherto pressed upon, and at this moment echoed from his heart. He held, apparently, the past, his childhood, in his hand; and this evening, at the concert, the invisible would be revealed from her cloud. His emotion needed no representation; every other would have chilled him.

He held, although upside down, the letter near his eyes. The paper was of a delicate blue-white, and, like the finest complexion, full of little veins. The reversed handwriting, so graceful and even! Wreaths of flowers were stamped upon the margin of the sheet; he examined every one of them; seeking the auricula he hoped to find, the last seven words of the last line fell under his eye. Shocked at himself, he immediately placed the sheet in its cover.

Although not read by Walt, the letter ran thus: "Of what avail any longer struggles, which are, perhaps, themselves sins? After your yesterday's conclusive words, I cannot be yours; for although I could easily sacrifice for you my life and future peace, I cannot sacrifice my religion. I shudder at the picture of a declared apostacy from my faith. Your religious philosophy may torment, but cannot change me. The church is my mother, and no knowledge that there are better mothers can tear me from the bosom of my own. If my religion, as you say, consists only of ceremonies, yet leave me the few more there are than in yours; for, in the end, all that is not thought and love is ceremony. If I give up one ceremony, I know not why I should retain another. Keep from my father, as I do, for I know how it would offend him, your severe demand, that I should abjure my faith. Ah! dear Jonathan, what more can I say? That silence, which you so often blame, is not caprice, nor coldness; but mourning at my own inferiority to your great worth. O, friend, is this beginning of our union the true one? My heart is only firm, but wounded. WINA."

Walt had at first resolved to give the letter to Wina herself, at the concert; but now, when he considered a little his luxurious day, his festival dinner, the evening concert, the whole a holiday, he could not conceal from himself, that, like the great, he had the whole day been turning giddily upon the wheel of pleasure; and that he should have also a night of intoxicating dreams, in which one constellation of joy would arise, as another went down; while there were other poor devils, who had nothing but dark, gray days, with obscured and gloomy nights. In this humor, he took his way, both head and heart full of Vult's flute-playing, the divine bride of the auriculas, the letter he was to restore to her, to the first concert he had ever heard. In Leipsic, he had never been able to spare the entrance-money; sixteen groschen would have been to him then a heavy expense.

No. 24. *Shining charcoal.*

CHAPTER XXV.

THE MUSIC OF MUSIC.

Holding fast his entrance ticket, Walt made one of the long procession whose course it indicated. The inpouring of the splendid stream, the lofty hall, the tuning of the instruments, and the fate of his brother, gave him a throbbing of the heart, like one intoxicated. He observed the stream with joy, and would have counted the waves which were to leave a washing of gold upon his brother. He looked in vain for him; he also sought Wina; but how could he find a diamond in a field covered with sparkling dew drops? By the result of his hasty calculation among the ladies before him, there might be forty-seven true Uranias, Cythereas and Graces sitting there in splendor, although, on account of their averted faces, there might have been as many more. He asked himself the question, "if this whole chain of birds of paradise should arise, and he had the power to bring one down with love's arrow, which should it be?" He could find no answer in his own heart, but this — "She who would sincerely press my hand, love nature, and myself." It did not enter into his calculation, that among these lovely feathered birds, unnumbered birds of prey, harpies and the like might also soar. He was only a young man, who would make his first love his first marriage also.

Pasvogel, the bookseller, chose the moment to address the notary just as Haydn let the unfettered power of his war-steeds break loose in the harmonious tones of his battle-piece. One storm followed another, but with warm sun-beams between; then came a dark sky, heavy with vapor, and suddenly, the cloud torn away, one tone only, like a beautiful veiled form, seemed in plaintive sounds to weep alone! Walt, whom a miserable cradle-song of the nurse had power to rock into Elysium, possessed, indeed, little knowledge or eye for music, but he was all head, all ear, all heart. The counter-play of fortissimo and pianissimo, was entirely new to him. Like that of human joy and woe, of prayer and curses in the same breath, thrown into a rushing stream of sound, he was carried along, overwhelmed, again raised, again overwhelmed, stunned, annihilated, and yet he felt himself free! Like an Epos, the whole of life passed before him; all its islands, and cliffs, and precipices lay open before him. It passed by in the low tones of age, the cradle-song, the jubilee of marriage mingling together; the same bell announcing both birth and death. He raised his arms to fly, not his feet to dance. He shed tears, but hot and passionate, as though he listened to heroic deeds; unlike his gentle nature, he was wholly wild. He was angry that they *hushed*, when a new musician entered; that many of them were as corpulent as their note books; that the audience took out their handkerchiefs and snuff-boxes in the pauses of the music; more especially with Pasvogel, that he struck the time with his teeth, and said to him, "truly an ear *repast!*" To him the expression was as offensive, as that which calls the nightingale *Schlauz*.*

"And yet the adagio and my brother must come," said Walt to himself. "The musician who is now led on," whispered Pasvogel, "is the blind flute-player, and he who leads him is the blind court-drummer, who is better acquainted with the ground than the other. The pair have grouped themselves very prettily."

The dark-haired Vult now came slowly forward, one eye covered with a black band, looking fixedly, with his head a little elevated, like one totally blind, and the flute at his lips, to conceal his smiles. He allowed himself to be placed by the blind drummer in the right place for bowing, and as all the fair talkers were silent and touched by his appearance, Walt could scarcely restrain his tears, not less on account of the music he had just heard, than for the thought that destiny might take the jester at his word, and the dreadful semblance of a blind brother might become a truth. It needed little to make him believe, with the whole audience, that Vult was really blind.

Vult gave, like a monthly magazine, and with the

---

* Villain.

insight of a true *artiste*, the best pieces first. He knows, that if the music that follows is bad, men yet hold fast to their first impressions; and for women also, if they are to be heard at all, the best pieces must be given first, as nothing wearies the delicate ear so soon as long-continued music.

The adagio rose like Luna, following the Titan. The moonlight of the flute revealed a pale shimmering world, and the accompaniment drew a lunar rainbow to hover over it. Walt suffered the drops to stand in his eyes, that they might impart to him something of the night of the blind. He heard these sounds, no longer eternally dying away, but approaching from distance to nearness, and the Hernhutt graveyard, together with all the sounds and scenes of the village evening, arose before him in the glow of sunset. As he dried and raised his eyes, he saw the last rays of daylight through the windows of the hall, and it seemed to him as if he felt the sun lingering upon distant mountains, and that he could understand the *heimweh*, the eternal longing for their distant home, the Alps, which, at every familiar tone, made the heart of the Swiss rush weeping through the cheerful blue sky, back to the dark and cloudy mountain, but reached it — never! Oh, pure, unspotted music! How holy is thy joy and thy pain! Thy jubilee and thy sounds of woe are not for any one circumstance in life, but for life, for existence itself; and nothing is worthy of thy tears, but eternity. Could, then, thy purifying influence prepare for thee a residence in the human breast, which has so long been filled with earthly thoughts, hadst thou not been earlier within us, and thy notes the echo of that heaven, which existed for us before our life began on earth?

As a spiritual enchantment, the adagio vanished, and the rude applause of the audience led on the rest of the concert, a continuation of the foregoing adagio, but how unlike it! A low comedy following, as in the English theatres, a sublime drama!

And yet Walt had not seen Wina! She might be the lady before him, who wore a celestial blue dress, and sat near one who turned her back towards him. From the motion of the feathers of the head-dress of the latter, he concluded she was praising the music, and she could be no other than Raphaela. Where then was Wina? Walt looked many times through that female starry firmament, and pressed, with his eyes upon his heart, first the dark dressed ladies, then those in white, and, at last, the more gaily dressed. The music increased, immeasurably, his interest in the unmarried. He imagined words of homage, that he would address to them. "Ah, beautiful pale one," he said to himself, without any timidity, "Ah, that I could adorn thee with the tears of joy, and of heaven; and thou, upon whose cheeks the roses glow, might I only dance this *presto* with thee; thou with the blue eyes! ah, if at this moment I could bless thee, they should overflow with joy, and thou shouldst draw from thy white roses the honey of pensiveness. *Thee*, gentle one, I would place before Hesperus and the moon, and touch thy heart myself, or some other, if —— *You*, little bright-eyed playthings, of thirteen or fourteen years! Ah! could I only present you wardrobes of dresses and beautiful ornaments. Oh, gentle, gentle maidens! were I only a little while Destiny, how would I love you and make you happy! Ah! how can stern time touch such sweet cheeks and eyelids! make them pale, and fill them with tears, and then half efface them." With this text, Walt accompanied the prestissimo.

For many years he had most devoutly wished to see a tear in the eye of a beautiful woman of rank and refinement, for he could not imagine a more beautiful water in such a diamond, a more golden rain, or a more splendid magnifying lens for the heart. He looked around the seats of the ladies for this descending light upon those celestial orbs, this eye of the eye, but he found, because ladies scarcely can weep, when full dressed, only the sign of tears, the handkerchief. But to Walt a handkerchief was always a tear, and he was entirely satisfied.

At last that moment approached, which occurs in every concert, and in every festival for the ear, that moment when the frost melts from the tongue and heart, when both can be loosed, and we feel that we are in a concert.* At this moment, when the whole

---

* A few lines are here omitted.

hemisphere of beauty arose and turned towards him, Wina must be discovered! Raphaela stood forward, but her celestial-blue neighbor remained quiet behind her. Walt at length gained courage to ask Pasvogel. "Next to the eldest Mademoiselle Newpeter," answered the court bookseller, "in celestial blue and silver, with pearls in her hair; she has been at the court. Now she stands up and looks this way. Can there be a darker eye, or a more oval face; although I very well know, that she is not regularly beautiful; that is, she has not a Grecian nose, nor the waving line of beauty in the closed mouth; but otherwise — heavens!"

As Walt looked at the beautiful woman, the power that directs the destinies of man, whispered to him: "This will be thy first, thy last, thy only love! suffer what thou wilt!" The poor mortal felt the thrust of the arrow, shuddered and trembled, while the wounded heart burned and swelled! It did not occur to him that she was beautiful, or of high rank, or that she had been the auricular bride of his childhood, or that she was now the bride of Klothar; he felt only that she, who had been forever adored, although enclosed within his heart, and hitherto had given to his spirit, blessedness, and holiness, and beauty, was now revealed to him by the arrow that had pierced him; that she stood beside him like heaven; yet, ah! how distant! (All too distant, yet all too near!) and there she must bloom forever, so beautifully, so celestially in the presence of that solitary, wounded spirit, which she had deserted, but which could not live without her!

Wina, with Raphaela, who had attached herself to her, from the vanity of appearing among the crowd who pressed around, as her confidant, now approached the place where Walt stood. As they passed close before him, he saw more nearly the deep, dark, enchanting eye, that in Jewesses only is as beautiful, but never as calm; not like a flashing star, but like tender moonlight, which timid love had half veiled with the beautiful eyelid. Walt stepped unconsciously back; a sharp pain passed through his heart, and it swelled almost to breaking. Ah! that everything on the earth should pass so wearisomely slow, except herself, and the Niagara of his heaven be scattered in a thousand little rain showers! Thus is a divine man like Walt, to whom, instead of the hundred altars, where lie the ashes of love and beauty, the phœnix bird himself, with outstretched golden wings, floats suddenly and from afar before him! The crowd soon concealed Wina and the path she had taken to her former place on the other side. Walt followed the blue dress with his eyes, and now regretted that, of the vanishing face, he had seen nothing but those dark eyes, so full of dreams and of goodness,—but *these* alone were to him enough! To men, the star of love is like Venus in the sky. In early youth it is a dreamy Hesperus, or an evening star, filling their world with a twilight of flowers and the songs of nightingales; *later*, it is the morning star of purity and power, that makes known the day; and they can be united so as both to become one star, only through the fit time of their appearance.

Walt now suffered his attention to fall upon the other ladies. They were all Wina's sisters or step-sisters, and her radiant sun shed upon all the constellations a more radiant light, also a double portion upon Saturn, the count, with his double wings of love and friendship. Wina seemed suddenly to interpose between their bond of friendship. The count, with her as his bride, was too exalted for the simple friendship of Walt. The opportunity and the right to restore her letter to her, seemed now to be passed; for, as he considered it more maturely, the baptismal name merely did not permit him to presume that she was the correspondent of the youth, nor authorize him to give the letter to her.

The music began again. If tones make a touched heart tremble, how much more one deeply moved! As the full tree of harmony, with all its branches, rushed over him, a new and strange spirit seemed to descend into his soul, that said nothing but *weep!* and he listened without knowing to what. It was as if heaven had descended upon him from an opening cloud, and he saw before him his own life, heavenly blue sunlight, and warm as a lovely day, and sounds became voices and faces, and to these sweet children of the soul Wina gave the sweetest names. *They* also wafted her on the gala ship of life to the shores of an Arcadian world. There, Walt's friend, her own beloved, received her in the midst of the songs of shepherds, and pointed out to her, all around the horizon, Grecian groves, shepherds' cottages, and villas full of beautiful waking and sleeping flowers. Cherubs drew near, wafted upon clouds of rose color, bringing flower incense, to shroud, within that perfumed twilight, Wina's first kiss of love, and then to speed far away, to whisper to the listening heaven that first kiss. As he thought for a moment upon this blissful dream, his brother dwelt long upon two high notes, making them tremble as they died away, like a long drawn sigh. Gottwalt also, trembling, wished that in this strange dream of happiness he also might die! The loud discord of applause now broke in, but Walt was so lost in emotion, that he scarcely heard it.

All was over. He strove, and not without success, to be the next behind Wina, not even to touch her garment, but to keep at a certain distance, and serve as a wall of protection from the pressure and contact of all others. But he still pressed to his heart, as he followed, the traces of her own hand, in the letter to Klothar.

At home, in the heat of the moment, the following *Streckvers* burst forth.

"THE UNCONSCIOUS."

"The earth brings forth, and displays the delicate flower in the presence of the sun, but conceals within her breast the hard and knotty roots. The light of the sun is reflected by the moon, but upon the earth we are only conscious of its borrowed and tender beams. The stars diffuse their refreshing dew upon the nights of summer, but withdraw ere it has been exhaled by the burning sun; and *thou* — thou, the unconscious! hast borne to me flowers, sunshine and dew, and art unconscious of thy gifts, although refreshing the world, also, with thy blessings. Oh, fly fly to her, thou whom she loves, and tell her, that through her alone thou art happy! And will she not believe thee, show her other mortals."

As he wrote the last word, Vult, without his bandage, and in the gayest humor, stormed into his room.

No. 25. *False emeralds.*

CHAPTER XXVI.

CONVERSATION.

"I SEE!" cried the flute-player, with a gaiety of tone in which Walt could not immediately sympathize. Vult requested him to listen, first, to the cure of his blindness, and then to talk of what he would. Walt was content. "It cannot be known to you," said Vult, "that to-day was the birth-day festival of the director of the orchestra; but from one example, myself, you may learn, that all concert-players excite themselves before they elevate their audience. The director's wine became to them a cure for hypochondria, and they imbibed so much of enjoyment from this well of truth, that the violinist looked upon his bass viol as a little heaven, while it appeared the contrary to others. A feeble spark of the succeeding war glimmered at the dinner, by the simple expression of a German, relating to the great German trio, of which he said Haydn is the Æschylus, Glück the Sophocles, and Mozart the Euripides in music. Another said, as to Glück, he agreed; but Mozart was a musical Shakspeare. The Italians now joined in the conversation, and, in order to please the director of the orchestra, who is himself an Italian, said, in Naples they knew something better than Mozart. In the short time I remained to receive my part of the receipts, (I have sixty thalers, of which here are thy ten,) the war broke out in full flame, and, as I looked back, both nations fought at cut and thrust.*

"The director being at last inexpressibly provoked by the city *Tertius*, a little *Mannlein*, reaching scarcely above his own knee, seized, and hung him up by his waistband; this turned the war into shouts of laughter.

"'What does all this laughing signify?' asked the blind court-drummer.

"'Herr,' I answered, confused by the tumult, 'the director has drawn the little Tertius from under the piano, and hung him up, like a pair of leather breeches, that a Berlinean is drying.'

"'What, *donner!* Herr!' exclaimed the court-drummer, 'you see again then!' 'Just at this moment,' I answered, retreating farther from the battle, lest I should get some blows, 'I think—I have, wholly unexpectedly, my former sight, although extremely short; too short to see the city and country again, through these distant galvanic shocks.'

"But, my dear Walt, is it not as if my best genius had given me this musical battle, as a wall, already

* Vult goes on to relate the *musical* war between the Germans and Italians, but as it consists of terms unintelligible to the translator, it is omitted, except the conclusion only, the circumstance that betrayed Vult's assumed blindness.

covered with fresco painting for our *Romance of the Heart*, apparently shoved it before our noses, that we may build it into our romantic Odeon, till it fits exactly where ours runs crooked? brother!"

"If all the personalities can be erased from it," answered Walt gravely, "good! It will be pleasanter to read than to see. Thank God, that you *saw* it only. But ah, we have to speak to-night of that which certainly belongs *not* to our romance."

"*Not?*" said Vult. "Speak on Walt." Walt was the first to recover himself, and to ask, earnestly, how Vult meant to play out his part of blindman in the city?

"I have at present," said Vult, "some little glimmering of light; my sight will improve, and I shall appear, at last, with a great short-sightedness."

Walt said, that he also rejoiced in the prospect of a happy futurity, when life would expand before him like a variegated flower. In the hope of surprising the *artiste*, he poured upon his part of the concert a spring shower of the perfumed waters of praise. But *artistes*, who travel about giving concerts, and who are always applauded, and hissed only after they have gone, are still vainer than actors, who are at least sometimes nipped and withered by a good monthly criticism.

"I, myself, venture," said Vult, "to boast a little, without injury to my modesty. But how did you listen? to the past and the future, or only just at the moment? People hear like animals, close to them, but never forwards or backwards. They listen to musical syllables only, but to no syntax. A good listener engraves the characters of a musical period upon his mind, that he may understand the beauty of the conclusion."

Walt declared himself wholly satisfied with both. He told the flute-player of the powerful deepening of the impression the flute made upon him by the presence of the ladies, and by Wina herself, without guessing from Vult's face, that the taste of this laurel was very bitter to his palate; on the contrary, he thought his discontent arose from the imperfect *Streckvers*, which Vult was just then reading.

He had taken up the poem, hoping it was in praise of his own musical talent, which he valued above all other beauty. "It is," said Walt, hesitating, "upon the count's betrothed; but I am not satisfied with many hard measures in it. I mean the *ditrocheus*; but heat is apt to harden."

"Yes, like beating! and eggs also," said Vult. "But, Ach Gott! How do thy human creatures listen! Should not one rather cut his flute into a blowpipe, or into shavings for his coffin, when men so horribly asperse the only divine experience that lifts us far above life's villainy. But I aim not at you. You only excite me to it. For hear only, how with every art, music, especially, is profaned. I will not speak of table music; that is as bad as the table sermons, that in cloisters they are obliged to take in with their food; nor of detestable, corrupting court concerts, where the divine tones must ring like billiard balls in billiard pockets, to excite people to gambling: a ball in a picture cabinet would not be more absurd; — but this is a misery, that I am compelled to go in vain to a concert, where every one has a right to expect something for his money. The cockney pricks up his ears upon two or three conditions; first, when a fortissimo suddenly whizzes up, like a flock of partridges, from an expiring pianissimo; secondly, when, with the bow upon the violin, one has drawn out, and danced, and wavered upon the highest note — head over heels he dashes upon the lowest; third, when both occur at the same moment. In such circumstances, the citizen is beside himself with rapture and applause. There are other hearts, Walt, that feel more delicately and egotistically. There are hours when I storm at a couple of enamored fools, who, if they meet with that which is elevated in poetry, painting, music, or even in nature, believe immediately that it has been made expressly for their particular momentary state of feeling; and that composer, or artist in finishing his work, calculated upon their sympathy only; that for them alone they take the rank of artists, and come back with the embroidered coronation mantle, or Isis veil of art upon them, merely for their gratification. One of Newpeter's associates would, at such a circumstance, look at night upon the galaxy, and say to a tradeswoman, 'Princess! receive that circle of stars as a ring and bride's girdle of our divine union?' "

"Ah, brother," said Walt, "you are too severe. What then can a man do when emotion swells his heart, whether it be excited by art or by great nature herself, and where do both dwell in such full and entire power as in humanity itself? Well may man then appropriate them, as though they were for him alone. The sun rises upon the battle-field of heroes, upon the little garden of the bridal pair, and upon the bed of the dying peasant, at the same moment. Yes, at the same moment it rises and sets for all, and each may dare to follow it, and draw it to himself, as though it shone for him alone; and made alone his joy or his sorrow. And I may also say, that exactly in the same filial manner every one calls upon God as if he were his *own*, while a whole universe prays before him. Ah, else were we miserable! Yes, we are one in God!"

"Good! Take the sun," said Vult, "but not the paradise rivers of art to turn your own mill. You would mingle tears and emotion with music? it is only because music is to you the servant, not the creator of emotion. Thus a miserable harmony, which, on the dying day of a beloved being, would soften your grief, would be to you good music. And what impression from art is that, which, like a nettle-sting, vanishes the moment the cold air blows upon it? Music is of all the arts the most purely human, the universal art ——"

"Therefore it embraces so much," interposed Walt. "Always must we bring a disposition to listen, why not the most favorable, the tenderest, so that the heart may become a true sounding-board? But I will not forget your lesson, always to listen forward and backward ——"

"What has happened to you otherwise?" asked Vult, sullenly, "for I shall remain by my opinion; that to knead the pure reality with the artistical, gives a mixture, such as I have seen upon wall paintings, where the perspective is made more like reality by the insertion of bass-reliefs of plaster."

Walt, who ascribed Vult's ill humor to his own unartistical manner of hearing, and over whom his own love held its heaven of forbearance, readily related how he had sought the count; had sat opposite to him at the Newpeter dinner (which he described), and in the affinities of the mind, and through his philosophical elevation above narrow views, and sectional prejudices, he had found him strikingly like the flute-player.

"You love duplicates, friend," said Vult, who, like a woman, was never pleased with the praise of resembling another; "but indeed here are none! Go on!"

Walt now showed the envelope of Wina's letter, which he hoped would serve as an introductory card to Klothar's apartment and ear.

"Ja, ja, very naturally," began Vult; "but in heaven's name do not call such low citoyennes, as the Mam'selles Newpeter, ladies! In great cities, in courts, there are ladies, but not in Haslau. I will be hanged; if you would not speak thus of many Mam'selles, that in the world, are, in understanding like the five foolish virgins in scripture. And what do you think of the virtue of these charming beings, the little rose-maidens, and the *prima donnas?* but that I already know."

"No," said Walt, "I am not afraid to acknowledge, at least to you, my brother, that till this hour I could not conceive the idea that respectably dressed, beautiful ladies, could sinfully forget their own honor. It is somewhat different with peasant women. God alone knows how sacred and tender they are in their inmost hearts! Who of us can ever know! *I* only know, that I would give my heart's blood for every one of them!"

The flutist sprang up as if entirely overcome with astonishment, walked about the room, snapping his fingers in sign of contempt, and repeated, nodding his head, "*respectably dressed!*"

We hope our female readers will excuse, if they will not justify, his astonishment, when they recollect the relations he must have been betrayed into in his extended travels, where, as already mentioned, there were few great cities, or high families, in which, as a celebrated master of the flute, he had not been invited to play — and this must also mitigate his guilt.

Walt was much offended at these mimic insinuations. "*Speak*, at least," he said, "for this does not refute me." But Vult answered, with the utmost indifference, "*De gustibus non*, and so on. But now of something else. Did you not say something like this before, that the Mam'selles Newpeter looked upon themselves as ugly, and that you manifested compassion for them?"

"So much the better," said Walt, "if they find themselves more beautiful for my admiration. Ladies may be excused for that, as they only see themselves in the glass, where their point of distance is more remote than that of another, and every distance, as you know, especially the optical, makes one more beautiful."

"So it appears," said Vult; "but for the sake of the joke, I will describe the three women as I learned to know them in Cornrose Valley. Engelberta, the mother, no, that is the daughter, but the mother may also come in for her share. Her heart is an old empty ancestor's chair; besides, she has inherited from the ancestral oyster, not the pearl only, but also the soul. Engelberta, only that she jokes sometimes, many call it slander, like the garrison in fortresses, she sallies out in bad weather, although she is not besieged. Raphaela, as you say, is susceptible. But I ask, is she more so than my nail or my heel? I acknowledge, indeed, that upon a sentimental lover's line, with the flexible angling rod of a poetical flower stem, she would draw a fish, what others call a husband, from the sea. The little Alsatian, Flitt, at her feet, willingly seizes the bait. He would willingly live upon the table, like a gold fish in a glass globe, and be fed by her beautiful hands with crumbs of cake. The others — but enough of them! Nothing would have pleased me at the dinner but the vintage of the south, the wine — *that* should enter no head except that of a wit's. It is a sin against the divine influence of wine, that it should flow for the loaded appetites of common men."

"Oh Heaven!" said Walt, "why so often and so angrily do you use that expression, '*common men;*' as though the common had descended voluntarily from a higher, and the uncommon had risen voluntarily from a lower grade; while you speak more mildly even of animals and savages."

"Wherefore? time, life, Satan!—all, embitter my spirit — especially — but what's the use? Greet the count heartily from me! the *honorable* and honest seven heirs, entirely against *my* wishes, have stolen from thee thirty-two garden-beds, but not apparently against thy own! In the mean time, adio," said Vult, and hastily departed, displeased at the little influence his worldly knowledge could exert upon the opinions of the inexperienced brother.

Walt said, "*good night,*" in a tender voice, but without embracing his brother, although he looked upon him only with love and compassion. He reproached himself, that, apparently through his own ignorance of art, he was unable to appreciate his brother, and also that he had lost *for him* the thirty-two garden-beds. "At least," he said to himself,

"I silenced the calumny against him, at Newpeter's table." Walt thought it was only admissible to praise, but not to blame, behind the back of its object.

No. 26. *Crystallized wood, from Snowberg.*

CHAPTER XXVII.

NEW RELATIONS.

In the morning, Walt hastened to the count's, with Wina's letter, but did not deliver it, for gilded carriages and liveried servants were at the door, and their lords in the visiting apartment. "What have I with these?" he said to himself, — and to the servant, "I will call again, when no one is within," to whom it sounded much like the declaration of a thief.

At the *table d'hôte*, he found upon the cloth the newspaper, containing Klothar's printed request, that the *honest* finder of his letter would restore it to him.

At the table, he heard that General Zablocki would allow his cook to celebrate the jubilee of his services. The comedian ascribed this festival to the general's good heart, an officer to his love of good eating, and added, "His cook is nearer to his heart than his regiment, or his son-in-law." Walt hastened again to the count's villa. The count was dining with the general. The hope of an interview, however, gave him spurs and wings, with which he flew through the garden-door of the count. It must be remembered, that the last evening's concert was in his head and in his heart, and that it was only an accessory thought, that the general was the half proprietor of Elterlein, and that he was himself a Lefter.* Although his brother would have condemned the whole, he could have wished to take his advice; but he reflected, as he went, that he should surprise him all the more in the evening, and perhaps shake him out of his ill humor, with the news, that he had been boldly to the Polish general's, and delivered Wina's letter into the hands of his son-in-law.

He went very late, and so as not to fall upon the dinner hour. Thus should every one avoid visiting the great in the morning, when mind and body are exhausted with yesterday's digestion; but go, rather, soon after dinner, when every one is most humane. Upon the way, and at the thought he should enter the house where, as a child, and a young maiden, Wina had so long dwelt, made his heart waver, like a flower-bed agitated by the west wind. In the last street, his plan was entirely decided. "I cannot, with propriety, do otherwise," he said to himself, "than first to ask for the general, as the count is only a guest in his house, and then apologize, by saying, that I have something to deliver to the Count Klothar's own hands, apart, but that he and the

* That is, born in the part of Elterlein which belonged to the general.

count's bride may be present, or not. — I shall, at least, see a general, yes, a Polish;" and he strove to anticipate no other joy than that of listening to a general. He had once, in Leipsic, stood three-quarters of an hour at the Hotel of Bavaria, to see an ambassador step into his carriage. His heart thirsted in the same manner for the sight of a Prussian minister. This triumvirate, he thought, must be the trident of power, refinement, and wisdom. How this state trio could say, "good morning," "good evening," and other common courtesies, without flowers of speech, he could not understand, or deem possible; as he believed, that to all who came in contact with them they appeared as Lewis 14th and Versailles do in the eyes of posterity. Only three persons, so to say, could be placed near them; namely, their three wives. He often dwelt upon the idea of an ambassadress, whether Russian, French, or English. "Ach Gott!" he said, "what a perfect goddess she must be; whether in point of the most delicate virtues and accomplishments, or the finest complexion, countenance, dress, and ornaments! But wherefore, poor devil that I am, have I never seen an ambassadress?"

At last, he stood before the Zablocki palace. The ascending steps and connecting chains of the pillars were seven mile boots for Walt's fancy; he rejoiced in the thought of the night, when upon his pillow he could think over, and reflect calmly upon this excited and timid hour. He entered the palace. On the right and left were broad steps, with iron banisters, and great folding-doors, near which waited a Moorish foot-boy, with a white turban on his head. Powdered men ran out and in, hither and thither. Doors above were opened and shut. It was difficult for Walt to find any one upon the lower floor who would carry his request, that he wished to see the general. He stood a quarter of an hour, hoping one of the people would turn to him, and that he could unfold his business; but all passed by. At last, he walked freely up and down, and once went half way up the stairs, bringing before his imagination all the great men of antiquity, that he might better know how to speak to a living one. At last, he asked a passing maiden for the general. She pointed to the porter.

Walt consoled himself with the thought, that heaven was entered by purgatory, as a palace by a vestibule, and that perhaps the whole learned world of antiquity had sweated thus at palace-doors. At length, a door near him opened, and there stepped an elderly, powdered, displeased-looking man, with a broad belt over his breast, bearing a stick with a heavy silver knob. It was wholly out of Walt's power to take the leather bandalier for anything less than an order-band, or the porter's staff for any other than a general's staff, and the porter for any other than the general himself; he therefore bowed low, and approached the door, the porter murmuring some polite words.

"*That* will not help you," said the porter, "his excellency is sleeping, and you must have patience."

No one, who has seen much of the world, will be surprised at Walt's mistaking the one for the other; for every respectable proprietor of a door, is himself door-keeper at a higher door. Either at the imperial, the royal, the princely, the ducal, or the trap-door; either as a knocker for those who would enter, or a ringer, to make known their wants; and each, like Janus, the god of the threshold, turning one face towards the street, another towards the interior.

Blushing deeply, Walt entered the gay domestic's hall, that scourging-hall of the needy learned. Servants are parasites to men—villages, where, as upon letters, the next post-station must be indicated; yet the Zablockish were good-humored, and, on account of the jubilee, princely drunk. Walt sat there undisturbed. "Where is the *bon soir*,* friend?" asked a lackey, as he entered. Walt thought he meant himself, not the light-killer, and that he had omitted this evening-greeting, and quickly answered, "*Bon soir, mon cher!*" In fact, he succeeded, at last, in finding a servant, who conducted him through ante-rooms, full of family portraits, through splendid apartments, to the door of a cabinet, that the servant opened and shut again, before he opened it to admit him.

The general, a stately, robust, but beautifully-formed and cheerful man, asked, with kind voice

* The last cup.

and expression, what were the demands of Monsieur Harnish? "Excellency, I demand," he began, and thought the repetition of the verb was the manner of the world, "to return to the Count of Klothar, whom I hoped to meet here, his lost letter." "Whom?" asked Zablocki. "The Herr Grafen von Klothar."

"Will you trust the letter with me? I can immediately restore it to him," said the general.

Walt had promised himself a much more agreeable termination of his visit; but now it would all come to nothing. How could he refuse to trust a father with the letter of his own daughter? As he gave it to him, he said, "The seal of the envelope is broken;" and added, delicately, "I return it open, as I found it." He wished to indicate, as gently as possible, his own integrity in not having read it, and his expectation, that this forbearance would be imitated by the father.

After a slight investigation of the writing, the general placed it carelessly in his pocket, and said to Walt, that he had heard so many praises of his flute-playing, that he wished much to hear it himself. Great men are as forgetful as curious, and Zablocki only asked for the sake of hearing some one talk. "I wish," said Walt, "I were not the substitute of another, or rather," he added, (for he recollected the wholly opposite sense in which his words might be taken,) "I wish I could be his substitute." "I do not understand you," said Zablocki. Walt explained, that he was from the same province of Elterlein, and that his father was the justice there.

Walt now believed, that he could recognize in Zablocki a truly benevolent man; much more, when he inquired, with a friendly expression, about the Van der Kable inheritance,—even asked, with much sympathy, to hear an exact history of the same.

This, Walt related, readily, with distinctness and warmth, and half dizzy with exultation at looking down, from the height of the palace, upon the spires of his native village, while he talked so long with its great man. With exultation, he recollected, that this benevolent heart had never sought the bondage of an order-ribbon, or to break a corner, or a jewel from the Polish crown, or to melt this crown itself, as a present for a beautiful head, that he might himself be known, through the acknowledgment of the present. As Walt had nothing except his eyes, by which he could express his love, he began to stroke the head of a tall greyhound, which sat with his nostrils high in the air.

"Have you a French hand?" asked the general, and immediately laid a paper before him, upon which he should make a trial. Walt said, he knew better how, in more senses than one, to write French than to speak it; and for this, he must thank his teacher. But he found it, at the moment, difficult to decide to which word, among the many thousands which the language possessed, he should throw the handkerchief. "What you will," said Zablocki. Walt thought again. "*Das Vater Unser*," the Lord's prayer, said the other. But, in his haste and confusion, Walt could not translate. Shomaker, who, for whole long years, had not been able to hold a French dialogue; first, because a second person belongs to a dialogue; and, secondly, a first is needed, of which he understood nothing; he, by means of mercantile letters and travelling agents, had brought French handwriting and forms of address to an extraordinary accuracy; perhaps, except Hermes and one other romancer, no author, of mental power, and without rank, had ever surpassed him; and Walt had learned both from him.

"Oh, excellent!" exclaimed the general, when, at last, Walt had written Wina's address to Count Klothar in French; "very good! Now, I have collected upon my journeys a pretty large packet of French letters, of different dates, and from various persons, which I wish much to have copied into a book; without this care, they are so easily scattered; if, then, you will consent to write an hour every day in this book (we will call it *Mémoires érotiques*), here in my house, —"

"Excellency!" said Walt, with flashing, eloquent eyes, as though upon this tender subject no *yes* could be tender enough. "Will it not suit?" asked the general. "Oh! the best," said the other, "and at any moment of my life." "I will collect the letters together, and let you know the hour;" and then Zablocki bowed, as though taking leave; Walt bowed slightly, and waited for what was to follow. When the general turned away, and looked out of the window, as after a leave-taking, Walt could not reconcile its abruptness with the previous warmth of their conversation.

Walt was now obliged to seek what was as difficult to find as the entrance had been, viz., the *exit* from the smooth and polished cabinet, within which, no door was visible. He pushed gently with his hand the seamless tapestry; for he was ashamed to ask how he came in. He tried three sides of the apartment with the palm of the hand, when, at last, in a corner, he perceived that a door was indicated by a golden cross. He turned it softly, and found the entrance to a cabinet in the wall; where, hanging at its whole length before him, was the blue dress Wina had worn at the concert. Astonished and delighted, he stood entranced before it; but the general, having heard Walt's efforts, turned hastily from the window. "I would find the exit," said Walt. "*That* is *here;*" and Zablocki opened a door, that really led through the tapestry.

Destiny had apparently contrived this little mortification to damp, in some measure, the consciousness of honor, medals, and pasha horse-tails, with which he traversed the apartments, that he might come out upon the street with some degree of moderation. At the same time, his esteem for the world was not lessened, as he concealed from himself how few there were, that could, without guilt, attain to such elevation!

With the intense desire, before everything else, to

lay upon Vult's table a faint sketch of this day's coronation and triumphal hour, he knocked at his door. It was fastened, and upon it was written with chalk,—" *Hodie non legitur.*" To-day there is no lesson.

No. 28. *Shell of a Sea-fish.*

CHAPTER XXIX.

DONATION.

After some days, the gardener from the gardens of Alcinius (such to Walt appeared the coachman of Count Klothar) came to invite him to the villa; and Walt built hastily a whole Philadelphia of brotherly love upon this friendly island; for he understood the invitation as a delicate reward for the restored letter. But the gardener came up again, and called through the half-opened door, that he must take his seals with him, as he was called upon notary business.

It was, however, in any case, *something*. Walt entered the rich country-house of the count at the same moment with the fiscal Knoll. But when he saw the splendidly bound books, the gilded ceilings, the luxury of the apartments of the count, they seemed to make him more of a stranger to Walt, than he had hitherto been, in the dwellings *of strangers*.

Klothar, slightly noticing the entrance of the others, continued his dispute with the church-rath Glanze, thus: "The will influences the opinions of a man much more than the opinions the will. Give me a man's life, and I shall know his system of belief. Tolerance of conduct includes within it tolerance of belief; no man is therefore completely tolerant; that is, he is not tolerant against intolerance." Glanze assented, merely because his *me* was described; but Walt, because he stood idly there, objected, and said, "No man is wholly intolerant; every one forgives little errors, without knowing it; but those who are limited in their views, those who dwell in a valley, see only *one* way; the dwellers upon mountains see the whole circumference."

"To enter the centre, *one* path only is requisite," said the count to Glanze, "to pass out of it, the paths are innumerable. Be so kind," he said, turning to Walt, "to place yourself, Herr Notary, at my bureau, and draw, in my name, the customary introduction to a donation-instrument, for the Fräulein Wina Von Zablocki. I am called Count Jonathan Von Klothar."

The names of Jonathan and Wina fluttered upon the ears of Walt, as though apple-blossoms had been showered upon them. He sat down, and wrote with pleasure,—"Be it known to all men, by this public brief, that I, Graf Jonathan Von Klothar, to-day, the —" Walt whispered to the jurist, "the 16th," answered Knoll, courteously. Walt would not take a new sheet, but began to erase the mistake of the old date. While he was erasing, he could not help listening to the thin, hairy Knoll's reading of the marriage-contract, near whom the beautiful count appeared to him like the noble Hugh Blair, in his youth, whose soul-elevating sermons had been, for him, wings to heaven.

A *contract* between Wina and Jonathan, a self-seeking *do ut des*, was to him a violently contradictory idea. One might make a contract with the *devil;* but with God — *never!* He made use of the time during the erasure of the date, as of a free moment, and said, boldly, — as something true and honorable, although timidly in manner, as if it had been the contrary, — "Although I am a jurist, Herr Fiscal, and a notary, yet in every marriage-contract I draw, I cannot but regret that *love*, the holiest, the purest, the most disinterested, cannot act without taking this coarse, juristical, selfish form, — like the sun-beam, the most delicate and celestial element, it cannot act with all its power, until it is united with the atmosphere of earth!"

Knoll listened with a sour aspect to only half the period; but the count answered with a pleased expression, and in the softest voice, "I do not wish a marriage contract to be made, only a *Donation Instrument.*"

A servant of the general's entered, bringing a letter. Klothar cut the seal, a second, but unsealed, lay within. When he had read some lines of the first, he gave the notary a slight sign to desist. He did not open the enclosure, but it appeared to Walt the very same letter he had found the day before. The count, with a nod of the head, dismissed the servant, and immediately after, with a request of pardon to the witnesses, and to the notary, said, "he was doubtful whether he now should wish them to continue — something had occurred which must prevent it." Some shadows, as of inward clouds, passed over his countenance. Walt saw, for the first time, a beloved person, although a man, under the influence of concealed trouble; and even a perfect stranger, when subdued with grief, was always to him subduing.

It appeared at this moment, to his pure mind, that it would be merely selfishness to remind the count, as he intended at first, that it was himself who had found and returned the letter, *unopened;* and, that it would be the extreme of indelicacy to ask if the father had also returned it, in the same manner, *unopened*.

When he took leave, the count would have pressed into his hand something harder than his own. Walt declined taking it. "My obligation is the same, my friend," said the count.

"I will take only the address" (that is, friend, which was little understood by Klothar, who half offended, continued to press him), "and my sheet, I should wish to keep," and he extended his hand for it. It had given him pleasure to write upon it, Jonathan Von Klothar.

"Herr Graf," interposed Knoll, "the sheet belongs to the seven heirs on account of the erasure."*

* It will be recollected, that for every mistake or erasure in an instrument, Walt forfeited a portion of the inheritance.

"Oh heavens! it shall be acknowledged," said Walt angrily; and with a scornful drop burning in his blue eye, he claimed the sheet for his own. To excuse and conceal this, he pressed Klothar's hand, and hastened from the house, in order to console himself and forgive others.

"Ah," he thought on the way, "how hard and long is the path from one kindred heart to another. How must the difficult way lead over costumes, orders, stars, and even time itself. I will love thee, Jonathan, as I love thy Wina, without even the hope of a return. It will perhaps be possible: but I shall wish for thy portrait.

No. 29. *Rough mixture of leaden ore.*

CHAPTER XXX.

CONVERSATION UPON NOBILITY.

Walt every day continued to deplore the absence of his brother. He could not account for this vanishment. Even the *eclipse* of the sullen spirit had become invisible to him. Sometimes he thought him drowned, sometimes travelling or eloped; at other times, that he was happy through some rare and fortunate adventure. He sought to combine the meaning of the double-sealed letter with this invisibility, and to draw some hope therefrom. Alas! how often was he compelled to observe, how inaccurately the best calculations for winning and losing are stated upon the dark reckoning board of life that hangs before us! What splendid pictures had he not already sketched, pictures that extended far into the future of that time, when they should live in the daily exchange of ideas and emotions, and in this growing knowledge of each other, they would be able, with a few freemason signs of relationship, to draw the count into their warm band of friendship. But of all these pictures, nothing was left but these sad thoughts. He had already in the history of nations, especially in the Peloponnesian war, as well as in his own life, observed, how little there was of unity (all reflective poets make unity a standard), how infinitely little of joy or sorrow occurs systematically, and therefore, to presuppose a dark or bright sequence for himself or others, from any former premises, was never to be relied upon. Over the whole historical picture gallery of the world, the greatest clouds change into the less, and the smallest become the greater; around the most splendid stars of life, dark halos are drawn, and the Invisible God alone can evolve the serious and true from the eternal play of life and of history.

The old errand-woman from Elterlein brought Walt the following letter from his brother.

"To-morrow evening I shall return. Come to meet me. Thy mother* profits by me, for I am at the inn at Elterlein. Since I left you I have blown the flute for money in some considerable market-towns. There grows indeed for me, more grass than flowers; but the former bears the latter. I speak of men. I will confess, that before my departure from Haslau, I was as untuned as a wind-harp, or the bell of a Brocken cow. I know not wherefore, but either a particular friend of yours, or yourself, had screwed all my strings across each other; in short, one, or both of you had offended me, and the sullen spirit took the ascendancy. By this I should have been untuned without the loss of the thirty-two garden

* Mother village.

beds, for which I should have roundly reproached him who robbed me. I should have thundered, hailed, lightened; *that*, as I said before, restores good weather. For nothing is more injurious to harmony, in the marriage or friendship of delicate souls, than a long and unexplained dwelling upon a false note, in the perpetually recurring, but mutual concert of all the tenderest duties of life; so that the simpletons jangle their cords without knowing how to extricate them. In every such discord, the delicate parties should think very eagerly of nothing else, until they have turned the *Zanke* upon which reconciliation alone rests. The manganese, by moderate heating, emits a suffocating gas; but make it of a glowing heat, and it gives out vital air. The charge is forced from the pop-gun, only through a second charge.

"But to return. My self-possession was restored by the free air, by riding, and blowing the flute, and writing; and I imagined tolerable things for our Romance of the Heart, only I wished them to be much better, and, on this account, I believed I must hasten to Elterlein. *There*, thy friend received light, I thought; why not his friend the same? I could also accomplish a duty long delayed. As I have often said that I had met the absconded young Harnish, Vult the flute-player, I could now give the old justice fine news, and letters also, from the wild fellow. I therefore invited the father into the Wirthshaus, and told the astonished man, that his son was my intimate friend. That when he was not to be found in the concert-room, he was usually well accommodated in a post-chaise; that he was as well off as myself, and that he had so splendidly altered, that if he now stood before him, he would scarcely know him; that the treble key of his rich voice had changed with the beard, and that as a bearded man he would now greet him.

"He answered, 'that it rejoiced him above measure, that so brave a gentleman as myself could say any good of his good-for-nothing son; that it conferred true honor upon him, and upon the fugitive.' I threw in some excuses for the good, absent man, and handed him a letter from the same to me, from Bayreuth, in which, after some musical complaints upon the ears of the age, he speaks only of his beloved mother. 'The brother also, the present notary, I know very well,' I added, and drew before his nose a slight sketch of thy heights and depths. 'The admirable man,' I said, 'has not lost more than thirty-two of the garden beds, struck off by a blow of the tuning hammer; and the city hold it more of a miracle, considering the strings that were under his hammer, that all of them did not give way.' This I said, in order to prepare him for your future news with the more lenient opinion of the world; but even the *heart* of the world could not enter his breast; he poured out upon you his ill humor, and closed with the words, 'I have little joy in my sons, and the devil may take the villains when he will!' I sent him quickly and haughtily away, with the remark, 'that he appeared to forget, that his twins, possessed, in some degree, my esteem.'

"In the evening, as I reclined upon the most beautiful elevation of the Zablocki garden, and composed for our romance, a satire upon nobility, I saw, as I looked in the angel eye of the sun, that it shone as lovingly upon a wretched village, as upon the courts of the great world; and then, above me, upon the light rose-colored clouds, many pictures of life shifted with their hues. Suddenly there fell upon my ear, a splendid, scientifically instructed voice, that banished from me all satires and dreams, and chased the setting sun into the ear, in whose labyrinths, as in the Egyptian, gods lie buried. The general's daughter sang. Like many educated ladies, she has the habit, when wandering in solitude upon her estate, (for the listening peasants are not more alive to music than the quiet flowers, or the birds in the hedges,) to express her whole suffering heart in music. She wept but softly; as she was alone, she did not dry her tears. 'Ought the noble Klothar,' I said, 'to clothe his bride in mourning, merely because it improves her beautiful form? Hardly *that*.' At last she saw me, but without fear or embarrassment, because the blind concert-player, for whom she took me, could not of course see her tearful eyes and wet cheeks. She, 'The Unconscious,' looked around for my leader, while she let her solitary song die away. Anxious for the helpless blind man, she drew near and began another, a lively song, so that as she approached me singing, I might not be embarrassed when she addressed me; but, although they were the most cheerful sounds, her eyes suddenly overflowed with compassion, so that she could scarcely address me. (Truly, a good creature! I would she were no bride, or already a wife!) Like a rose in the evening sun, her kind feelings bloomed upon her child-like face; and when I considered the soft dark crescent, above the most beautiful dark eyes; I know not which most to admire, the eye or the eyebrow. But how can a man say to such a beautiful creature, 'Marry me and my estate,' for *I* would lose through marriage, as through Eve, paradise and all its rivers; all, except the bird of paradise itself, that flies sleeping. But, ah! to be able to secure a heavenly voice through the marriage contract! *That* is reasonable. Especially as the voice, like singing birds, always returns again; but the beauty of the face, once lost, never! The voice has also this advantage, that it is not perpetually, but only at times, present with the lover. Do I not know many married men, who have become yellow, as Elfin bones become white, by being constantly worn on a warm heart? while the lovely voice of the wife, like the Italian air from warmer climates, would melt and thaw the polar ice of long years of marriage.

"Wina, as though ashamed to be able to see in the presence of a blind man, took little notice of the path of the sun. She ceased singing, and immediately told me who, stood before me, and asked, as though it were a thing of course, who had conducted me. It was impossible for me to embarrass her with the acknowledgment of good eyes, and I answered, that my eyes had much improved; that in the sunlight I saw very well, and only in the night were my perceptions indistinct. While waiting, she began to praise my flute-playing, which, she said, seemed not to belong to the breath, but the sounds seem to come from a distance, and rise as if to the heavenly stars of life. But how can sensibility endure the perpetual emotion of the flute; sounds that appeal to feeling, like those of the harmonica? '

"One who sang as well as herself, I answered, would best know, that art must learn to hold itself pure from all personal emotion. That was all I could say, for I can never succeed in expressing my thoughts. 'An artist,' I continued, 'while he plays from within, must restrain all inward emotion. Emotion may be excited by emotion, but not art perfected.'

"She was silent; as much surprised as you would have been. Then she removed some briars from the path, that I might not be wounded by the thorns, and lingered, as though unwilling to leave me; while I saw, by the frequent motion of her eye-lids, that tears were there, though I knew not why.

"At length, she said she would go and send me a leader from the mansion house. I stood up, and told her it was unnecessary; and as she perceived

I was going, she turned back, and told me to wait—she would go before me to the Wirthshaus, and inform me of every obstruction, and of every impeding stone. The friendly creature did so, and went on, with her head half-turned round, to see that I met with no evil. At length, we overtook a young peasant behind his plough, to whom she gave a piece of money, with the request, that he would lead the blind gentleman to the Wirthshaus. Most kindly, she said, 'good night,' and the long eyelashes too quickly hid her beautiful eyes.

"The devil fetch (pardon the curse) Count Klothar, if he ever causes the smallest, slightest tear to flow from the beautiful eyes of this precious bride. You know with what anger and bitterness of soul, I always enter a nobleman's village. If, under the Romans, a whole population had to vote for the scourging of one man, here, on the contrary, as you know, one man may oppress a whole village. But in Wina's Elterlein, I thought mildly of every one.

"In everything,—in betrothal, even, more than in marriage,—as in music, we dwell longer and louder upon the prelude, than upon the principal note; in short, may not Klothar fail in his prelude? In the inn, I began a *Streckvers* for Wina, in your manner.

"'Art thou Philomele? no! for thou art incomparably beautiful, although thou hast the voice of the nightingale.'

"Thus, you see, you are imitated before you are printed.

"After supper I went around in the village. I thought so much of that first evening, so well known to you, that I added it upon my reckoning board to others, so many of which are like that, passed away. Hasten to meet me when you receive this letter, which will be exactly at three o'clock, for thus have I agreed with the errand woman. Ach Gott! I think often of many things! What is life, but an eternal *ci-devant.* Is not the purest trumpet of joy crooked, and is it not filled with tears, merely through continually blowing in it? Must not the longest stairs to heaven, which are indeed shorter than those to hell, be placed firmly beneath, upon the mire, although they may reach above, to the constellations or the pole-star?

"In the mean time I look for your answer, namely, the verbal, with which you will hasten to the tavern with the sign of the tavern, to meet the well known, or *what God will.*

"QUOD DEUS, ETC.

"P. S., Walt, we might be *real* brothers, yes, twin brothers. The family name already chains us —and yet far more!"

Walt took wing. His heart was full and heavy. All that a knight-errant on horseback vowed to do for one loving woman, he was ready to do on foot for all women, and for Wina inexpressibly more than all.

Upon the way to the Wirthshaus, he met Newpeter's daughters on Flitt's arms. "Perhaps," said Raphaela, "as you are from Elterlein, and write at the general's, you know what has happened to my unfortunate Wina, and whether the beloved girl is still there." Walt could, from sudden emotion, scarcely stand. "She is yet there," he said, "I have just heard so. But I do not yet write at the general's. Ah! why is she then unfortunate?"

"It is now known that an innocent letter of hers has been betrayed into the hands of the general, and her engagement with the count will be broken off. Ah, the angel!" added Raphaela, and wept a little in the high road. Her sister was highly displeased at this display of tears, and grand acquaintanceship in the street, while the Alsatian, looking at the sky, said, "from the appearance of sultry clouds, it threatened rain."

Raphaela had not failed, at the table, to return Walt's compassionate expression with a sympathizing glance. To love, as to fermentation, belongs two conditions, warmth and moisture; and Raphaela began with the latter. There are female beings — at least, they call themselves such — who enjoy nothing so much as pity for the sorrows of others, especially for feminine sorrows. They *wish* to seek their friends upon the principle of suffering, that they may awake, through sympathy with other souls, an equal sympathy in their own tears. This virtue, indeed, may be so much increased with use, that it becomes like the hedge-sparrow, who never sings so gaily as before rainy weather sets in. Mendelssohn, who places pity among the mixed emotions, considers it, for that reason, a less agreeable virtue.

The double unhappiness of his friends penetrated Walt deeply and sadly; although a good angel did not suffer the suspicion to occur to him, that the letter he had confided to the father was the cause of separation between Wina and Klothar. He sympathized with Klothar, rather than with Wina. With Klothar, indeed, he felt the deepest grief, and could think only of his loss of the beloved bride.

He arrived, full of melancholy thoughts, at the inn with the sign of the inn. Vult was not there. Even in this short interval, time, with his ready sickle, had mown down much that he had left there. First, the hay had been cut from the blooming God's acre of the Moravians. Secondly, that forget-me-not, that honey-suckle of memory, the broken western wall of the Wirthshaus, where he had supped with his brother, had been restored.

Vult arrived. In all the ardor of deep emotion, they flew into each other's arms. Walt made known to his brother how he had longed for him, how he desired to know the history of his absence, and how much he needed a kindred heart, in which to pour the mingled feelings of his own. The flute-player would relate his own history last, and desired first to hear that of the other. Walt related backwards; beginning with Raphaela's information about Wina, then united the donation-deed of the count with the letter of the daughter, as the cause of the rupture of the contract; lastly, he informed Vult of his own good fortune with the general, and closed with concentrating all the warmth of his longings in one great, ultimate desire, that of becoming acquainted with Klothar.

During the relation, Vult's countenance presented many changes. When it was ended, he gave the horse an extraordinary blow, that sent him into the stable, and bade Walt to walk to Haslau with him, and not mind the rain.

He assented: Vult put his flute together, and blew occasionally a lively refrain; then held his face under the warm-dropping, evening cloud, to efface the traces of tears; then blew again in the mild air.

"Now, my good friend, that you know all, *decide*," said Walt.

"Dearest, most poetical florist, what, then, shall I decide? (Cursed rain! the sky, at least, might be dry.) I mean, how can I judge, if we cannot agree about any one?" said Vult.

"I often blush, "continued Vult, "that I, a man who has only just passed through some few city gates, some few palace doors, should be right, and you, a courtier, wrong. You, who, to say truth, have been in all courts, and in all *ports*; in fortunate and unfortunate; in all the coffee and tea houses in Europe; in Belle-vue, in Laide-vue; in Mon-plaisir, in

Ton-plaisir and Son-plaisir, and so on, where I have never been!"

"Do you seriously ridicule my poor situation, brother?" asked Walt.

"Seriously! no indeed; mere sport. What the general desires, I can tell you. That which you call benevolence, is merely the love of anecdote. In learned Germany, no water is considered deep, especially by the nobles, that is not also smooth and broad. The general, from mere ennui, would have long and broad histories from you, even if he already knew them. Friend! we book-men, who by the faithfulness of the press are daily and hourly in conversation with the greatest men of antiquity, and who know so much of the most important events of the world, the great men, who have nothing else but their table, would place us between themselves and the hound Ennui. They thank God upon their knees, if they hear an anecdote related that they have already heard. But I know not what you will say to this!"

"Upon opinions," said Walt, "we can easily receive and trust the opinions of others; but not upon persons. If the whole world were to censure you, could I believe it, rather than myself?"

"Of course," said Vult, "as to Wina, what she desires is perfectly plain to me. She wishes to draw her tender finger out of the betrothal ring. I also predict, that the *mésalliance* of souls between you and the count will never take place."

Walt became excited, and asked, anxiously, "Wherefore?" Vult blew some running notes, and was silent. Walt added, that since the loss of Klothar's bride, he had attached himself still more warmly to the youth, and asked again, "Wherefore?"

"Because," answered Vult, "you are *nothing;* nothing but a publicly sworn attorney, and the count — is a *count.* You would not *to him* be greater, if after the old fashion you called yourself a *tabellior,* a *protocollista,* a *judex chartularius-scriniarius-exceptor.* "Impossible," said Walt. "Is in our days a philosophical Klothar proud of his nobility? I myself heard him commend liberty and equality, and the French revolution."

"So do we citizens praise collectively the scavenger, and his moral worth, but none would wish him for a father-in-law, and would lead no *mâitresse des hautes oeuvres et des basses oeuvres* to the dance. Heavens! when shall the disgust cease with which I hear people tattle of the absence of pride in the nobility? Be so polite Walt as to permit some little impoliteness against them. Ach Gott! what then do you know of them, of the nobility? or of all that has been written of it? I wish you would remain a little longer crouched in that shepherd's cart, and listen to me. I will finish the satire upon nobility, that I began at sunset, in the Zablocki gardens. It is now extremely apropos."

"The pride of ancestry, if placed in anything but

in the personal merit of our ancestors, is wholly childish and *foolish*. For who then has no ancestors? None, but our sovereign God! *from* whom immediately descended citizens. A newly-created nobleman must have at least a citizen for his ancestor; for if the emperor have presented him with four backward receding noble ancestors, of whom the first needed *his* four ancestors, yet the original can be only a citizen. But a nobleman thinks so little of merit, that he would rather present himself at court, or at the bishoprick, or at the diet, as the descendant of sixteen honorable robbers, adulterers, or drunkards, than to be the honest scion from three-score of the vanguard of citizens. What the devil does the nobleman pride himself upon? Upon his gifts — as thou and I, and all geniuses do; as the millionaire upon his inheritance, as the born Venus upon her beauty — as the born Hercules. No man is proud of his *rights*, but of his *prerogatives*. The last I think the nobles have. So long as in every court the noble alone is allowed to wait upon his Lord; has exclusively the right to dance, to give the princess his arm, and the soup, to deal the cards; (according to the German history by Hoberlin, a pair of *citoyenne's* feet have never been thrust and withdrawn from under the Sunday court table, let the government newspaper say what it will); so long as the army, the church and the state, refuse to suffer their highest, richest fruit-branches to be plucked by the hard hands that heap the manure about the roots that nourish the tree, so long will the noble be a *fool*, I say, if he is not proud of such privileges.

"Citizens, like plants in the old system of Tournefort, are classed by their flowers and fruits; the nobles, much more simply, after the method of Linnæus, by their races, their sexual system; and in this way there are no errors. The class of nobility is united through the whole of Europe by equality of privileges. It consists in a beautiful family of families; like Jews, Catholics, Freemasons and Corporations, they hold themselves together. The roots of their ancestral trees filiate themselves through each other, and the woven filaments run sometimes here, under the feudal fields, sometimes there, up to a throne. We citizen simpletons, on the contrary, never know each other. The rank of citizen, among men, is about the same as the rank of Germany as a land — namely, subdivided into innumerable single parts. No Harnish in Vienna asks after a Harnish from Elterlein; no Legationsrath in Coburg after one in Haslaw or Weimar.

"Therefore, the noble sails in a ship wafted by full-spread canvass; the citizen toils in one with oars. The former arrives at the highest posts in the state, while the latter, like the sloth, is slowly toiling for the summit. And what is left to us poor devils? If we should possess inexpressible merits, *these* cannot ennoble us. We must be ennobled by something, or somebody else; and then we may be made use of as ministers, and even sometimes raised to other honors.

"Oh, silence! a little longer. It is true, some people think the pride of the nobles is diminishing, because one and another prince dances with a citizen's daughter, as I, spite of my learned rank, with the daughter of a peasant. Or, that a prince sometimes invites a learned man, or an artist, like the tuner of his piano, or like his master tailor, to visit him, not to his social circle, but in private. 'My people,' they say of their servants, *Mes gens*, to distinguish them from we other people.

"Why do you wish to climb and sit upon one of the highest branches of the heraldic tree? That I should sit above in my place as Herr Van der Harnish has its reasons. I look from my pinnacle above, down upon the citizen mob, and elevate what is worthy from your ranks. No one can boast of having so offended the nobility as I have. In cities where my birth was not acknowledged, they have offended me, when under the pretence of valuing my person, they have invited me to their tables to save the expense of a flute. *Then* I did not play, but thought 'I will pipe you something,' and tired them out. But this I now avoid."

Walt replied, "I will answer your half sportive, half serious remarks with perfect openness. The poet against whom no situation is barred, and all ranks are open, may dare, I think, aspire to the highest; not *there* to make his nest, but like the bee who may rest on the blossom that waves on high, as well as upon the flower that creeps beneath. The higher ranks, that like constellations, shine around the sunny zenith of the state, are, through the poetry that surrounds them, removed from the heavy, dark realities of life. Ah what a beautiful elevated life it were, were it only in the imagination that they must avoid everything low and mean. This would keep up a spiritual elevation; for happiness cannot rest till it has created for itself a claim to happiness; thus the parodox becomes truth, that whoever esteems himself, is esteemed of others. What a glorious position. All, possessing the same freedom, all, in the the triumphal car of honor, which each is bound to protect."

"It is pitch dark," said Vult, "but indeed I do not laugh."

"*Theirs* the only consecrated names in the books of heraldry, registered and shining forth like stars, (while the names of common people are excluded, or melt away like dewdrops,) they shine like stars in the sacred neighborhood of princes, who treat them tenderly in exchange for their representation of themselves as ambassadors, chancellors, or generals. They stand near the state, whose great sails they draw up and direct, while the people only work at the oars. Like the high Alps, they are surrounded, only with great and elevated objects; behind them only the shining royal line of the old knights, whose high deeds, like banners, wave them on, and into whose sacred castles *they* may enter like their children."

"Believe me, upon my word, I do not laugh," said Vult.

"Around them all the splendor of riches, of estates; the court and a blooming future in prospect, with that free, unrestrained culture, that forms them not to a rough-hewn angular limb of the state, but to completely finished men, polished by travelling and social joys in the midst of pictures, music, and, yet more than all, accomplished beautiful women, whose charms no weight of indigence nor work has ever crushed, or robbed of their free and graceful play, so that the nobility form the Italian school of painting, and the poor people the Dutch."

The flute-player had hitherto, although with a suspected voice, assured Walt that he had no disposition to laugh; he resolved still to conceal his smiles with the darkness, and again repeated that he was not the man to laugh, but was as serious as the death angel. However, at this comparison of the opposite schools of painting, he sang out clearly, and said, "think nothing of my laughter; but to return to the count, now that you have come to this picture illustration, and hold him for a Raphael and yourself for a Teniers, how would your respective figures unite upon one canvass?"

Walt was wounded and silent, for he did not look upon himself as a Teniers, but rather as a Petrarch, and Vult pressed him warmly to devise any means of union with the count upon which he could rely.

"I believed I could effect this union by loving him sincerely," said Walt, humbly and gently.

Vult was touched, blew upon his flute, but remained inflexible. "To trust to your love alone to draw such a gentleman to you, you must, modest as you appear, hold yourself for nothing less than a second Karpser."

"Who was he?" asked Walt.

"A barber in Hamburg, for whom the Karpser street in that city is named, because he dwelt therein; a man of such refined manners, so full of experience from life and from reading; so enchanting, that princes and noblemen who came to Hamburg found their first and greatest satisfaction, not, I will venture to say, not in the pesthouse, in gambling-houses, or in the Schul-allee or Alster walks, but in the knowledge that the barber was at home, and would admit them."

Walt, who looked upon himself as an incipient Petrarch, and who might not have placed the barber so high above himself, merely answered, exhausted as he was by the afternoon's contest, "How happy is a nobleman, he can love where and whom he will! Were I *one*, and an honest, common notary gave me but one warm sigh of his love and truth, I would soon understand him; I would not torment him even the length of a moment. I believe indeed I should be more proud towards my equals than towards him."

"Heavens! do you know what? I have an excellent project!" broke out Vult, in a wholly different voice. "In fact the very best; for it will make everything plain, and if he is such as you imagine him, unite you and the count delightfully, and forever."

Walt expressed his pleasure and the curiosity, which would hardly allow him to wait. But Vult answered, "to-morrow or the next day I will explain all."

Walt besought, as they were near the city gate, and the time of taking leave, to hear his project to-night?

Vult answered peevishly, "this much I will say, that I never say *proschekt*, but either *projèt* in French, or *projectum* in Latin."

Walt said, "do you not perceive my joy at the mere proposal of this plan, and will it not be much greater at the disclosure?"

"Certainly," said Walt.

But the project belongs to another chapter. This is finished, and good night.

No. 30. *White pebbles from Saxony.*

CHAPTER XXXI.

THE PROJECT.

"PURZEL agrees!" said Vult, as he rushed violently into the apartment of his brother.

"God grant it! and what then?" said the other.

"Purzel is the theatre tailor and my landlord," said Vult, humour flashing from his eyes, as he drew out the essay he had made upon the nobility, for their double romance. "You will acknowledge, that you need a needle, a diamond-eyed needle, to stitch together your union with Count Klothar. That my project will be. All moralists agree, that actions form the direct path to the heart; they are level shot right in the breast, while words are only diverging, or arched shots. Should you purchase a watch-key, or strike a bargain for a friend, it opens more easily the barred entrance to his heart, than thirty *dejeûners* in a month of thirty-one days.

"Thus, if you could only throw a stone into the count's window, or upon his shoulder-blade, you would immediately come into contact with him; and easily, after that, into a nearer union. If, in the dark, you were were to fall upon him, seize him by the coat, and not let him go, because you mistook him for the brother that you love so inexpressibly! But as this cannot happen,—so listen. My landlord, Purzel, has many festival and dinner dresses in hand; that is, turning and mending for the theatre: I will furnish you with one completely suitable to appear before the count; but as I am acquainted with him, I will write a note before, and say that I wish much to blow the flute with him upon a certain evening, and to bring you with me (do not speak yet); thus, you can allow yourself, without an articulate lie, to pass for a nobleman in his presence, merely because you are my friend, and we appear together. Then it is impossible, that the parchment of nobility can be any longer a fire-proof wall of division, a stove screen drawn before the flame of your friendship; and if the count is not an ice island, with as much ice beneath the water as there is above, I foresee that under the shelter of the flute, you can say and prove all; perhaps stand united with him upon the altar of friendship, while I have gladly been the grafting knife. Now speak!"

"Glorious! glorious!" cried Walt, and embraced his brother. "I shall stand upon the starred car of friendship, and roll through heaven! But if I should win his friendship, I must instantly, yes, the same evening, tell him my ignoble name. I must present him, not only a warm, but an open heart. And then nothing can change."

But now, the variegated and enchanting vapor with which his romantic spirit had shrouded the adventure, drew off, and sank down. Conscience, with her balance and scruples, placed herself coldly before him; although he had resolved immediately to efface the deception, he could not find it right to *begin* a friendship with one. Vult assured him he would merely say, that he was a relation of the same name, and appear, in the hurry of speaking, to forget the *Van*. "But if I should, at last, say, I am your twin brother, what could you then answer?" asked Walt.

"'Herr Graf,' I would say, 'he is in *everything* my brother, yes, the twin brother of my heart; a spiritual or canonical relationship, in my opinion, is the best.' Even our God establishes one in common with us creatures of clay, and allows us to call him father! Is not this affinity true?"

Walt shook his head!

"What!" continued the flute-player, "if it were not so! — If we were *not* brothers in spirit? Ah! twin! who then is related, think you? If bodies complete souls, and unite hearts, then I should think a pair of twins, who become brothers earlier than other children, even in that double-bedded cradle of their first unconscious sleep; participating in the earliest and most important influences of their life; two hearts beating beneath one, in a partnership that can never again happen; sharing the same nourishment, the same inconveniences, the same and equal joys, the same waxing and waning — if in such circumstances, where, in an especial sense, two bodies unite in one soul, as the eldest and first Aristotelian, namely, Aristotle himself, desired in friendship — what, the devil! if, in such circumstances, one twin dare not say he is spiritually related to the other, where then, Walt, can there be relationship upon the earth? Can there then be, thou methodical fratricide, an earlier, nearer, older, more careful friendship than with such twins? Oh God! you laugh at my emotion," he added, and struck his whole broad hand over his brow, ——

"I should deserve hell, if I did," and Walt drew his hand away, to cover his own wet eyes. "Oh! brother, brother! wilt thou never know that I understand thee, and see thy tender spirit under thy roughest jokes? Ah! how beautiful and mild is thy inmost being, and why cannot the whole world know thee thus? But what should I be, if, on your account, I consented to that which you would venture for me with Klothar? No! we may accept from others sacrifices to save us from martyrdom, but never to purchase a joy! the thing cannot be — dear Vult!"

But Vult was already down the steps. Meantime, the more Walt reflected, the more unwilling he found himself to purchase this heaven of friendship at Vult's expense. At length, he wrote him decidedly, that his conscience would not allow him to consent!

A few hours after, Vult returned the following answer: — "Dear Sir, *Fratercul!* I received the count's *consent* at the same moment when I received your *refusal.* You must go with me; my honor is pledged. Come, and fly early to me. Your dress, or masquerade, lies ready upon the chair; the hair-dresser is sent for; spurs and boots stand ready. Believe me, a habit is prepared for you that simulates only, not dissumulates. It would be very different, if I were to present you as a mountaineer, or in a monk's cowl, or in a bishop's consecrated dress, or in the uniform of an English captain, or like the *devil* and his *grandmother;* but, on the contrary, you will only appear in a proper dress for yourself, and, therefore, suitably and truly. Visit him with me, in your Polish coat, and in the mantle of your love for him. Purzel thinks well of it, and I long inexpressibly for the joke! The evening will disguise you sufficiently; powder is not to be thought of, that must be left out.* In the beginning, I had naturally invited the good count to a little light supper in Rosenthal, but without mentioning you. He preferred to invite us to his garden. Come resolved; for this evening will decide the conditions of a friendship which will last during forty or fifty thousand future evenings. I write with much emotion. Garrick knew how to repeat the alphabet merely, in such a manner that the people wept. All that touches the heart in description is made out of alphabets. Hearts are like

* Walt, as a notary, was obliged to wear powder.

goose-eggs, those that will not move in warm water are good for nothing, tainted, and dead. Heavens! how I shall play this evening! how make the flute speak! Indeed, I am too happy!

"P. S. I would not at first, but I must now inform thee, that thy future friend, Klothar, will journey to-morrow, at five in the morning, as *he* says, to Dresden, but as *I* say, to Leipsic; for the purpose of gaining, through the Protestant mother, a hearing from the Catholic bride. So, if you are not a complete Shomaker second, you will come to-night, and strike, although only a citizen, the pedal triller of friendship with a nobleman. For where is the deception? if I do not say (without which you cannot contradict), that you are noble; but say only, at first, that you are my friend, and then, at last, that you are a notary. Where? I ask!"

"Ah! I will indeed come," Gottwalt wrote back.

No. 31. *Pill stones.*

CHAPTER XXXII.

MISANTHROPY AND REPENTANCE.

THOSE who read in print, Vult's old, and yet unsealed letter to Walt, will probably penetrate, at once, his secret aims, completely disguised as they are to the guileless notary, and find they are two-fold. The first object of Vult was to make himself more angry than he had yet been, and while witnessing his brother's proffered friendship to the count, and perhaps even its return, he would himself be driven to that angry and stormy outbreak of feeling, without which, according to his well known opinion, there can be no reconciliation.

The jealousy of friendship is much stronger than that of love, as it cannot, like love, bring itself to despise its object. The second concealed aim of Vult could only be founded upon probabilities; either that the count (if the notary should let fall the noble plumage) would drive him from his heart and garden, like a plucked crow; in that case, Vult would again win his brother, or be reconciled to the count (as one crow does not pick out another's eyes), and if he should thus quarrel with his brother, he could trust to his love for a reconciliation; and in the third place, — but there is no third.

Walt came, apparently undecided and unhappy. "Here," said Vult, "lies the misanthrope, *Meinau* from Kotzebue's Misanthropy and Repentance," and pointed to a coat of the finest broadcloth, a long napped round hat, and spurred boots, and a neckcloth three ells long, to keep down the bloom of the complexion, and underdress of silk.* But that which before had wavered in the ether of imagination, now stood immediately before Walt in unchangeable reality, and the undefined wrong became a positive sin.

"The devil!" said Vult, and untied the little notary cue from Walt's hair, "do you yet scruple? as if this could not be a *dress*, instead of a disguise? Can a pair of boots and spurs make a nobleman? Do not make me angry!"

A hair-dresser appeared. The whole hair must be rolled into innumerable curls. Afterwards, he was hermetically sealed in cloth, and his own sound kernel enveloped in a gentlemanly shell.

Upon the way, Walt assured him, that, on account of the twilight, he would be unknown; and the great, also, such as the count, never remembered a peasant's face. * * * *

They arrived at the park, and the count came to meet them, with his simple, earnest, dignified man-

---

* As this was published in 1802, the dress was that of the French fashion of the time, and could not be considered a disguise.

ner. "It is my friend and relation, of the same name;" thus Vult introduced his brother; "his love of the flute impels him to come with me."

Walt, instead of making excuses, as his brother had advised, merely bowed, rather boldly. Vult had said, the count knew too much of the world, when he had invited him to his garden, to catechise him at the door.

Walt thought too nobly and honestly to condescend to disguise his weakest thought from the count, — with the exception of his person — nothing.

Vult had been right in saying that the count, like the great, who in travelling and at courts have seen armies of men, would not easily retain in his memory a trace of the notary. Klothar looked at him a little thoughtfully at first, but in the twilight did not again recognise the curled, cueless, and thickly neckclothed cavalier. His *Meinau* disguise was also a little too narrow for him. Disguises are represented in romances much more agreeably than they in reality are.

As the weather, within doors, is always the first subject of remark, so, in the open air, beautiful nature is the luck-penny and savings-bank of conversation. Walt did not conceal from the count that the place where he had stood, near the waterfall, with the statue of the vestal, and the distant hills behind, and listened to his music, had great and true charms for him. Klothar affected to think little of them, and assured him that every park pleased only once, and wearied ever afterwards.

The flute-player was as avaricious of words, and as polite, as the count himself, and spared his humors and his tongue for his flute.

The brothers were regaled with wine, pressed rather from the leaves than from the grapes. The count would not drink; Walt, a little only, — as the smith pours water to increase the fire. *Vult*, angry at the sour wine, and at everything else, walked quickly backwards and forwards without playing. Klothar left him to his own humor. At last he began his flute concert, and blew with contempt for the count's musical taste, fragments of tunes, phantasies, gallopades, musical fancies, half sunshine, half shadow; then seized powerfully the flute strings with the breath, as the storm-wind lays its hand upon the Eolian harp.

Both the cavaliers were by this melo-dramatic throwing off of the flute agreeably launched into conversation. The English park was a post-packet, by which they were both transplanted to England, and both were of one mind in their observation and admiration of that country. Count Klothar commended the British reserve and unsociableness. "To certain faults," he said, "belong certain advantages." "Flowers *only* sleep, not the grass," said Walt, who through poetry and imagination easily translated the opinions of others into his own. He who seeks the south or sunny side of everything, easily finds light and warmth. Klothar asserted that friendship acknowledged no difference of rank, as the soul no sex. Walt managed his answer so that it expressed the idea, that in striving to forget their inequality, both friends were at least equal; but his pronunciation was a little rustic, and his eye, instead of delicately glancing, overflowed with the excitement of his feelings.

The count rose calmly, and said he must withdraw a moment to order his carriage for his departure half an hour later, and acknowledged, that he were rarely so easily understood as upon this evening.

With inexpressible delight Walt said softly to Vult, "Thanks! thanks! my Vult. Ah! we should never take the behavior of a man towards us, were it ever so frosty, for a mark of his worth. How many rich souls are lost to us, through pride. I can now tell him *all, Vult!*"

"But the wine," said Vult, "might have been a little better. Acknowledge that! Shall I then no longer consider him a self-seeking egotist, an iceberg, a frost conductor? He knows nothing more of your face, or of the rapid cure of my well known blindness! But that may be a mere matter of memory; and that a stranger is less to him than himself. Without waiting for an answer, Vult poured his irritated feelings into his flute; but as the count returned, played exquisitely.

The latter heard him out, but said nothing. Walt could say nothing; he had the moon, the count, the flute, the wine in his head. The moon had risen above the windmill-crowned heights, and flooded the whole plain with light. The notary saw by the moonlight, upon the face of the youth, an earnest, deep melancholy. The flute appeared to him like the post-horn in the distance, that was bringing him the sweetest future, with a new friend. "But where can *he* again find what he has lost, and must ever mourn, a bride like Wina?" thought Walt. He could no longer restrain himself; he must tenderly press the count's hand. He was so inexpressibly delicate (he hoped even, that he went beyond the old French romances, and the present French women), that he would not allow himself the most distant hint, that he knew the mainspring of Klothar's bridal carriage was broken.

"We should have known each other earlier," said the count, and pressed his hand, "before the sphinx, as a very clever poet describes love, had shown me the claws." Walt had been himself this clever poet. He pressed the other hand upon the one which held the count's, and said nothing of his poetical paternity, but—"Noble count, I knew you early, and have sought you long." "Blow, good Vult (he turned suddenly to the player, who stormed up and down, between heaven and hell, in sounds that were like hysterical laughs); blow milder,—shepherds' songs, lute tones, or sacred songs."

Vult played five or six carouses, stormy finales, and then ceased entirely; as it seemed to him too absurd, too ridiculous, to set the deep disappointment of his own heart, the running text of his own emotions, to music.

"I also," answered the count, "recollect your appearance, but imperfectly, but I would not desire to break your incognito."

"It is already broken," cried Walt; "I am Harnish, the notary, from Elterlein, the same who found the letter of the Fräulein Wina, in the park, and delivered it to ——

"*What?*" said the count, slowly, and rose like a king. But he immediately recollected himself, and said, calmly, "I ask you very earnestly for your name, and especially, with regard to the open letter, how far the contents of that letter were unfolded to you?"

Walt, shocked at the excitement of the count, said he trusted he had said nothing that was unpleasant to him. He looked round for his brother, who had withdrawn; and as he heard a loud noise, like fighting, behind the shrubbery, he cried, "God, what has happened to my brother?"

"There is no danger in the park," continued the count; "but go on! go on!" Walt related briefly the finding of the open letter in the park.

"What! Monsieur," cried the other, in a tone that nearly silenced the waterfall; "what! *he** can degrade himself by delivering *my* letter, which he has found in *my* park, to the general, that he may ingratiate himself with him, because the general is the owner of Elterlein, Herr!"

* The use of the third person expresses the utmost contempt, and is only used to servants and inferiors.

Walt was struck at once by a double flash of lightning, charmed and destroyed. With a mild and failing voice he answered, "Ah, Heaven! that is too unjust! Misfortune upon misfortune. I am indeed entirely innocent of a thought of treachery. No indeed! such injustice is far from my conception. It was also in Newpeter's park."

Vult heard Klothar's excited voice, and came from the moss hut, where he had retired in displeasure, and after his old manner had been lost in a boxing game with his own passions. Walt stood by the statue of the vestal, who looked down upon him as if he had been her husband. The flutist saw by a glance, that the incognita was broken, that the noble caterpillar's shell had fallen off, and he hung an immovable chrysalis. He requested immediately from tho count an explanation of his displeasure.

"It lies in the thing itself," cried the other, without looking at him; "but *this* I do not understand, how they can have the boldness to seek the person whose letter they have read, and usurped the right to betray into false hands, that which was expressly forbidden in the letter."

"I have read nothing! I have done nothing!" said Walt; "but I will willingly endure your severe expressions, if I have been the unconscious cause of bringing such misfortune upon you."

"Herr Graf," began Vult, proudly, "I can venture to say, upon my word of honor, that Mr. Harnish has read nothing, although I do not know what is the subject of dispute." "Herr Van der Harnish," turned Klothar quickly upon him, "I have an especial explanation to demand from you. In how far have you presented *this notary* to me under a stranger's name?"

"I presented him as my friend and relation; *that* he remains. I could also have presented him as the probable heir of Van der Kable's inheritance. Is any other explanation requisite?"

"I would demand another," answered the count, "if I were not this moment to step into my travelling carriage."

"I am ready to step into it after you, and there to explain to each other, or otherwise, as you will;" and Vult, much offended, followed the count.

"O, listen to me! spare me!" besought Walt. "You know not how I have injured him!"

"The fool shall not speak so warmly; and you are one, also," said Vult. "Herr Graf, you owe me an answer!"

"Indeed, none! But I ask, are you brothers?"

"Father and mother must you ask, not me," said Vult. The unfortunate notary could not lift the coffin lid under which he heard these noisy preparations for a duel.

"If you have presented no one under a false title but yourself, I require no explanation; and from *peasants* I demand none;" and the count sat coldly in his carriage. Vult would hardly suffer the door to be closed, and cried within it, "Cannot there be *two* noble *fools?* or indeed *three?*" The carriage rolled on, and he remained, with defeated heroism, behind.

Walt could not *express* to the count his wishes for a happy journey; he, whose heart he had robbed of the greatest happiness, how could he wish him happiness?

Silently, with his silent brother, he left the garden, to him a lost garden of Eden. Vult saw that his brother was bent under the deep, low hanging thunder-cloud of regret, but he said no word of consolation. Walt took his hand as if he would hold himself upon the brother's heart, and asked, "*Who* then can I love?" Vult was silent, and held his own hand as if it were paralyzed. Walt said no more. He went silently through the gay evening streets, at the side of a brother, upon whose jealous breast, tears, like petrifying water, would have formed only a stony rind.

"Why did you take my part," said Walt, at length; "I was much to blame. Do you know the whole history of the letter?" Vult coldly shook his head. Walt's earlier account of the affair had been, from mere modesty, like everything that related to himself, short and cursory. But Vult, from his cultivated histrionic talent, was accustomed to consider every occurrence under every light, and to discern the smallest advantage that he could draw to himself to influence the present or the future. Walt possessed nothing of this court talent. He looked and thought straight forward. He described a fact, and had nothing more to do with it. Walt now told his brother of his unfortunate transfer of Wina's letter to her father. "Ei! the devil!" cried Vult, entirely softened, for he now guessed *all*, and was frightened at the intrigue into which he had led his brother. "Take the disguise off," he said, "*there*, above." "Yes," answered Walt; "and although I do not anticipate immediately any misfortune, I intend to see the father and the bride, and to explain *all!* Ah, who can say, in this many-sided and confused life, '*I* am guiltless.'" "Fate," he continued, as he ascended the steps to Vult's apartment, "in some accidents, holds the magnifying glass of our littleness distorted before us. Ah! above unmeaning words, above the lowest complaints, there stands a quiet, concealed height, from which they unconsciously draw down the avalanche upon them."*

"Take yourself immediately out of that dog's shell," said Vult, gently, as they entered the quiet chamber, filled with clear moonlight.

Silently, Walt raised the Kotzebue hat from his brow, and stroked his locks again back from his forehead.

"*I*," said Vult, placing himself behind his brother, "will make thy cue. Take the ribbon, at least one end, between your teeth." He did it, but reluctantly and ashamed. As Vult, with his brother's back towards him, took the tender, curling hair in his fin-

---

* A word, a sound, the striking of a clock, sometimes causes the avalanche to fall.

gers, he could very easily imagine him dead, or distant, or forever separated from him; and this linear perspective of the heart affected him with a strange sorrow. He held the head so closely between his hands, that Walt could not turn round, and Vult said to him, in a voice thick with the tears that he would not shed, "Gottwalt, do you still love a certain Quod Deus Vult?"

There was something in his voice so touching, that Walt turned hastily around, and cried, as he let go the hair-ribbon, "Ah Vult! do you love *me?*" "More than any, or all the other villains upon this earth, and that is the reason that I croak like a hound, or a woman. But bite the ribbon again." Walt turned quickly round, and was pale as death, when he saw tears running over the agitated face of his brother; "O God! what has happened? what is the matter with thee?" he cried. "Perhaps nothing, or something of no consequence," said Vult,—perhaps *love!* . *So*, that cursed word has come out. I was jealous of the count. 'Is it not evident,' I said to myself, 'that my brother so reveres, and hunts after this man, that he is more to him than any one else? a man of whom, in fact, I think as badly, as a Father of the Church thinks of the Grecians and Romans. And this brother must not imagine, that he can satisfy me with a ragged, divided love.' My young life is already very dry. The sea has left the open haven of my heart, and no *boat* can ever again anchor there. Brother! I often have days of agitation, and nights of paroxysms of heart agony. Ach Gott! I wept one night till half-past twelve o'clock." Vult was obliged to restrain himself, the agitation of his brother became so visible. "What troubles thee so?" asked Vult, as Walt shook his head, and, walking backwards and forwards, took unconsciously, sometimes a glass, sometimes a book in his hand, and then, to wipe secretly away the hot tears, looked out upon the clear moonlight. "We will be again as of old, *friends*," and he embraced him warmly. But Walt withdrew quickly from the embrace. He afterwards recovered his self-possession, and said in a sorrowful tone, "Must I then occasion the unhappiness of all with whom I am connected? Then my brother will complete the three figures of my dream." Vult, in order to withdraw him from his painful recollections, and the thought, that he had unconsciously injured the count and Wina, asked pressingly to hear the dream. Walt, though reluctantly, related it.

"Veiled forms," he said, "passed before me, and asked why I was not sorrowful and pale, like the others. One after another, came, and asked; at length, I trembled before a veiled, colossal form. Three beautiful angel children descended from heaven, and looked at me with kind, encouraging glances. 'Give me your white hands,' I said, 'and raise me towards heaven.' They did so, but I tore their arms from their breasts, and they fell dead before me — and as I awoke, I saw where they fell a funeral procession. My dream is fulfilled."

Vult, now that his angry pain was charmed away, made every exertion to soothe his brother. He looked at every event upon the bright side; complained of that poisonous, that sultry corner in the left side of his breast, where a sullen dwarf, a true wolf-hound, housed, and looked angrily out. He drew the silvering from the poisonous pill that his letter had enclosed, and made his own strange nature known, that was never tractable without a previous quarrel, like the hooded lark that will never sing except when it grumbles. He swore that Walt was not the first he had tormented, nor would be the last, unless his infinite amiableness should have power to cure him.

But Walt did not easily listen to reason; he considered it merely sacrificing tenderness, and asked why he had defended him so warmly before the count, if he wished to bar the way to him.

"From anger, dearest," he said, "and somewhat of pride — nothing else. Here is the proof," he said, and took out a letter closed with two seals; "here I have explained all, and justified you and myself to the count."

Walt would not open the letter. He said he would rely upon Vult's word, and that now, at length, he understood him, and felt happier. Vult was consoled, pressed his brother to his heart with that long-delayed, warm embrace that revealed his own wild nature. And the brother was happy, and said, "We will remain brothers!"

"Montaigne says, 'a man can have but one friend,'" said Vult.

"Oh! only one," sighed Walt, — "one father, one mother, *one love*, — and only one — one twin brother!"

Vult answered, wholly seriously, "Yes, indeed! only *one*, and in the heart of each must dwell love and justice!"

"Joke again, as formerly, good Vult, as a proof of reconciliation; (I shall certainly laugh as well as I can,) your seriousness cuts me to the heart."

"If you wish it, I can indeed joke," he said. "Ah no! by heaven, no! The Kamskadales believe, according to Steller, that if there are twins, one has a wolf for a father. I am indeed this wolf's bastard.

"Now that we can speak openly of this intricate affair, I will venture to tell you, that you have acted throughout the whole business truly and justly towards Klothar. But you have too little egotism to perceive egotism in another. Klothar is indeed a great egotist. I will not attack him now; but I know no one, at present, of your sort. The philosophers, the young at least, are, by heaven! *all* egotists.

"Their maxims of benevolence and morality are, as thou knowest, merely quackery. A light is not a fire; a lantern will not warm like a stove. Yet the philosophical mob throughout Germany think, as soon as they have taken their tallow candle in their heart, and placed it on the table, its light will heat both apartments."

"Dear Vult," said Walt, with the most touching expression, "excuse me from answering; I dare not to-day, at least, judge the unfortunate Klothar, for I have been the means of taking from him the loveliest creature upon this earth; and now, solitary, and in the night, he journeys, with a heart filled with night, into a darker future! Thou art guiltless. *Thou*, not I, may speak of him."

"Walt! I say, the philosopher has this night taken care of *himself;* and when spiders do that, it is a sign we shall have fair weather. Apropos — dress yourself; but better — more physically."

That Walt did; the other held him, as he placed the bootjack before him. "How the moon laughs around the chamber!" he said; "place thyself in the lovely light; snd take again the hair-band between thy teeth; now I shall twist thy hair with wholly different emotions and fingers than, before — splendid curled pate!"

Afterwards they separated, their hearts filled with peace, and full of affection for each other.

No. 32. *A half-digested Farthing.*

This last chapter has been somewhat abridged. — *Tr.*

Translator's Notes, omitted at the foot of the page.

Page 63. "Meister-Sänger, from Nuremburg." The corporation of Meister-Sängers was of great antiquity, dating far back in the middle ages; Nuremburg being the principal metropolis of their song-craft. They were originally called the corporation of the twelve wise masters, which was composed of artisans from all parts of Germany. There is a particular account of the Meister-Sangers in the Introduction to German poetry in Longfellow's "Poets and Poetry of Europe."

Page 148. *Currend* or running boys, are the pupils of charity schools, who wear some distinguishing badge, and sing in companies, through the streets to collect charity. What is thus thrown them pays for their maintenance and instruction. Luther, the great reformer, began life as one of these *running* boys.

CPSIA information can be obtained
at www.ICGtesting.com
Printed in the USA
LVHW040339110522
718423LV00001B/290

9 783375 003487